tell me no lies

LISA HALL

HarperCollinsPublishers
1 London Bridge Street
London SE1 9GF

This paperback edition 2017

First published in Great Britain by
Carina an imprint of HarperCollins*Publishers* 2016

Copyright © Lisa Hall

Lisa Hall asserts the moral right to be
be identified as the author of this work

A catalogue record for this book is
available from the British Library

UK & Can ISBN: 978-0-00-820519-5
USA ISBN:978-0-00-822879-8

Set by CPI - Group(UK) Limited,

Printed and bound in the United States of America By LSC Communications

17 18 19 20 LSC/C 10 9 8 7 6 5 4 3 2 1

LISA HALL

loves words, reading and everything there is to love about books. She has dreamed of being a writer since she was a little girl – either that or a librarian - and after years of talking about it, was finally brave enough to put pen to paper (and let people actually read it). Lisa lives in a small village in Kent, surrounded by her towering TBR pile, a rather large brood of children, dogs, chickens and ponies and her long-suffering husband. She is also rather partial to eating cheese and drinking wine.

Readers can follow Lisa on Twitter @LisaHallAuthor

For my Granny and Grandad Langford – for always being there.

PROLOGUE

They say everything happens for a reason. That a person comes into your life at a certain time, whether their intentions are good or bad. I used to think it was a load of rubbish, that we are in control of our own destiny, but now, knowing what I know, I'm not so sure. Sometimes people aren't what they seem. Sometimes people set out to destroy everything you hold dear. And sometimes, that person is you.

CHAPTER ONE

I heave a box from the back of the van, taking care not to stretch too far. It's not heavy, and I shift it in my arms as I turn and look up at the house. A fresh start, that's what it is. It's not just a house, it's a chance for Mark and I to put straight everything that has gone wrong this year, to give Henry a happy family home instead of the war-torn existence full of accusations and blame that he's had to put up with this year. This imposing, statuesque Victorian townhouse is going to make us feel like a family again, with its large rooms set over three floors, a garden with enough room for Henry to run around in and impressive trees that line the street outside. It's a step up too, from our cramped two-bedroom flat in Crouch End, to this beautiful house in Blackheath, that's almost so big I don't know how we'll ever fill it. And Blackheath isn't *that* far from Crouch End, not really. A movement to one side catches the corner of my eye and I turn slightly to see Mark walking towards me, holding out his arms.

'Here, give me that.' Dark eyes twinkle at me, in the way that captured my heart six years ago, and I swallow hard. Twinkly eyes or not, forgiveness is not quite that simple.

'I'm fine. It's not heavy. And I'm not made of china.' I shift the box again in my arms, but he insists and tugs it gently away from me.

'You're carrying precious cargo there.' Mark smiles down at me and I manage to muster up a small smile back. Surreptitiously, I run my hand over the small swelling of my stomach, still almost invisible to anyone else. Mark strides towards the house, and after one last look at its imposing front, I follow after him.

He heads straight for the huge, airy conservatory at the back of the house, a stunning addition that lets vast amounts of light into what would otherwise be a gloomy, shadow-filled, Victorian kitchen. He adds the box to a pile that has already been off-loaded and turns to me.

'Nearly there, Steph. Only a few more boxes to go and we're done. You can start unpacking if you want, make it look like home a bit before Henry gets here.' I give a small nod, and Mark pulls me towards him.

'Honestly, Steph, it's a fresh start. We can say goodbye to all that's happened and try to start again. Or we can carry on dwelling on it all and let things really disintegrate. We can do this, Steph, I know we can.' Hearing the slight sense of desperation in his voice, I lean into him and feel his chin rubbing against my hair as he rests his head on mine. Pulling away I look up at him, trying to see the man I married, instead of the man who broke my heart.

'I know, fresh start. I'm trying, Mark, really I am. It's just a bit overwhelming, that's all. Everything's changed, everything that I thought was solid has turned out to be ... liquid. I'm just finding my foundations again. Give me a bit of time.'

'I'm sorry, Steph. You know that, I've never been more sorry. We can get over this; it'll be hard but we can do it.' He tugs me back into his arms and I rest there for a moment, squashing the queasiness in my stomach, and trying to ignore the stench of decay that still surrounds our relationship.

Two hours later, the removal lorry is finally unloaded and I've managed to find mugs and the kettle. Henry's bed has been made up, and I feel like maybe this wasn't the worst idea we've ever had. Maybe we have done the right thing, getting away from everything that went wrong, trying to start again somewhere new where there are no memories. Surveying the mass of boxes in Henry's room I take a deep breath – I just need to get over the anxiety that hangs over me in the wake of all things new, and remind myself that this *is* for the best. I'm just smoothing the bed covers on Henry's bed when the doorbell rings. Hoping it's my parents bringing my little boy home, I run lightly down the stairs. I can hear

Mark in the conservatory, swearing under his breath, obviously attempting to put a piece of furniture together or unpack something that is clearly getting the better of him. Swinging the door open, my 'Hello' dies on my lips as I realise it isn't who I am expecting. Instead of my mother standing on the doorstep, there is a tall, redheaded man in a Christmas jumper, despite the fact that it's not even the middle of November yet. There is a vaguely familiar air about him, as if I think I have met him somewhere before, but nothing comes clearly to mind. This isn't unusual; my memory for faces isn't the best even when I'm not pregnant.

'Hello?' I lean on the doorframe, aware that I must look a sight. My T-shirt is crumpled and filthy from cleaning Henry's room before setting up the bed, my hair a tangled bird's nest. The man on the doorstep smiles, showing off a perfect set of gleaming white teeth, and holds up a bottle of red wine.

'Sorry, I know I'm probably intruding hugely, but I just wanted to introduce myself. I live next door – I'm Laurence. Laurence Cole.' He holds out a hand and I shake it without thinking, before glancing down at my dusty palms and wiping them surreptitiously on my jeans.

'Hello, Laurence Cole. You're not intruding as such … It's nice to meet you, but perhaps now isn't a very good time.' I glance behind me, where swear words are pouring from the kitchen.

'Steph, is that the chap from next door? I told him to pop over; show him in.' Mark's voice floats out from the kitchen and my heart sinks a little. I'm really not feeling up to visitors; the house is a tip and I look a fright. But I rustle up a smile, taking the wine bottle from Laurence and showing him into the kitchen where Mark has just about given up on putting a cabinet together. As a television producer it's safe to say DIY isn't his forte. Getting to his feet, Mark wipes his hands over his jeans and holds one out for Laurence to shake.

'Sorry about that.' Mark swats his dark hair out of his eyes and turns to me. 'Laurence, this is Steph, my wife. She's a journalist too.'

'Hardly a journalist, Mark.' I look down at the floor, before raising my eyes to meet Laurence's. 'I don't really think interviewing minor celebrities for trashy magazines is journalism.'

'Oh, I don't know.' Laurence smiles at me. 'I wouldn't mind interviewing a few celebs. I'm at the far more boring end of the scale, I'm afraid – I'm a financial journalist. I bring you all the doom and gloom from the financial quarter.'

'There's probably more juicy gossip your side than there is at Steph's end.' Mark gives Laurence a wink as I cringe. Mark doesn't always think before he speaks, not realising that sometimes he comes across as brash and embarrasses me, even when he's trying to be complimentary. Busying myself opening the bottle of red he's brought over, I don't realise at first that Laurence is speaking to me.

'I'm sorry, what?'

'I said that must be where I know you from.' Laurence accepts the glass of wine I'm offering, his hand brushing mine as he reaches for it. I pull back, not sure if I imagine the tiny fizz of electricity that sparks on my skin where his hand glances against mine. He takes a sip of wine, his eyes never leaving my face. 'From the magazine. I think you interviewed Sasha Ronan after she got caught having an affair with that London banker – the one who embezzled a ridiculous amount of money and then spent it on his mistress. It was one of those trashy magazines that picked up on it all and gave her the chance to tell her story.' My cheeks burning, I fill the kettle to make myself a drink, seeing as how I can't drink the wine, no matter how much I want to.

'Well, you know, it pays the bills.' I avoid looking at Laurence; he is ridiculously good-looking and obviously my pregnancy hormones must be going crazy, my face hot with the force of the blush that spreads across my cheeks.

'Sorry – I didn't mean that the way it came out. I just meant that that was where I'd heard your name before. It caused a bit of a scandal in my office, and we talked about it for weeks. It made a change to read the other side of the story for once.' He smiles at me, and I feel the hot flush of my cheeks subside.

'Chill out, Steph, he didn't mean anything by it. We don't want to fall out with the new neighbours before we've even settled in.' Chuckling, Mark perches on the kitchen stool next to me and picks up his glass of wine, patting my hand in that clumsily affectionate way he has. I slide my hand out from under his and spend the next hour listening to him and Laurence trading stories, like they've been friends for years. They don't seem to need much input from me, thankfully, and I can tune out and think my own thoughts, random and spiralling, taking me somewhere far away.

We see Laurence out some time later, after an impromptu takeaway suggested by Mark, following a call from my mother to say that Henry has fallen asleep after a busy day and she will keep him for another night, allowing us to settle in properly. Standing at the end of the garden path, watching Laurence fumbling with his door key to get in, Mark puts his arm round me and pulls me in for a hug. I breathe deeply, inhaling the scent of him, the smell of clean laundry and Hugo Boss aftershave, with a slight tang of sweat.

'See, I told you everything would be OK. We've made a friend already – it'll be nice living next door to someone we get on with, who we can have a curry and a bit of a laugh with. And I'll feel better when I'm working away, knowing there's someone nearby if you need them.'

'Hmmmmm. Yes, Laurence seems nice. It was very kind of him to bring us a bottle.' I wrap my arms tightly around him, wanting to believe that what he's saying is true, that everything will be all right. Walking back up the path together, the curtains in the living room of the house on the other side of the street twitch slightly, and I can't help but feel an unexplained but overwhelming sense of unease.

CHAPTER TWO

I am sitting at the kitchen table, sipping a cup of mint tea, when Mark hurries in, simultaneously wishing me a good morning, tying his tie and flicking the switch for the coffee pot. It's still dark outside, crisp swirls of frost patterning the kitchen window. The kitchen is warm, the heating having come on half an hour before, and I loosen the belt of my dressing gown a touch, now that the early morning chill has abated slightly. We have only been in the house a week and it's beginning to feel more like home, but now the furniture is all in place and only the very lightest boxes remain to be unpacked, Mark has no choice but to leave me to it and go back to work – he starts production on a new series in a few weeks and he can't put off his return to the office any longer. He pours himself a cup of strong coffee and the smell of it makes my stomach roil in protest. I swallow hard, pressing down the bile that sits at the back of my throat.

'What time will you be home?' I sip at my tea, hoping to stop the morning sickness before it really grabs hold.

'Late, probably. I know it's not ideal, but after sorting the house out last week I need to make inroads into the new production. It's not going to be an easy day. Are you sure you're going to be OK?' His eyes search my face, and I swallow back the urge to ask him to stay.

'I'll be fine, I promise.' I give him a small smile, the smell of coffee in the air making the sick, queasy feeling in my belly worse. Oblivious to my nausea, Mark leans over to kiss the top of my head, breathing coffee fumes into my face.

'Jesus, Mark!' I gag, and sprint to the downstairs bathroom, only just reaching it in time. A few minutes later I hear the beep of the central locking on Mark's car as I sit back on my heels, wiping my mouth with a tissue. I was hoping that, this time around, the morning sickness wouldn't be as bad as it was with Henry, but it looks like I'm in for a rough ride again. Hauling myself to my feet, I am already feeling drained and exhausted and it's not even seven a.m. yet. Reaching the kitchen, I hear footsteps scurrying around upstairs that sound like an army of tiny mice, telling me Henry is up and ready for another day. Mark has left, his empty coffee cup turned upside down in the sink to leave a dark, tannin stain on the enamel, the dirty coffee pot left unwashed on the side, burnt-coffee aroma filling the air and making my cheeks fill with bile again. A hastily scribbled note on the kitchen table reads, 'SORRY, HAD TO LEAVE. SEE YOU TONIGHT. I LOVE YOU.'

Pushing my hands through my hair, I ignore the wreck of the kitchen and head upstairs to find my son.

A few hours later, Henry has been safely dispatched to school; I have waded through the dirty dishes in the sink and unpacked the last few boxes. I have an article due in two days on 'What He Thinks About During Sex' for a controversial women's magazine, and have no clue where to start. How about the other woman he wishes he was sleeping with? I probably wouldn't be the right person to write this article at the best of times, given the way things are between myself and Mark, and now, after what has happened in our marriage, I would say I'm the last person who should be writing articles on the subject. But, as I said to Laurence, it pays the bills and that's what counts. I have just deleted the opening sentence for the fifth time and started to bash out another version when the doorbell rings. I sigh in frustration, glancing at the clock on the kitchen wall, as I only have an hour before I have to leave to collect Henry from school. Opening the door, I am surprised to see a petite, dark-haired woman on the doorstep, someone I definitely don't know.

'Hello?' I smile quizzically at her, not having a clue who she is.

'You're Steph, right? I'm Lila – your neighbour!' She gives me a wide, toothy grin and looks at me as though I should recognise her.

'From next door? Oh, you must be Laurence's wife. Nice to meet you. Sorry I haven't been over to introduce myself; things have been a little hectic here.' I pull the door fully open and hold out my hand for her to shake.

'Oh, silly! Honestly. I don't live next door; I live across the street with my boyfriend, Joe. I've been meaning to pop over and introduce myself, but you know how it is. I wanted to come over the day you moved in but Joe said I should wait a bit, let you get settled.'

I wonder if this is the curtain twitcher from the first evening, when Laurence came over? Feeling a little on the back foot, I give her a tiny smile, thinking that maybe I should invite her in – Mark would want me to invite her in for a cup of tea, at least.

'Well, it's nice to meet you, Lila. Would you like to come in? I mean, I don't have long, I'm working … I work from home, you see.' I'm rambling, so I stop talking and wait for her response, half wishing she would refuse the invitation.

'That sounds lovely – I bought you this, as a little house-warming gift.' Lila holds out a foil-wrapped package and, with one delicate, porcelain-white hand, peels back the foil to reveal a home-baked coffee cake. The smell hits me before I even realise what it is and I reel back.

'Oh, Jesus. Sorry.' I clasp my hand over my mouth and sprint back into the house, running for the downstairs bathroom before I am sick again.

Coming out of the bathroom ten minutes later, as I wipe my hand across my mouth, I remember that I left Lila on the doorstep. Now, it seems she has made herself at home in my kitchen, the foil-wrapped package tightly resealed and stuffed deep into the bottom of the bin, and the kettle boiling merrily away as she busies herself taking down mugs and finding teabags.

'Sorry about that.' I sit down heavily into the nearest kitchen chair, legs still shaky after the vomiting.

'Nonsense. Don't worry about it. I should have realised that coffee cake is not the best gift for a pregnant lady suffering from morning sickness.' She smiles at me and hands me a cup of steaming mint tea.

'How did you know?' I ask, taking a small sip. 'I could have just had a virus.'

'Your husband … Mark, isn't it? He mentioned it when I introduced myself, last week.' Lila sits at the table next to me. 'Now, drink that slowly. You don't want to be sick again, do you?'

'Mark mentioned it?' Mark never said anything to me about the fact that he had met our other next-door neighbour. He never mentioned anything at all about meeting any of the neighbours.

'Yes, Joe and I were on our way back indoors after we'd been out and your husband was in your front garden – he is your husband, isn't he?' I nod, and she carries on: 'I introduced Joe and myself. Mark said then that you had a little boy and that you were expecting another.' Lila sips her tea, her eyes darting all around the kitchen as if looking for something. 'Where is your little boy?'

'At school.' I watch her carefully, this strangely overfriendly woman who seems to have just barrelled her way into my home, although my dashing off to be sick and leaving her on the doorstep didn't really leave her much choice, I suppose. She must be quite a bit younger than I am, maybe twenty-eight or so, with dark, almost black, glossy hair falling in soft waves to her shoulders. Her skin is pale, alabaster-white, set off by a pair of striking green eyes. She is most unusual looking, almost like a real-life version of Snow White, and far more glamorous than I am, sitting here with my rusty-brown curls tied in a knot on top of my head, yoga pants with a small yoghurt stain on the right thigh where Henry flicked his yoghurt spoon at me this morning, and presumably the scent of sick on my breath.

'Well, I can't wait to meet him, you lucky thing. I'm so looking forward to when Joe and I have a baby,' she breathes. 'It's going to be so lovely to have a nice family as neighbours, especially after the people that lived here before.' Lila makes a little face, before giving me a broad smile as she pats my hand, and I hope that a little of her sparkle and fizz will rub off on me. I don't know anything about the family that lived here before us, only that they left in rather a hurry, possibly something about a job abroad.

'Lila, it's been lovely, and I'm so sorry about the cake. It's just the coffee thing. I can't seem to stomach it at the moment; even the smell sets me off. I'm hoping that in a few weeks it'll wear off.' I set down my mug and get to my feet. I don't want to be rude but I have a deadline to meet, and my boy to collect in just under twenty minutes.

'Of course! I'm sorry to keep you. We didn't get off to the best start, did we?' Lila also gets to her feet, still smiling. She makes me feel like I must have a permanently miserable look on my face, compared to all her shine and glitter. I see her to the door, holding out my hand once again for her to shake. She bats it away and steps forward, enveloping me in a huge hug. I stand there stiffly, feeling ever so slightly awkward. I'm not a hugger, and certainly not one of those people who will scoop up someone she's just met for a giant squeeze. Lila hugs me tight, until I give her the tiniest of hugs back.

'I'll pop in during the week, shall I? Just to check on you, OK?' Lila says, buttoning the front of her pea-green coat. 'Someone needs to take care of you while Mark's working away, don't they? It's going to be so lovely having someone my age living across the street! I don't know if you've noticed, but they all seem to be a bit *older* than us around here.' She laughs and gives a little wrinkle of her nose. 'And I promise, no more coffee cake. We're going to be *great* friends – I can just feel it.' She gives me a wink and one last twinkly smile, before marching off down the path towards her own house, leaving me standing on the doorstep, feeling slightly bemused.

I walk back into the kitchen, intent on finishing the last bit of the article I was writing, only to find that the Word document I had open on my laptop is completely blank. I must have clicked on the delete button in my haste to get to the front door. Sighing, I close the lid of the laptop, and as I'm shrugging on my coat to walk up to the school to collect Henry, I realise I don't remember telling Lila that Mark worked away. Mark must have told her when he met her in the garden, I think, and I wonder why he never mentioned it to me.

CHAPTER THREE

I make it to the school with seconds to spare, the walk taking me a little longer than I had anticipated. I should have driven, really, knowing that I was under pressure to get there on time, but the lure of fresh air and a brisk walk proved too much to be able to resist. This is my favourite time of the year, those few weeks between the start of a fresh new school year (odd how, even twenty years after leaving school, the first week of September still feels like a fresh start to me) and Christmas – all the giddy excitement of preparing for the festivities, made all the more fun since the arrival of Henry. The perfect time for us to re-evaluate things and make a go of our marriage after all that has happened, giving ourselves a clean slate and a chance to start over. It's the best kind of day too – the kind that starts crispy and frosty, swirls of ice on the windowpanes and car windscreens, blades of grass turned white and crunchy with the frost. The kind of winter's day where, even though there are bright-blue skies and sunshine overhead, the temperature doesn't lift a degree or two above freezing, so all day long your breath puffs out in little dragon clouds as your boots slip and slide on the glittery, icy pavements. The best kind of day to pull me out of the thick, suffocating darkness that threatens to suck me under sometimes.

By the time I arrive at the school, the bell has rung and children are beginning to stream out of their classrooms, looking for their mothers waiting patiently in the playground. Half of the parents there don't seem to pay any attention to the children pouring out of the school, not looking eagerly for their offspring, preferring instead to catch up with the school gossip with the other yummy mummies congregating in the playground. I stand to one side, away from the gossiping masses, my nose red from the cold, my cheeks flushed from the race to get there on time, and unzip my thick winter jacket as pregnancy and the brisk walk make me warmer than I should be. As I push my hat further back on my head I see Henry come out of his classroom, holding tight to his teacher's hand. I feel my heart squeeze at the sight of his little face, a serious frown crossing his brow as the teacher leans down to speak to him. As she stands, she catches my eye and beckons me over with one finger. My heart sinks a little; today has obviously not been a good day for Henry. I make my way across the playground, dodging small children on scooters, their mothers still yakking away about nothing to their playground counterparts. I reach Henry and Miss Bramley, and lean down to give Henry a quick squeeze and a kiss on the cheek.

'Is everything OK, Miss Bramley?' I ask, knowing full well that something will have happened today at school. Henry is only in Year One, and this is only his first week in his new school, but he doesn't seem to be settling in as well as they would like him to.

'We just had a slight incident today with Henry, Mrs Gordon, nothing too serious, but I thought we should let you know.'

'What is it? What happened? Henry, are you OK?' He gives a small nod and a sniff, not raising his eyes to meet mine.

'It seems Henry was pushed over by another child in the playground today, Mrs Gordon. It may have just been a little rough play that got out of hand, but I did think I should make you aware of it. Henry wasn't hurt, just a scraped knee, and this is not the kind of behaviour we at the school condone, I assure you.' Miss Bramley almost looks embarrassed at having to tell me my child has been hurt at school, her eyes looking everywhere but at me.

'Henry, is that what happened? Was it just playing?' Henry nods, a small, slight nod, and I look down at him helplessly. 'OK. OK, fine. Thank you, Miss Bramley.' I take Henry's hand and lead him away towards the black railings at the far end of the playground, to collect his scooter and get us out of the gate before I can speak to him properly. Henry is a sensitive boy, much more like me than Mark. I think when he was born, Mark thought he would be getting a rough-and-tumble boy, one he could play football with in the garden and take to the green to play cricket in the summer. A boy who would appreciate vigorous play, wrestling on the living-room carpet with his dad, instead of one who preferred to sit quietly, drawing or painting. Since he started school and discovered the joys of reading, he has become a voracious reader, devouring all the picture books I collected and read to him when he was tiny and clamouring for more every time we venture into a bookshop.

As we begin the walk back down the hill towards home, he scoots a little ahead, using his school shoes as a brake – something that would normally infuriate me, but today I don't mention it. We cross with the lollipop lady, a cheery soul who stands there morning and afternoon in sunshine and torrential rain, always with a smile on her face. She waves to Henry and hands him a lolly as he crosses, which brings the first smile to his face that I've seen today.

'Henry, wait!' I shout to him as he whizzes along the path, narrowly missing a lady walking a yappy Chihuahua that snaps at Henry's legs as he passes. He slows and I catch up with him outside the small convenience store, panting slightly. 'Leave the scooter there. We need milk. And some hot chocolate, if there are any good little boys about?' I peer around and Henry giggles, his laughter tickling my skin like summer sunshine, pulling a smile onto my face. Henry chatters on as I fill my basket with milk and other little bits we've run out off. I am only half listening, concentrating on packing my shopping bag as the man behind the till scans the items.

'Eight pounds forty, please.'

I smile at the man behind the counter and give him a ten-pound note. He hands me my change before reaching under the counter and popping a small purple packet into my hand.

'Your change. And a treat for the young man.' He winks at Henry, and I give him a small smile, nudging Henry into a 'Thank you' before adding the bag of chocolate buttons to the rest of my shopping.

A short while later, via a small diversion to the green, leafy park that we pass on the way home, we let ourselves in and Henry busies himself putting away his scooter and tugging off his school coat. I wait until he's finished and then follow him through into the kitchen.

'So then, hot chocolate?' I ask, turning to the shopping bag and pulling out a large carton of milk.

'Can we have marshmallows?' he begs, his face lighting up. 'And squirty cream?'

'Well, of course,' I reply. 'Is there any other kind?'

He giggles and I pour the milk into a saucepan and set it on the hob to boil.

'Is everything OK at school, kiddo?' I ask him, watching his face carefully for any clues. He is just like me, so insular. Neither of us likes to open up unless we have to, both of us preferring to keep things bottled up and deal with them in our own way, something I've started to realise is not always healthy. I want to encourage him to start to be more open, to let him know that I'm his mum, that he can always tell me anything and I would never judge him. Something I didn't have growing up, which I think has contributed to the way I deal with things. I have to encourage him, even though I know it means I'll have to force myself to do the exact same thing.

'Yeah. Mostly.' He carries on scribbling away, colouring in a drawing of a tiger. I turn to the milk pan, catching it just before it boils over and splashes all over the hob. I wait a moment, leaving him a chance to expand, but he carries on colouring, taking painstaking care to make sure he doesn't go over any of the lines. I pour the milk, whisking in the cocoa powder, topping them both off with squirty cream and marshmallows. It turns out that baby number two is far more partial to horrifically calorie-laden hot chocolate with all the trimmings than he or she is to coffee. Placing the mug in front of him, I try again.

'Just mostly?' I ask, nudging him gently. 'Why just mostly? Is it something to do with what happened in the playground today?'

'No.' He grasps the hot chocolate in his hand and blows gently on the top, like I showed him. 'That was just silly. Bradley doesn't know how to behave himself. He always *GOES TOO FAR*, that's what Miss Bramley says. He's not my friend, anyway. I don't care if he doesn't want to play with me any more.' Henry takes a sip of his hot chocolate, managing to slurp up several of the mini marshmallows dotted on the top at the same time. I give him a small smile and pat his hand, turning back towards the kitchen sink to blink away the tears that rush to my eyes.

Later that evening, once Henry is safely tucked up in bed, I tell Mark about Lila coming to visit.

'She seems nice,' I say, neglecting to tell him how my first instinct was to close the door in her face. 'She said she had met you already.'

'Hmmm?' He looks up from his laptop, pushing his glasses back on top of his head. 'Come here.' He pats the sofa next to him and I slide along until our thighs are pressed together. 'That's good – you know, that you had tea with her and everything. It'll be good for you to have a girlfriend; you don't seem to have anyone close, not since Tessa left for New York.' He puts his arm around my shoulder and pulls me towards him.

'So, you never said you'd met Lila already.' Although I know we said it's a fresh start, I can't help the spark of … what? Jealousy? Mistrust? I don't even know what it is that flickers inside of me. Mark rubs his hand across his forehead, tiredly.

'I didn't really think about it, to be honest. She introduced herself and I told her about us, that we had a little boy and a baby on the way. Nothing exciting. Now come on, up to bed with you, you look exhausted. I'll be up in a minute. I just need to send a couple of emails.' He kisses my head and I shuffle off the couch to head upstairs.

While Mark is downstairs finishing off emails or whatever else it is he has to do on the rare occasions he gets home from work before midnight, I sit in bed and slide my hand between the bed frame and the mattress to pull out my diary. I used to keep a diary, years ago, when all the bad stuff happened, but once I sorted myself out and met Mark I let it lapse. Now, though, following on from everything that has happened between Mark and myself, including after Henry was born, and on the instruction of the counsellor Mark found, I've started to write in it again. The counsellor, Dr Bradshaw, recommended I document how I feel about certain things that happen, in an attempt to keep at bay the dark feelings that threaten to overwhelm me sometimes, so now I sit in my pyjamas and write about today. I write about how sad I feel for Henry, as he struggles to fit in at school with the other kids; I write about how I wonder what Mark is doing downstairs –

he says he's checking emails but how do I know that's really what he's doing? I write about Lila – about how she brought a little bit of sunshine into my day today with her bouncy demeanour and her vomit-inducing coffee cake, and about how, maybe, after so long avoiding making new connections and new friends, I should learn to trust other people again. Maybe I should make an effort to make a new friend. Maybe if I pretend for long enough that everything is going to be OK, it *will* be OK. *In fact*, I write, *I think Lila might be good for me.*

CHAPTER FOUR

I push my way through the crowded restaurant towards the table at the back, the one Belinda always favours and somehow manages to bag, no matter how busy it is in there. She has arrived already, which is no surprise seeing as how I'm fifteen minutes late. I seem to be running at a pretty constant fifteen minutes late since I fell pregnant again, the morning sickness that lasts all day always appearing just as I am about to leave the house. Belinda sits at the table, eyes constantly scanning the room for people who might not want to be seen, permanently on the lookout for her next story. She puffs rapidly on her Vape, her nicotine addiction still as strong as ever. The day the smoking ban came into effect was a dark, dark day for Belinda. She tosses her icy blonde hair over her shoulder, squinting towards me in the dim light of the restaurant. Then, as she realises that it is actually me approaching her, she gets to her feet and waves at me enthusiastically, cigarette and all.

'Darling. I was beginning to think you'd stood me up.' Belinda's voice is husky from far too many cigarettes, late nights and bottles of fine whisky.

'Sorry. I felt a bit … yeuch. You know how it is.' I lean down to kiss her on the cheek, inhaling the familiar waft of Chanel No. 5 and cigarette smoke, the signature scent that is Belinda.

'You know damn well I don't, and I never want to either. No offence, darling, but babies are *not* for me.' She takes another deep drag on her fake cigarette, squinting at me again in the half-light.

'None taken. I do think it's time for you to dig out the specs again, though, Bel. You're squinting at me like mad, and I don't know why you choose this restaurant every time – the lighting in here is awful.'

'That's precisely why I choose it, darling.' Belinda lets out a cackle, drawing the attention of two older gentlemen dining at the table next to us. 'Soft lighting makes me look twenty years younger, plus no one can see the bags you're carrying under your eyes. Speaking of which, is everything OK, Steph?' Speaking her mind as ever, she eyes me with concern. Belinda may be a tough old bag, but she has been a huge support to me since I first met her. She was, and still is, the editor of a very successful magazine – not as posh as *Tatler*, but a few steps above the trashy weekly gossip mags. I did work experience with her, way back when I was doing my journalism degree, and never expected to even cross her radar, but it seemed I was the only one in the office who could make her coffee exactly as she liked it, and she took a shine to me. She took me under her wing, showed me the ropes, and eventually, once I got my degree, gave me a job as a features writer. Fifteen years older and infinitely wiser than me, Belinda taught me everything I know, and now, since having Henry and not wanting to work full-time, she still passes me interviews and features to write in a freelance capacity.

'Yes, Bel. Honestly, everything is fine. Just a bit exhausting at the moment, what with sorting the house out and being pregnant. I'll be fine.' I take a sip of the sparkling water on the table as Belinda takes a hearty gulp of cold, crisp Chardonnay. Lunchtime is drinking time to Belinda, and no doubt she'll carry on until late in the evening. Apparently, she writes all of her best features half cut.

'And Mark? What about him?' Belinda's nose turns up a little as she mentions Mark's name. She doesn't know what happened between us earlier in the year, and I want to keep it that way, but she doesn't like him and never has, and she's never told me why. I don't like to ask.

'He's fine. He's back to work and starting on a new project. Some wildlife, adventuring programme thing. Think Bear Grylls crossed with David Attenborough. Apparently he and the crew are travelling to some far-flung place next week to start shooting some footage.'

'Bear Grylls slash David Attenborough, eh? Impressive.' Belinda raises an eyebrow as she takes another gulp of her wine.

'Oh, come on, Bel. Don't be like that.'

'Well, I just don't like it, Steph. He leaves you and the baby on your own for weeks at a time. Anything could happen. He's lucky you don't find someone else to take care of you while he's not around.' She raises an eyebrow at me as I shake my head, a smile on my lips. Despite a tough exterior and a reputation for being a hard-nosed bitch, on the inside Belinda is as soft as spun sugar.

'It's fine, Bel, honestly. I knew what I was getting into when I married him.' To some extent, yes … his behaviour six months ago, not so much. Belinda pulls a face and I think it's best to change the subject. I don't want to talk about Mark, about how he's up and leaving me and Henry again just a few weeks after moving into a new home, a few weeks after promising me a fresh start. I don't want to think about who will be travelling with him, or what he'll be doing while I'm not there – that way madness lies. I'll end up driving myself crazy wondering what's going on, which is the reason why I took Belinda up on her offer of lunch today. I'm hoping she's got some work for me, something a little more upmarket than 'What He Thinks About During Sex' and other such exciting features.

'So? Why am I here, Bel? What have you got for me?' Our starters arrive, steaming-hot, tiny bowls of creamy pasta with a Parmesan crisp sticking out of each one. I don't know why Belinda bothers to order anything; it'll just get pushed around her plate, while I will eat everything and then feel like a heifer afterwards.

'I've got a great interview for you.' As expected, Belinda swirls a forkful of pasta around her plate, before taking another sip of wine and letting the pasta fall from the fork before she's even lifted it. 'A TV star turned entrepreneur. Trashy-mag fodder turned rival to Alan Sugar. Darling of the reality-TV phenomenon turned bona fide business tycoon. It'll be fabulous.'

'Sounds intriguing.' I shovel a forkful of pasta into my mouth, the morning sickness having left me famished. I have to eat while my stomach allows it; who knows how long it will be before the queasiness returns? 'So, who is it?'

'Melissa Davenport. You know, the girl that won that desert-island reality-TV thing? You must do; I'm sure you said Mark worked on that. She's started her own lingerie business; it seems to have really taken off. Everyone's going crazy for it, so I'm thinking we strike while the iron is hot. While *she* is hot. She's kept a low profile lately – obviously she's been working on this business idea of hers – but if we can get an interview with her now, before it all takes off, then we've got the scoop on all of the others. What do you say? Steph?'

The pasta has turned to ash in my mouth and I feel the blood draining from my cheeks. *Melissa Davenport.* Just the name alone is enough to start my stomach roiling in a manner far, far worse than morning sickness ever could. Saliva squirts into my mouth, heralding the fact that my stomach is about to revolt. Making my excuses, I jump up from the table and race towards the restaurant bathrooms.

Heart hammering, I make it to the ladies' room just in time to watch the small amount of my starter, that I did manage to eat, come back to haunt me. Splashing cold water on my face, I raise my eyes to the mirror, not at all shocked at the fright staring back at me. My face is pale, dark circles surrounding my eyes. My fringe lies flat on my forehead, no sign of the sheen and bounce I carefully styled into it before I left the house. Sighing, I pat my face dry with a paper towel and make some effort to look normal by patting some powder onto my cheeks and adding a dab of mascara to my eyelashes. Satisfied I can pass Belinda's inspection, I make my way back to the table. Belinda is on the phone and abruptly ends the call as I reach my seat.

'Darling. Are you OK? Is the morning sickness really that terrible? Thank goodness I never found myself in the family way. I'd *die* if I had to get sick in a public place.' Belinda wrinkles her nose in distaste and roots in her handbag for her Vape, dragging it out and puffing furiously. She's not good with illness, or sympathy for that matter. I sit down, leaning back in my chair as the waiter fusses around our table, removing the plates. Belinda waves him away impatiently.

'I'm fine. I'm sorry to spoil lunch. I don't know what came over me.' I sip at the glass of water next to me, avoiding Belinda's stern gaze.

'Don't apologise – you can't help it. If anyone is to blame, it's Mark.' Belinda puffs and gives a short bark of a laugh. If only she knew how true that was. 'So, what do you think about the Davenport girl? Is she worth an interview? We could make her the cover – she sells magazines by the bucket load.'

'I'm sorry, Bel, I don't think so. I'm sure she'd give you a brilliant interview but I just don't think I'm the right person for the job at the moment.' Just hearing her name makes my stomach flip over. There is no way I would be able to stand being in the same room as her. *Melissa Davenport*. The woman who slept with my husband. The woman who tried to steal Mark away from me. The woman who tried to destroy my life.

My mother has agreed to collect Henry from school today, so that I can have a long, leisurely lunch with Belinda. With this in mind, I take a slow walk home instead of jumping on the tube. Belinda is incredibly understanding about my not wanting to do the Davenport interview, blaming my hormones and the pregnancy (and Mark), and I am thankful I never told her what happened between Mark and Melissa. He says it was a one-off, a reaction to how I was after Henry was born, that it was a mistake and that it is only me he loves. *She*, on the other hand, didn't say much at all, only to beg me not to tell the papers, as it would destroy her career – she was concerned about being seen as a homewrecker (as well she should), although it's just unfortunate that that didn't cross her mind before the affair began. I've told no one, apart from my best friend, Tessa, about what happened between them, shame and humiliation making me keep silent. I told no one about how I found messages from her on his phone, messages that were anything but the innocent texts he said they were. I stomp angrily home, her name beating a tattoo in my head, the rage and hurt still as white-hot and fresh in my mind as it was the day I found out.

Lila is in her front garden as I make my way down our street towards my own front path. She raises a hand to me as I pass, pulling off a pink gardening glove as she straightens up.

'Steph! How are you feeling?' She smiles at me, a perfect row of white teeth gleaming, and for some reason I feel even crappier than I did before, imagining my teeth slicked with the vile taste of vomit.

'Hey, Lila. Not great, I'm afraid. Morning sickness still kicking in at the moment. I'm just going to go and have a lie-down before my mum brings Henry back.'

I barely look at her as I fumble in my bag for my door key, juggling my phone in the other hand.

'Oh, bless you, you don't look too well. Go and rest up. I'll be home if you need anything, just give me a shout. In fact …' She pulls out her mobile and holds her hand out for mine, before inputting her number into my phone. 'You just call me if you need anything, OK?'

I nod wearily, half raising a hand to her as I cross the street and let myself in. I need a hot bath, pyjamas and my little boy snuggled on the couch next to me.

Two hours later, when I go to the front door to let my mum in, Henry jabbering away nineteen to the dozen about the Christmas fair she took him to, I notice a tiny bunch of winter flowers tied together with a piece of raffia tucked into the corner of the porch. A small slip of white paper attached to the raffia reads, 'Just a little something from my garden to cheer you up'. A smile touches the corners of my mouth. Even though I was so rude to her earlier, practically ignoring her in my haste to get indoors, to get away from everyone, she still thought about me. She still cared enough to leave me a gift to cheer me up. The thought of it is warming, and I resolve to fight against my instinct to push her away, to make more of an effort to let Lila in properly, as a new friend.

CHAPTER FIVE

Mark calls later that evening to tell me not to wait up. It's always like this the few hectic weeks before he and his crew go off on location to start shooting – meetings that start after hours and go on long into the night as they plan what equipment they need to take, which routes they'll travel along and which flights they need to catch. For once, he calls early, just as I am about to put Henry to bed, so he says goodnight to our son and waits patiently as I finish tucking Henry into bed.

'Hello? I'm back,' I say, as I fold my legs beneath me and get comfortable on the couch. Despite not managing to eat any lunch, I'm not hungry yet and decide not to eat until later. 'What time do you think you'll be back? I haven't eaten – I can wait for you.' I say this in the hope he'll tell me he's leaving soon.

'No, no. Don't wait. I think it's going to be a very late one. That's why I'm ringing; they've decided to pull the whole thing forward.' Mark's voice is low, barely above a whisper and I realise there must be other people nearby.

'Pull the whole thing forward? What do you mean? You're not supposed to be leaving for another two weeks!' My voice is shrill, and I take a deep breath to try to calm myself. I should have known that the 'fresh start' wouldn't last for long – Mark is a workaholic, the lure of the camera and all the excitement that goes with it pulling him away from Henry and me time and time again, no matter how many times I beg him not to go.

'I'm sorry, Steph. I know I said a fresh start, and that I wouldn't go if it wasn't absolutely necessary. But it is necessary. I have to go, and the sooner we leave the sooner we come back.' He carries on, making his excuses to me about how this is a once in a lifetime opportunity (it always is), and how if they leave now they'll miss the worst of the rainy season, blah, blah, blah. Always the same old reasons.

'So, when do you go?' I ask, biting down hard on my tongue. He knows I'm upset – of course he does; you can't spend six years with someone without knowing them inside and out, can you? I refuse to lose my temper, refuse to shout and beg him not to go. I used to. I used to get cross and shout and tell him he loved his job more than he loved me and Henry, but after the affair with Melissa Davenport I don't feel like I can. That maybe the reason he did what he did was partly my fault – my fault for being a nagging old shrew.

'Please don't be upset, Steph,' he says, his voice breaking a little, and I melt a tiny bit inside. 'We leave in two days. I'm sorry, you have no idea how sorry, but this way we can be back in plenty of time for Christmas. I'm gutted that I have to leave so early. You know I didn't want to leave you alone, but at least this way I won't miss it. I'll be there on Christmas morning when Henry wakes up.'

This does go some way towards softening the blow, as Mark knows I want him home for Christmas. Of the five Christmases that Henry has celebrated, Mark has missed all but two of them, and one of those was his first Christmas, when he was just two months old and didn't really take part in any of the festivities at all. I reassure Mark that it's all OK, that we will be fine without him, and when, with a sigh of relief in his voice, he asks if I have had a good day I decide not to mention lunch with Belinda, or the fact that she wants me to interview Melissa Davenport. If he is going to be leaving me, the last thing I want on his mind is her. He says goodbye and assures me he'll be home as soon as he can, promising to take Henry and I out for dinner tomorrow night as it's his last night before he leaves. I agree, and hang up, knowing in my heart that there's little chance of his making it home before midnight tonight, and probably little chance of us seeing him properly at all before he leaves us again.

I am just making myself a bowl of scrambled eggs when there is a light tapping at the front door. Nervously pulling my dressing gown tightly around my middle, I go to answer it and am relieved when it is just Lila standing on the doorstep, bundled up like a snowman. The temperature has risen a couple of degrees since the arctic weather this afternoon, but it is still bitterly cold outside and the inky night sky is full of clouds, pregnant and heavy with the first snowfall of the season.

'Lila! God, you must be freezing. Come in.' I stand to one side of the front door to let her squeeze in, her bulky winter coat making her face seem like that of a petite china doll, peering out from underneath her fur hood.

'It is freezing out there; there's definitely snow on the way.' She grins at me, pushing back her hood with one hand, her other hand clutching on to what appears to be a black sack filled with something oddly shaped.

'How are you feeling now?' Lila follows me through into the cosy living room, hanging her coat on the stair banister as she passes. I have lit the open fire that sits in the centre of the room, and Lila stands to warm her hands in front of it, the smell of coal and the pine cones I chucked onto the open flames filling the room.

'Oh, better.' I smile. I shed a few – OK, a lot – of tears after my phone call with Mark, the thought of the next few weeks alone almost too much to bear, what with finding work, although I know Belinda will help where she can, making sure Henry is settling in

OK at school and, obviously, the seemingly never-ending rounds of morning sickness. That, and spending my evenings alone, in the dark, without Mark there. It doesn't matter how many times he goes away; it never gets any easier. 'It just sneaks up on me a bit at times. It turns out that morning sickness is not just confined to mornings.' I don't elaborate any further, not wanting to discuss Mark's imminent departure or to delve into the deeper side of how I am feeling about this pregnancy, the nervousness I feel about what happens next, once the baby is born. How I don't want a repeat of what happened when I had Henry.

'Well, I'm pleased you're feeling a bit better. I was a bit worried about you earlier, you looked so peaky,' Lila says, leaning forward to squeeze both my hands. 'I have a little something for you and Henry, something I hope you're going to like.' She reaches down by her feet to the large black sack I noticed her carrying earlier. 'I made it myself, from the plants I have growing in my garden. Anything else that I didn't have growing I went out and picked. It's unique, made just for you and there's not another one like it in the world.' She is like a small child, her enthusiasm glowing across her face and her dark hair shining in the glow of the firelight. I can't help it – her eagerness is infectious, and I lean forward, suddenly desperate to see what is in the sack. A broad grin sweeps across Lila's face and I find myself mirroring it back to her as she slowly withdraws a hand-made Christmas wreath from the sack. It is exquisite, a perfectly woven circle of moss, holly, ivy and mistletoe, with a few winter flowers peeping out here and there to give it some extra colour. It is absolutely perfect. Tears spring to my eyes as I hold my hands out for it and Lila lays it gently in my palms.

'Oh, Lila. It's gorgeous – and you made it all yourself? You are clever. It's beautiful and Henry is going to be so pleased when he sees it.' I turn it over in my hands, spotting more flowers tucked in underneath. It really is a work of art.

'Oh, don't be silly. It's nothing, just a little something I knocked up.' Lila smiles at me bashfully, a faint blush staining her cheeks.

'It's not nothing – it's gorgeous. You should sell these; you could make a fortune.'

'No. No, I don't want to sell them. I just thought… well, I knew you weren't feeling too great. It's just a little something; call it a welcome-to-the-neighbourhood gift. This is the first one I've made this year.' She leans over to tuck in a stray piece of wayward mistletoe. Her words make me smile, and the way she is so enthusiastic about things reminds me a little of Tessa.

'Well, I'm touched, Lila. I really am. This is a really lovely gift; it's so thoughtful of you.' I lean forward, surprising myself as I give her a small peck on the cheek. Not a Steph thing to do at all, but maybe I am learning to open up to others; maybe I am making an effort to make new friends. I resolve to make sure I note this feeling in my diary later; the warm feeling that comes from a budding new friendship. It's been so long I've forgotten what it felt like, to let someone new in, to start trusting again.

'I just thought maybe you needed a bit of cheering up, that's all,' Lila says, sitting back on her heels where she is perched on the floor in front of the fire. 'You looked really miserable when you came home earlier, and I thought maybe the morning sickness was getting to you a little bit.' She is bashful, looking down at her hands, and I lean over and give one a quick squeeze.

'I'm fine, honestly, but I do appreciate the sentiment. I was feeling a bit miserable earlier, you're right, but you already left me something to cheer me up. I got your little posy and the note when Henry came home. It was a lovely thought, thank you.'

Lila cocks her head at me quizzically, as if I have said something that makes no sense to her whatsoever.

'What do you mean, Steph? What posy?'

I laugh a little nervously, and stand to walk through into the kitchen where I have left the small posy of flowers in a vase on the windowsill, still tied together with raffia, the note tied to one side.

'These.' I put the posy down on the coffee table in front of where Lila sits. 'They were on the doorstep when my mum brought Henry home from her house.

The note says "a little something from my garden to cheer you up". I just assumed it was from you as I had seen you in the garden when I came home.' I look down at the innocent-looking flowers, laid in the small circle of water that has dripped from their stems, a cold shiver beginning to prickle at the base of my spine. Lila inspects the posy before she turns to me, a serious look crossing her perfect features.

'Sorry, Steph. They're not from me. I was out in the garden when you came home, collecting holly and ivy for the wreath I made you. I've never seen these flowers before in my life.'

CHAPTER SIX

The thought of the small posy of flowers weighs heavy on my mind all the next day, or rather the idea of someone who isn't Lila leaving gifts on the porch while I was sleeping does. After reassuring Lila what felt like a hundred times that I was OK, that the idea of someone sneaking on to my porch while I was asleep and leaving a present for me did not creep me out in the slightest, she left, promising she would keep an eye out to see if anything else was left.

'Honestly, Lila, it's fine. I promise I'm not concerned about it in the slightest. It's just odd, that's all, that I saw you, then when I woke up the posy was on the doorstep and I just immediately assumed you had left it for me.' I brush her concern away as best that I can, although inside my mind is racing, fearful that the one person I don't want to find me has found me.

'Well, I kind of wish I had now. At least then you wouldn't need to be worried.' Biting her lip, Lila tries to smile at me, as she stands on the doorstep to go home.

'I'll keep a look-out, OK? You don't need to worry about anything, especially if Mark's not here.'

Despite her reassurances, though, the posy sneaks into my mind on and off all day. Is it not just a little bit weird? That whoever left it didn't sign their name? Could it be *him*? Is it Melissa, trying to freak me out? I scribble a quick note in my diary, just a few sentences documenting how I feel about it, how uneasy the idea of it has made me, in the hope that if I write it down it might get it out of my system a little bit.

Mark gets home before six, a hugely unexpected surprise despite his reassurances last night that he would be home in time for dinner. I am trying to wedge a huge black sack of rubbish into the outside bin when he parks alongside the kerb, giving the horn a little toot. I smile as he gets out of the car and immediately drops his bag on the pavement to help squash the black sack into the bin.

'Thank you.' I kiss him. 'You're my knight in shining armour.'

His brow creases and he looks apologetic.

'You might think that now, but not for long. I booked us a table at that swanky pub on the other side of the Heath tonight as a surprise, but my sister can't babysit now. Jacob's got chickenpox. It was meant to be a surprise. I'm sorry, Steph. I wanted us to have a really nice last evening together to make up for my leaving early, but it looks like I've cocked it up again.'

He looks so disappointed. I reach for his hand to tell him it doesn't matter when a voice calls, 'Steph? How are you feeling?' Lila appears from the other side of the hedge that shields one side of our front garden from the road. 'Hello, Mark – nice to see you.' She flashes a quick smile at him and leans over to peck me on the cheek.

'I'm fine, feeling much better actually.' I smile at her, and hope that she won't mention the posy before I have a chance to speak to Mark myself. 'Mark was just saying he'd booked us a meal out tonight, but the babysitter has cancelled. It's his last night before he leaves for Paraguay,' I explain.

'Well, don't miss out on an evening together for the sake of a babysitter! Why don't I sit with Henry for you? It'll only be for a few hours, won't it? You two should spend your last evening together, go and have a good time. Honestly. I don't mind.'

'What about Henry?' I ask, a frown creasing my brow. 'I mean, I'm grateful for the offer, Lila, but Henry doesn't know you that well. And he'll want to see Mark.' I know he wants to spend Mark's last evening with him as well. He's sensitive, and every time Mark goes away it disrupts his routine for days on end. It's always much easier if we have all spent the last evening together.

'We'll stay home and put him to bed together like usual, then we can go out for dinner on our own, just the two of us.' Mark snakes an arm around my waist and smiles at Lila. 'Thank you, Lila, we really do appreciate the offer. Steph, don't worry, Henry will be fine – we'll make sure he's settled before we leave. Come on, let Lila and I do this one thing for you.'

Lila nods at me, and that's it. Settled.

Mark is so pleased with himself for arranging tonight; I don't have the heart to tell him I don't really want to go. I know if I make excuses about not knowing Lila that well, or that I'm tired and would rather stay home, he'll start thinking I'm slipping back into the way I was before, when everything was an effort, and it was easier to let the black clouds blanket me from the outside world. I make my way upstairs, feeling crappy about getting so irritated with him. He's tried his hardest to sort out a lovely evening out, even booking a table and sorting the babysitting out with Lila – normally the things that I have to arrange – so why don't I feel more grateful? Because he's only done it because he's leaving us for weeks at a time? Because he asked Lila, someone who Henry really doesn't know that well, instead of just letting us have an evening at home? Because he cheated on me and broke my heart, and try as I might I just can't seem to get over it? I sigh, mentally kicking myself for being such a bitch and stand for a long time under a hot shower, trying to wash away my blues.

Henry is settled, Lila arrives on time and so does our cab. Before I know it we are sitting opposite each other in a restaurant that tries to model itself as a homely, English pub, but instead of dishing up the more traditional plates of fish and chips or pie and mash, it serves everything on wooden boards or pieces of slate, chips balanced up like a greasy, dripping tower. I have resolved, while I was getting ready, not to mention the posy of flowers to Mark, worried he'll think I'm being paranoid, but now, sitting here in the cosy pub, firelight glowing and filling the room with warm orange light, I decide I don't want to keep it a secret from him. I don't want him to leave for weeks with a secret between us, however small and insignificant it might end up being.

'Mark … yesterday someone left something on the doorstep.' I watch him carefully, to see how he reacts. I'm always conscious that he does have a tendency to think I jump to the wrong conclusion all the time, especially as he knows my history. He spears a forkful of salad before replying.

'Something? Like what?'

'Well, flowers. With a little note.'

'That's nice. Who were they from? They weren't from me, I'm afraid, babe. You know flowers aren't really my thing. I'd buy you something far more exciting than a bunch of flowers. Sorry, I'm starving.' He shovels the forkful of food into his mouth and I have to turn my face away for just a second.

'That's the thing. I don't know who they were from. I assumed they were from Lila, but she said she'd never seen them before in her life.' His eyes meet mine across the table and he gently lays his fork down.

'Maybe you've got a secret admirer?' He takes my hand in his large, warm one. 'Are you worried about it, Steph? Is that it?'

I sigh, and try to shake my head.

'I don't think so. Maybe. Why would someone leave them on the porch, when I was home asleep, instead of just knocking on the door? I just worry it might be somehow connected to what happened … you know … before.' I suck in a deep breath and blink back tears as I tell him exactly what the note said. He fiddles with his wedding ring, twisting it slowly around his finger. He must have lost weight; it never used to move so easily on his hand.

'Maybe they didn't want to wake you. It just seems to me like someone genuinely being nice, that's all. Steph, you worry too much. It's not to do with Llewellyn Chance, I promise you. Whoever it was just wanted to cheer you up, that's all. The sender might have even got the wrong door for all you know; they might have been meant for Lila. Please try not to worry.' I drop his hand. Maybe they were meant for Lila, but something inside me says they were meant for me, and that's not necessarily a good thing.

'Maybe I am reading too much into it all. Maybe you're right. I'm sorry; let's not spoil your last night at home. Let's order dessert.' Not wanting to talk about it any further I pick up the dessert menu and study it carefully, until Mark gently pushes it down away from my face.

'Do you want me to check? Make sure that he's still inside?' His eyes search my face and I shake my head gently.

'No. No, it's OK, they would have told me if he wasn't. Please, Mark, let's just leave it.'

'Steph, you are still seeing Dr Bradshaw, aren't you? You'll keep seeing him while I'm gone?'

'What? Yes, of course.' My face flames and I dip forward, allowing my hair to fall over my face. I have cancelled my last two appointments with Dr Bradshaw behind Mark's back. I don't really need to see him, I'm sure I don't. I am feeling much better and writing in the diary helps a lot.

'Please make sure you keep going, Steph. It's important, especially after last time. I don't want us to have to go through it all again, and I know you don't want to. I love you, Steph. I just want you to be OK.'

'I said, yes, didn't I?' My tone is sharp and Mark seems to realise that it's time to drop it. Mark calls Dr Bradshaw a counsellor, but we both know he's not. We both know he's a therapist, a head doctor, whatever you want to call him. We both know that Mark wants me to keep on seeing him because, even though I know he loves me, even though I know he regrets what he did, deep down Mark thinks I am still a *teensy* bit crazy. The mood changes after that and we decide not to bother with dessert. Arriving home earlier than planned, Mark tries to give Lila some money for babysitting, but she waves him away, laughing, saying it was her pleasure and that she doesn't get out enough as it is. I smile weakly at her and use checking on Henry as an excuse to make my way upstairs, out of the way of their banter, too tired to pretend tonight.

As I tiptoe into Henry's room and perch on the end of his bed, the nightlight casting a warm glow over his perfect features, he opens his eyes and smiles at me.

'Hi, Mummy,' he says, rolling over to face me.

'Hey, baby.' I lean down and kiss him on the forehead. 'What are you doing awake? You should be asleep by now.'

'I woke up and I couldn't get back to sleep. Lila made me a hot chocolate and read me some stories. Next time she says she's going to teach me how to play dominoes.'

'Well, that was very kind of her. You need to go to sleep now, sweetie – it's school in the morning.' He makes a face as I pull him in tight for one last hug, inhaling the sleepy, biscuity scent of him. A noise in the doorway startles me and I turn to see Mark's profile outlined in the shadowy hallway, so I stand and walk over to him, leaning my head on his broad chest. He wraps me in his strong arms and we gaze down at our finest achievement, our sweet, tiny boy, who gives a little sigh and slips easily back into sleep.

'I'm sorry for bringing up Dr Bradshaw tonight, Steph. I know you're still seeing him and I know you're much better, I just can't help worrying about you, that's all.' Mark says to me as we get into bed.

'Honestly, Mark, you have nothing to worry about, I promise.' I fluff my pillow behind me and change the subject. 'Henry seems to have hit it off with Lila, that's a good sign, right? Maybe it'll be good for us when you're not here, having Lila across the street. I won't feel so isolated.'

'Definitely. And I know we weren't going to talk about it any more, Steph, but I really do think that your friendship with Lila is a sign that things are going to work out OK. The fact that you're willing to let someone new in speaks volumes, after everything we've gone through together. After everything *you've* gone through. I'm proud of you.' He kisses the top of my head, and although I want to ask him to elaborate, to tell me how everything is going to work out OK in the end, I relax into the kiss and murmur my agreement. I can sort of see what he's getting at – after what happened before, then after Henry and the problems that I had, followed by Mark's indiscretion (oh, it was so much more than an indiscretion, but how can I say any more than what I have done already?) I shut myself off completely from the rest of the world. I was so terrified that if I let someone new in that they would somehow end up hurting me that I just stopped doing it. I pushed away all the friends that I did have, and refused to make any new ones, cutting myself off from the outside world. The only one who stuck with me is Tessa, my oldest friend. The one who already knows everything that there is to know about me, who knows all about the darkness that surrounds me and refuses to budge no matter how hard I push. She was the one who was there to hold my hand and help me pick up the pieces when everything fell apart around me when I was fifteen. She was the one I went to when I couldn't talk to my mum about what had happened. She was the one who held me as I cried, when I thought I would never ever feel normal again. So maybe Mark does have a point – maybe my friendship with Lila does show that I'm starting to open up again, that I'm ready to let people in, but the posy still plays on my mind. I decide to make an appointment with Dr. Bradshaw first thing tomorrow morning, just to keep Mark happy.

CHAPTER SEVEN

Dr Bradshaw's office is cold in both senses of the word. I sit in the reception area, avoiding eye contact with the other patients waiting for their turn to be seen. The heating is switched off, as is usual for this office, despite the fact that it's December. It's been snowing on and off for the last week, the first snowfall just having had time to turn to slush and ice before the arrival of the next deluge. I shiver slightly, pulling my thick cardigan tighter around my body, and give a small smile as the receptionist does the same, pulling the sleeves of her jumper down over her hands. The décor doesn't help the chill either – walls painted with a pale, frosty light blue add to the chilly feel, and hard, plastic chairs mean no one sits comfortably while they wait. You would think for the amount of money Mark is paying there would be a little bit of luxury awarded.

'Stephanie Gordon?'

I look up as the receptionist calls my name and gestures towards the closed door at the far end of the corridor.

'Dr Bradshaw will see you now.'

I smile my thanks at her and start the walk down the brightly lit corridor, painted with the same chilly blue, my heart beginning to hammer nervously in my chest. I hate these appointments, constantly feeling as though each one is a test I must pass to be able to carry on with my life, even though Dr Bradshaw is always perfectly pleasant. I give a tiny tap on the door and push it open, making my way inside.

'Steph. How are you?' Dr Bradshaw swivels around in his chair and gives me a warm smile. Around my age, with warm, crinkly eyes and a neatly trimmed, bang on trend beard, he is ridiculously good-looking for a psychiatrist – not at all what I had imagined when I first began seeing him. Not at all what Mark would have expected either, if he had ever managed to come along with me.

'I'm OK, I suppose.' Handsome or not, I am always nervous when I see him, anxious to make sure I say the right thing so he doesn't decide to cart me off to the loony bin.

'You missed your last two sessions – is there any reason for that?' He picks up a smart, leather-bound book and a fountain pen, poised and ready to write down my answers. When I asked him once why he didn't get with the times and use an iPad, he told me he preferred to do things the old-fashioned way, conscious that some of his patients might be put off by the modern technology. Another point in his favour for being so considerate. Handsome AND kind, I'm sure he's made someone a wonderful husband.

'Just busy. Henry has started school and I'm still working freelance so everything has been a bit hectic. No other reason.'

'And what about the pregnancy? How's that going?'

I purse my lips at him. I didn't even know I was pregnant the last time I managed to make it to an appointment.

'Mark told you, didn't he? Whatever happened to patient confidentiality?'

'Well, Steph, that works one way, I'm afraid. Mark is welcome to give me any information he thinks is relevant to our sessions, but you can be assured that anything that you say to me in here stays in here. I won't discuss anything said here with anybody else.'

I sigh, reluctant to speak about it, but now Dr Bradshaw knows about it, I know he won't let it lie.

'I'm scared, OK? I'm scared that what happened after I had Henry will happen again.' Tears spring to my eyes and I reach across his desk for the box of Kleenex that he keeps, just for these moments. Dr Bradshaw eyes me coolly from across the desk – tears mean nothing to him; he must see them all day long.

'There's nothing to be scared of, Steph. We know about it this time and we can deal with it. There is no need to spend this pregnancy in a state of fear. I'm here to help you, Mark's here; we're all ready to support you and make sure we treat the post-natal depression before it manages to get a hold of you, OK?' I nod, shredding the tissue between my fingers.

'Are you still writing in the diary?' he asks, as he scribbles in his posh journal and I nod. 'And how are you feeling in yourself? Are you worried about anything else, aside from the new baby?'

I take a deep breath, knowing the decision I make now could affect what happens next. It could affect whether Dr Bradshaw decides to prescribe more pills for me (no, thank you) or whether he lets me try to make sense of it all on my own, with his help, some cognitive behaviour therapy to talk it all out. I decide to bite the bullet. It's just one event and, now I think about it, in the safety of the doctor's office, it's not even that much of a big deal.

'Someone left something on the doorstep. Some flowers. I thought I knew who they were from, a new friend I've made.' *See*, I want to say to him, *I am trying, I'm trying so hard to be normal.* 'I asked her about them but she said she had never seen them before, that they definitely weren't from her.'

'And what do you think?' He raises his eyebrows at me, steepling his fingers and resting his chin on them in a typical therapist *listening* pose.

'*I don't know*,' I stress, searching his eyes to see if I can tell what he is thinking. 'I want them to just be a goodwill gesture from someone who is concerned about me. I don't want to think there's anything sinister about them but … it made me feel uneasy, that's all. They were left on the porch while I was asleep. I don't like the thought of someone creeping around outside the house while I'm there – why not knock on the door? But I'm sure it's fine, probably a neighbour or something.' As I speak I realise I sound paranoid, so I quickly backtrack, trying to convince the doctor (and myself, if I'm honest) that it really is no big deal. A bubble of anxiety rises in my chest and I swallow hard, trying to force it back down.

'OK. Steph, we've been through this before, haven't we? People know now that you are pregnant, correct? And Mark tells me you've been quite poorly with it – so, I think it probably is a case of someone having heard you've been a little under the weather and just wanting to give you a little boost, something to cheer you up. It's easy to see things that aren't there, especially when you've suffered with depression issues before and have battled through it.' He gives me a sympathetic smile, and resumes his scratching in his notebook.

I nod, blinking back the last of my tears. I must be seeing things that aren't there, if Dr Bradshaw thinks it's innocent. I realise this is the reason I made my appointment – I wanted reassurance from someone who isn't Mark that I'm not going crazy; that there is nothing in it, just a kind gesture from someone who would prefer to remain anonymous. I thank Dr Bradshaw, making a show of looking at my watch to say our time is up – usually his line, but today I'm taking advantage of it and getting out of here.

Ten minutes later I'm standing on the pavement outside the doctor's office, wrapping my coat around me against the bitter chill of the wind. I have made another appointment in two weeks' time, but I'm honestly not sure if I'll keep it. I feel a lot better now I've had some reassurance that the posy is nothing to be scared of, and Dr Bradshaw seems to believe my assertions that I am OK dealing with things. I feel lighter than I have done in days. As I step off the kerb I hear someone shout.

'Steph! Steph, wait!'

I turn, my hair whipping across my face, and see Laurence striding towards me, cheeks reddened by the cold.

'I thought that was you! How are you?' He stoops to kiss my cheek.

'Laurence. I didn't see you there – I'm very well, thank you. Just on my way home.'

'Me too. Let me walk with you.' He looks back over his shoulder towards the building I have just left, and I feel my cheeks flush red as I hope Laurence doesn't realise where I have just come from. To my dismay he nods towards the building,

'Have you just been in there?' he asks. 'Research, I'm guessing? From what I've heard he's a right old quack. I'll be interested to see what article you write on him.' He gives a little laugh and grasps my elbow gently as we cross the road. It's been a long time since Mark remembered to do anything as gentlemanly as that.

'Erm, right, yes. Research. That's it.' I feel flustered, both by his words and the fact that his hand is burning right though my coat to my skin. As we reach the other side of the road and he pulls his hand away, I fancy I can still feel his touch, branded onto my elbow. We walk slowly together towards home, and I feel odd, as I did the first time I met him, like there's something comforting and familiar about him. Like he knows me completely already, while I know nothing about him. I realise after a moment that he has been talking and I've not taken in a word he has said.

'I'm sorry, what did you say? I was in a world of my own.'

'I said, Mark has asked me to keep an eye on you and Henry while he's away. That's if it's OK with you? My being next door and everything.'

He looks down at me, eyes searching my face and I feel yet another blush rise to my cheeks. What the hell is wrong with me? Without thinking, I prickle back at him, 'I'm a grown woman, Laurence; I hardly think that anyone needs to keep an eye on me. I've managed on my own for years without Mark around, so I'm sure I can manage another three weeks or so.'

'Right, OK. Well, the offer is there if you need anything.'

Immediately, I feel like a bitch for snapping at him, disappointed in myself for letting things slip, for giving in to the natural instinct to push people away. Mark obviously wants to make sure we're OK while he's not there, and Laurence has very kindly offered to help. It's not his fault I feel so resentful towards Mark for leaving us so soon after promising me a fresh start, even though I know deep down that Mark doesn't want to leave.

'Listen, Laurence, I'm sorry. That came out all wrong. I'd be glad to have you keep an eye on us while Mark is away.' The words come out before I can even think about stopping them. 'Why don't you come for dinner tonight? I can cook us something, nothing too fancy, and you can update me on all the scandal from the financial world.' He gives a laugh, and tucks his arm into mine as we turn into our street.

'Sounds perfect. I'll be there.'

I am nervous before Laurence arrives, making sure the beef is turned right down low so it doesn't burn and fussing with my hair, which has been flattened by the wind on our walk home. At eight p.m. sharp the doorbell rings, and smoothing my hair down for the fiftieth time I pull the door open, not expecting to see the person standing on the doorstep.

'Lila! What are you doing here? Is everything OK?' I stand in the doorway, instead of pulling the door wide open as I usually would.

'Yes, everything's fine. I just brought this over – I thought we could chill out together this evening, girls' night in?' She waves a DVD in my face, and makes as if to come in. I hold out a hand, resting it gently on her forearm.

'Lila, wait. I'm sorry but … I can't. Not tonight.' Lila's face falls, and I feel terribly guilty. She has been so good to me and I hate to let her down, but even so, we hadn't made any arrangements.

'Oh. That's a shame.' She gives me a small smile. 'I just thought that … well, I thought maybe you might quite like some adult company while Mark's away. But it's fine, another time.' I go to explain myself, to say it's nothing personal, but before I can say anything, Laurence appears behind her. Lila turns, and seeing him behind her, gives a little nod. 'Oh, I see,' she says, in a flat voice. 'You've already made plans. I'm sorry, Steph, I didn't realise.' Dejected, she turns to leave.

'Lila, wait,' I say, feeling like a total heel. 'We're just having dinner. Laurence is looking after us while Mark is away, that's all. How about you join us? Or you and I could get together tomorrow evening?' It'll be the last thing I feel like tomorrow. After Laurence coming over this evening and two articles to write tomorrow the chances are I'll be exhausted by the time tomorrow evening rolls around, but I hate seeing the disappointed look on her face.

'Oh, no, don't be silly, it's fine. It was only a DVD and a bar of chocolate. But tomorrow, yes. That'll be lovely.' Lila turns on her heel and I watch her make her way back up the slippery, icy path, glittering with frost, before gently closing the door.

CHAPTER EIGHT

I wake up early the next morning, the previous evening with Laurence on my mind. I had forgotten how nice it was to spend an evening with someone who is mentally present, as well as physically. Mark always has to rush off to check work emails, or make phone calls, leaving me feeling as though our spending a quiet evening together is inconveniencing him, forcing him to take time out of his busy schedule. It didn't feel like that with Laurence – he listened to me without comment, without making me feel as though I needed to weigh up every word before I spoke. I am always so conscious of what I say to Mark, wary of saying the wrong thing in case he thinks I'm sliding backwards to how it was before. There was none of that yesterday evening – I felt relaxed, not at all on edge. I forgot how nice it is just to be Steph, not Mark's wife, or Henry's mum, just me, spending the evening with someone who wanted to be there, who didn't have a million other things he needed to be doing. I leave the house early, in the hope I can catch Lila before she goes out anywhere. I'm still not entirely sure what she actually does for a living. Despite us becoming so close over the past few weeks, every time I ask her she brushes me away, saying her job is terribly boring and often changing the subject. I've come to the conclusion that either she has a terribly rich family and has no need to work but is too embarrassed to tell me, or she really does have some rubbish boring job, like stuffing envelopes from home or something.

I ring her doorbell, even though it's only eight a.m., and keep an eye on Henry as he whizzes backwards and forwards on his scooter across the garden paths. I am about to turn and walk away when suddenly the door is wrenched open and Lila appears in her dressing gown, hair tousled as if she has just got out of bed.

'Oh, God, Lila, I'm sorry, I thought you would be up – did I wake you?' I pull an apologetic face, feeling awful. There's nothing I hate more than being woken up. She smiles at me, pale-faced, pulling her dressing gown tighter around her body.

'No, it's all right. Are you OK?'

'Yes, it's just ... well, I just wanted to apologise about last night. I would have loved a girls' night in but I had already invited Laurence for dinner and didn't want to be rude. I didn't realise you were home alone or I would have invited you too. How about lunch today?' Sod the two articles, I think, I can write them tonight when Henry is in bed if I meet Lila for lunch.

'Oh, don't be silly, you funny thing.' She smiles at me, a broad grin filled with perfect white teeth, at once much more her normal self, and pats my arm. 'I just had horrendous PMT and thought we could indulge ourselves with a chocolate-filled girly night, but it's fine. I came home and ate the chocolate myself!' She gives a little chuckle and leans against the doorframe, her stance making it clear she's not going to invite me in. Although she seems her normal chirpy self now, there is an air about her that's a little off and I guess she is still a bit miffed about last night, even if she says she's not. I give her a small smile back, before I say, 'Well, good. I was worried I had offended you. Shall we meet for lunch? Or are you busy?' I realise I really am worried that I have offended her – now that we seem to be getting along so well I'd hate to have upset her.

'Gosh, no. It takes far more than that to offend me!' She gives another tinkly laugh. 'And I'm sure poor Laurence needed the company far more than I did. Listen, I don't want to be rude but I must dash, I'm late as it is.' Lila reaches to close the front door, still not responding to my invitation to lunch. I decide not to mention it again – maybe she is offended, despite protesting otherwise?

'OK. Well, as long as we're OK? I'll let you get on. I need to get Henry to school.' I move reluctantly from the doorstep and make my way down the path to where Henry is waiting impatiently, scuffing his feet backwards and forwards.

'Oh, and Steph – how about one o'clock at the Hole in the Wall?'

I look back and grin, relieved that Lila is not cross with me after all.

'Perfect.'

I drop Henry off and am threading my way through children and parents, out of the playground, when a hand lands on my arm and stops me.

'You're Steph Gordon, aren't you? The new mum?' A woman moves in front of me, blocking the path ahead, so that I have no option but to stop and speak to her. She is petite, with hair in a shiny, black bob and a full face of perfect make-up, despite the early hour. Straight away she makes me feel grungy and lazy, with my curls once again bundled up in a topknot and no make-up on.

'Yes? Errr, I mean, yes, that's me.' I have no idea who she is, presumably the mother of one of the other children, hopefully a child that Henry has made friends with. She sticks a hand out for me to shake.

'We haven't been properly introduced. Jasmine Hale. Head of the PTA.'

'Oh, right. Nice to meet you. I'm sorry, but I'm kind of on a deadline …' I go to walk past her but she effectively blocks my way again.

'The PTA are always on the lookout for new members, you know. I'm sure you would bring some marvellous qualities to our little group. The school needs all the support it can get.'

'Oh, I'm sorry, I don't really think—'

'We raise a lot of money for the school; it's so nice for the children to have lovely equipment to play on, don't you think? But of course, we all have to pull our weight and make sure we do our bit. You'll be at our next meeting, a week on Wednesday, won't you? We are in *dire* need of some new blood and I just know you'll be perfect.' She looks at me expectantly, waiting for a response.

'Well, I'd love to, but the thing is … well, I work from home and my husband works away a lot. I'm not sure I would be able to commit—'

'Oh, don't be silly; everybody can spare an hour here and there. It's not a huge commitment, and of course it benefits the *children*. All of the children.'

She is so bossy and confident I'll do what she wants, completely ignoring the fact that I am desperately trying to turn her down. She's like a dog with a bone. I try to take a bit of a firmer stance with her.

'Jasmine, thank you for the invitation but I'm really not in a position to commit to *anything* right now. You know, Mark not being home and everything ...' I trail off. She smiles at me, head on one side.

'Oh, you poor thing. Yes, that must be terribly tough on you and … Henry, isn't it? It must be especially hard for him, poor little boy, not having his daddy home every night. Well, I'm sure we can come up with something. It is *so nice* to see all the PTA children playing together, and they all become *such* good friends. Catch up later.' She leans forward and kisses the air next to my cheek, sweeping off to join a gaggle of yummy mummies in the corner of the playground, all of whom have been watching our exchange with goggle-eyed interest. I watch as they close ranks around her, all except one, a slim woman with dark hair who stands a little way off to one side. She gives me a small smile and I smile uncertainly back, still unsure as to what actually just happened. Did Jasmine just insinuate that Henry doesn't have any friends, and now that will be my fault as all the PTA children play together and my refusal to join means Henry won't be included? Or am I just being paranoid? The gaggle of mums all turn simultaneously as I turn to leave the playground, Jasmine waving one gloved hand at me as I leave.

I am still unsure hours later when I walk into the Hole in the Wall to meet Lila. This is only Henry's first year at school, so I am feeling my way a little bit when it comes to playground etiquette, especially when it comes to things like joining the PTA. Maybe I should have just said yes, if that's what all the other mums do. Anxiety about being seen to fit in playing on my mind, I take a deep breath as I walk into the pub, casting my eyes about quickly to see if Lila has already arrived. She is sitting at the best table in the pub, a tiny booth in the far corner, near the roaring open fire, her coat hanging on the back of her chair and a glass of red wine in front of her. She smiles as she sees me and gets to her feet.

'You look frozen, you poor darling. Here, take my seat, it's closer to the fire.' She gets up and kisses me on the cheek, then shuffles round to the other side of the table and I gratefully take her seat. It's only a short walk to the pub, but outside the weather is still below freezing, an icy wind cutting through to my bones.

'It's much warmer in here – I'm so glad we could get together. And I'm sorry about yesterday evening.' She waves my apology away as I pick up the menu and quickly glance over it before opting for my usual jacket potato – it's all I can keep down at the moment. While we wait for our food to come, I tell Lila about my morning, and how Jasmine Hale had accosted me in the playground.

'She sounds like a perfect horror.' Lila laughs, as I come to the end of my story. 'Don't worry, Steph, Henry is a delightful little boy. He'll make friends. It just takes a while at that age. She sounds like she's just a bit enthusiastic, that's all.'

I bask in the glow of her reassurance, relieved we seem to be back on track and that she hasn't taken offence at my turning her down the previous evening. I realise Lila is talking to me, and I've missed what she's saying.

'I'm sorry, what was that? I was in my own little world for a moment.'

'I said I was just like Henry as a little girl. Quite insular, not the most popular girl in the class. I was shy and really struggled to make friends, and my family wasn't exactly the most … well, never mind. Look at me now – totally different.' She takes a sip of her wine. 'I have a lovely house, a gorgeous boyfriend and I'm having a glorious lunch with a good friend. Winning at life, don't you think?' She grins at me and chinks her glass against mine.

'Speaking of which, how is Joe?' Despite the close friendship we have developed, I am still yet to meet Joe. He's rarely there, spending even less time at home than Mark if that's possible, and when he is there, he seems to leave the house and return at odd times, meaning I haven't quite managed to spot him yet. I'm guessing that Mark has met him, after Lila's reference to her and Joe talking to him in the garden, but the man remains a mystery to me.

'Oh, he's fine.' Lila waves her fork around airily. 'Busy, busy. You know. He's working hard, as usual. I told you he's a photographer, right? He goes away on location for shoots, kind of like Mark. That's why he's not around much. You'll meet him next time he's back, I'll make sure of it.' Another thing we have in common, although I didn't realise Joe was a photographer. The conversation moves on to our respective other halves and how easy it is to seem to go for days without seeing them, they are so busy. We finish lunch and I realise that, for the first time in a long time, I have enjoyed myself. I don't feel sick; I've laughed until my stomach hurt at Lila and her witticisms; and it's been lovely not to feel so anxious about everything, just for a brief time. It's like how things used to be between me and Tessa, when she still lived close by, and I realise how much I've missed having a close girlfriend. We split the bill and Lila surprises me by telling me she is going to come with me to pick Henry up from school.

'Are you sure? You don't have to, you know.'

'I'm coming.' Lila's voice is firm as she winds a colourful scarf around her neck. 'I want to see Henry, and this afternoon has been so lovely, why shouldn't we string it out a bit longer?'

'Why not, indeed?' Smiling, I link my arm though hers, and as she pushes her hair behind her ears I notice she is wearing a pair of beautiful tiny diamond studs.

'Beautiful earrings; I have a pair just like them,' I say, smiling at her as a faint blush rises to her cheeks. One thing I have noticed about my new friend is that she is not very good at accepting compliments, and blushes like a fiend every time she receives one. It's sweet, really.

'They were my mother's,' she says. 'They're the last thing she gave me before she died. Now, come on, let's go and get Henry.' Lila gives one of her tinkly laughs, and we stride out of the restaurant, down the hill towards the school.

Henry is delighted to see that Lila has come with me to fetch him and shows off on his scooter, doing little bunny hops and jumping on and off the kerb while she claps her hands in delight. He takes her over to meet his teacher, who seems utterly charmed by her, just like everybody else, and I can't help but feel a little bit of pride that this shiny, beautiful, dazzling creature has chosen me – dowdy, permanently sick, tired me – to be her friend. As we leave through the front gate, I point out Jasmine Hale to Lila, discreetly of course, but Jasmine spots me and jogs over.

'Steph – lovely to see you.' She air kisses my cheeks on both sides. 'Have you had any more thoughts about what we talked about this morning?'

'Sorry, Jasmine, I haven't had a chance. Let me wait until Mark gets home. I might be able to help then?' I cross my fingers inside my coat pocket that I have said the right thing.

'Oh, of course, I forgot that your husband isn't around. Such a shame. Well, we can maybe speak about it then, if you have time, of course.' She smiles sweetly, before jogging lightly back to her friends, while I am left wondering whether she meant it, or if sarcasm laces her reply. Lila shrugs at me, and we walk out together, her arm tucked through mine.

At the bottom of the hill, Henry waits outside the little convenience store, chocolate smeared across his mouth.

'Henry,' I scold, 'I told you not to scoot down the hill without us!'

'It's OK, Mrs Gordon, I kept an eye on him.' Mrs Spencer, the lollipop lady, appears next to me, lollipop in hand. 'He said you were just coming – got carried away, I expect.' She gives a little chuckle before returning to her post on the opposite side of the road.

'Henry, come here.' I crouch down to his level, meeting him face to face. 'That was naughty – you must *never* scoot away like that again.' Tears fill his eyes, making me feel awful, so I pull him in tight for a hug. 'Don't cry – it's done now, but you must never do it again. What's that around your mouth? Chocolate? Did Mrs Spencer give it to you? You shouldn't really take sweets from people, baby, even if you know them.'

'It wasn't Mrs Spencer, Mummy.' Henry's tears are forgotten now, and he takes his scooter back from where Lila stands, holding the handlebars in one hand. He starts to scoot slowly ahead of me, towards home. 'It was Mr P. You know, the shop man.' I turn back towards the window of the small convenience store, where the man who served me the other day, *Mr P.*, stands watching us through the grubby glass.

CHAPTER NINE

I am just getting ready to leave for my next appointment with Dr Bradshaw when the phone rings. I'm in two minds whether to answer it or not, seeing as I'm already well on my way to being late, but snatch up the receiver at the last minute in the hope that it's Mark. I've barely spoken to him since he left, what with the time difference and the fact he has to use a satellite phone in the more remote areas he finds himself in. It means he quite often can't get a signal, but we have emailed backwards and forwards when we can and I have managed to reassure him that, with Lila's help, everything at home is running smoothly in his absence. I pick up the receiver quickly before it can ring out, but it's not Mark's voice on the end. Instead, the warm, honey-rich tones of my best friend come down the line, immediately bringing a smile to my face.

'Tess! What time is it for you? It must be early … is everything OK?' I tuck a stray curl behind my ear and put my door keys back in my bag. Depending on what's going on with Tessa I'm probably not going to make it to my appointment. Too bad, but things are going really well and I am pretty sure that skipping this appointment won't make too much of a difference in the grand scheme of things, as long as Dr Bradshaw doesn't tell Mark.

'Everything's good, sweetie, really good. I just wanted to check in on you, what with Mark being away and all the rush up till Christmas. I know you hate doing all that stuff alone.' Her voice has picked up a slight transatlantic twang after living in New York for the past two years, something that still surprises me every time I speak to her. I'm so used to hearing the South London accent I grew up with, it's strange to hear the way she pronounces certain words after being away for what feels like forever, but in all honesty is really not that long.

'I'm OK. Mark's due back before Christmas and I can sort out presents and stuff. I'll be OK, I promise. I've made a couple of friends … they're helping.' I fall silent and wait for Tessa's reaction – she knows how hard I find it to let people in. She witnessed me fall apart, as a teenager and again after I had Henry – it was she who put me back together again. She was the one I went to when not even my own mother could talk to me. I miss her so much.

'Really, Steph? That's brilliant! I'm so glad you're settling in OK. I've been worried about you after everything that's happened, then Mark dragging you halfway across town. Tell me about these new friends.' I get Tessa to hang on the line a moment while I take my coat off – I definitely won't make it to Dr Bradshaw's office in time for my appointment now, but I make a mental note to call and make a new appointment as soon as I'm done talking to Tessa. I don't want him telling Mark I haven't been coming, not when we've both said we will make an effort to get our marriage back on track. I head into the kitchen and flick the kettle on as I tell her all about Lila and how we seem to have really become close these past few weeks. I tell her all about how good Lila is with Henry, and how supportive she has been, popping in and keeping me company while Mark has been gone. I realise as I'm speaking that Lila seems to be filling the shoes Tessa stepped out of when she left for New York. Then I mention Laurence, and she seizes on it.

'Laurence – who is he? You haven't mentioned him before. Is he handsome?' I laugh; Tessa has always been the same, completely incorrigible when it comes to men even though she has been in a stable relationship with the wonderful Pierre ever since moving to New York.

'Yes, handsome. But Tess, I really do like him. I mean, there's something about him, something that I don't think I should like, but I do. Like, in the wrong way.' The line goes quiet as Tessa abruptly stops laughing. I sigh, hating myself for feeling like this about Laurence, but Tessa is the only person I can talk to about it.

'Shit, Steph, that's massive. What are you going to do? What about Mark? I know Mark is a total shithead and there's nobody who dislikes him more than me but … God.'

'I know, I know. It's just silly – there's something about him that feels safe and familiar. He's a genuinely nice guy, I think. Mark went away and Laurence came over for dinner and he was just so … kind. He gets on so well with Henry; he even played some video game with him last night so I could finish off the dinner in peace. Mark never has time for that stuff with Henry at the moment. And he listened to me, Tess. He listened to me and he didn't tell me I was imagining stuff, or that I was being paranoid or overreacting. He didn't ask me if I had missed my appointments with the doctor; he just listened, and made me laugh. I enjoyed his company, that's all, and it seems like it's been a long time since I enjoyed Mark's company.' A single tear rolls down my cheek as I voice for the first time how I really feel about everything. I love Mark so much, and I desperately want us to work, but he ripped my heart out when he had the affair with Melissa. Tessa sighs, and I can picture her sitting at her desk, even though it's only seven o'clock in the morning for her, a coffee steaming in front of her as she runs her hands through her short, blonde hair.

'Steph, you've had a nightmare year. Mark's affair with Melissa pulled the rug out from under you in a split second, and then Mark moves you halfway across London for a "fresh start", away from everything you feel safe with – which he then decides is all sorted and buggers off to bloody Peru or wherever the hell he's gone. No wonder you're feeling a bit up in the air.

Add to that the fact you're pregnant and no one would blame you for feeling confused. You know Mark isn't my favourite person, but I do really think he loves you. He just made a mistake.'

'It's Paraguay,' I whisper into the phone, as tears course down my cheeks. Tessa always has a way of putting everything back into perspective, making sure I know that everything that happened was in no way my fault, and I love her so much for this.

'Paraguay, whatever, they're all the same to me. Now, don't worry. I don't think you're in love with Laurence or anything; you're just feeling a bit vulnerable. Just enjoy having someone around to look after you while Mark is gone. If he hadn't been such a prick in the first place none of this would ever have happened – you'd still be living in your old house with none of this upheaval. Is it all still hush-hush? I'm surprised the papers haven't got wind of anything.' Tessa is disparaging towards Mark – she always has been a bit. She always thought he was a bit stuck up, but since his affair with Melissa Davenport she really can't abide him. I suppose this is because she worked so hard to help me get back to my old self, especially after Henry was born and I was lost in a swirl of post-natal depression, then had to witness me fall apart again. I reassure her that nothing has got out in the papers, that hopefully it never will. I couldn't stand the smug looks disguised as sympathy at the school gates. Who could stand comparison with Melissa Davenport?

Certainly not me. I tell her about my lunch with Belinda and how the subject of interviewing Melissa came up.

'Oh, God. What did you say?' I hear the sharp intake of breath as Tessa lights a cigarette.

'I said no, of course, but it was tricky. You know Bel – she's always suspicious of everybody and everything. She caught me on the hop a little bit, but then I was sick, so she was more than happy to accept my excuse that I was too pregnant and poorly to do the interview.'

Tessa's laughter pours into my ear and I can't help but smile. It does seem quite funny when I look back on it – Bel asking me to do an interview and me rushing off to vomit. If only it hadn't been about *her.*

'Well, Lila sounds delightful too. It's been a long time since I left, Steph. I'm glad you've found someone to look after you while I'm not there.' Tessa's voice is quiet now, serious, and I know she really does care about me. She worries when I'm on my own, especially after she has been through so much with me.

'She is, she really is. But don't worry – she'll never replace you.'

'As if anyone ever could.'

With Tessa's laughter still ringing in my ears I hang up. I feel better for speaking to her; I always do. Friends since junior school, Tessa has always been the one to look after me, hold my hand when exam anxiety hit, reassure me that Mark really did like me in those early days (despite the fact she really wasn't keen on him), squeeze my hand and tell me I looked beautiful before following me down the aisle on my wedding day. Helping me through my darkest days, the first time everything fell apart around me, and then again years later after I had Henry and the post-natal depression hit me hard. I dial the number for Dr Bradshaw's office and make another appointment before I can change my mind – I owe it to Tessa, and to Mark, to try my hardest to make sure it doesn't drag me down again this time.

I notice a white envelope peeking out from underneath the front doormat as I am pushing my arms into the sleeves of my coat, ready to go and collect Henry from school. A shiver of alarm washes over me – I have been sitting at the kitchen table following my conversation with Tessa, trying to get my article finished before the deadline that is looming over me, and I never heard anybody approach the house. *This is just like the posy again*, I think, before shaking myself and giving myself a virtual slap on the cheek. *Don't be silly; it's just an envelope, a note, that's all it is.* Taking a deep breath, I bend to pick it up, sliding my fingernail under the flap and easing out a piece of cream card. Casting my eyes quickly over the typewritten font, I breathe a shaky sigh of relief and give a small laugh.

'Dear Mrs and Master Gordon,
Mr Laurence Cole requests the pleasure of your company
this afternoon (after the school run)' [I laugh at this, a

cheeky little aside into what is a very formal invitation]
**'for afternoon tea. There will be French fancies, and fizzy
pop for those of us that do not wish to take tea. Please
RSVP on your way past.'**

I splutter with laughter as I search for a pen to scrawl
across the back of the invitation. Everything I said to
Tessa is true – Laurence is a genuinely nice guy who's
just keeping an eye on things for us while Mark is away –
but my heart does beat a little faster at the thought of
seeing him later on today. I scribble a response on the
back of the card, sliding it back into the envelope and
writing 'For the attention of Mr L. Cole' on the front.
I quickly run upstairs and smooth some product through
my hair in an attempt to calm my wild curls, and slick
a quick pout of pink lipstick across my mouth. Satisfied
that this will do, and not wanting to look as though
I have made too much of an effort, I rush out of the
front door and up the garden path to Laurence's. As I
slide the envelope into his letterbox I see Lila watching
from her front room window. She smiles and raises a
single hand to me, as the shadowy form of a man appears
behind her. I wave, trying to get a glimpse of who I can
only assume is Joe, but she turns and walks away from
the window, towards the shadowy figure, gesturing
wildly. I shrug, thinking to myself that Joe must have
been calling to her, and, checking my watch, realise I'm
going to be late for Henry if I don't get a move on.

CHAPTER TEN

I hum under my breath as I walk into the playground, the invitation from Laurence cheering me up and pushing away any lingering bad feelings I have after my telephone conversation with Tessa. It always unsettles me after I hang up the phone on her, the sense of missing my best friend always a little overwhelming. She has been like the other half of me for as long as I can remember, our friendship starting in a tiny classroom when we were not much older than Henry is now. This feeling is compounded when Henry runs out of his classroom, hand in hand with a little girl with beautiful, blonde, corkscrew curls. They run into the playground together, until Miss Bramley calls them back to line up, and then they dutifully fall into line against the playground wall, still clutching each other's hands tightly. I wait patiently for Miss Bramley to spot me, blowing on my cold hands to keep warm. She sees me and gives a little wave, before saying goodbye to Henry and pointing him in my direction. I watch as he turns and says something to the little girl before dropping her hand and racing across the icy playground towards me, cheeks red from the cold and a smile lighting his face.

'Careful there, champ,' I say, steadying him as he crashes towards me, school bag flying. 'Did you have a good day?' I wait, not wanting to push him on the subject of the little girl, wanting him to tell me of his own accord.

'I made a friend, Mummy.' He smiles up at me, big brown eyes shining with happiness. 'She's called Izzy, and she has lovely hair, and she told Bradley off today for being mean to me. We sit next to each other in the classroom and she helped me with my maths today. She's very kind – that's her, over there.' He points with a gloved finger to a corner of the playground where the little curly-haired girl is standing with her mum, the slim, dark-haired woman who smiled at me the other day. She doesn't appear to be a part of Jasmine's PTA gang, which is a huge relief.

'That's lovely, darling, I'm so pleased. Maybe she could come to our house for tea one day? Would you like that? Speaking of tea, guess what we're going to do now?' I bend down to whisper in his ear about our afternoon tea invitation to Laurence's and, as expected, Henry is completely thrilled at the thought of visiting with Laurence. He thinks for a minute and then says, 'Will Lila go for afternoon tea as well?'

'Well, no, probably not. I don't think so anyway. I think the invitation was just for us.' I pause for a moment; it had never even occurred to me that Lila might have been invited as well. 'Why do you ask?'

'I just thought Lila might like it as well. She seems a little bit sad sometimes, that's all.' Henry skips off towards the cycle racks to collect his scooter before I can ask him what he means by that. I wind my scarf a little tighter around my neck to avoid the icy cold wind that slices into us across the playground and am walking over to the racks to help Henry with his things when I find my path blocked, once again. Jasmine stands in front of me, a smile on her face.

'Hi, Jasmine—' I begin, but she cuts my words off before I can finish speaking.

'Stephanie, darling. How are you?' *Air kiss, air kiss.* 'You're looking … well. Gosh, some people really do show early, don't they?' She gives my belly a little pat.

'Oh. Yes, I suppose they do.' My cheeks burn scarlet. 'Jasmine—' Once again, I am cut off before I can finish my sentence.

'Of course, I should have invited you *properly* the other day.' She pats my arm.

'Invited me?' Confused, I'm not sure what she's talking about – I can't remember being invited anywhere, but then pregnancy is pretty much wrecking my memory at the moment.

'We're still going ahead with our planned meeting next week, but it was suggested to me that perhaps you're a little shy? So, we'll be in the Hole in the Wall on Friday evening. Be there at eight o'clock sharp. You can come early and sit next to me, and then you can meet everybody before the official meeting next week. We don't dress up, but we do like to look … smart.' She glances over my outfit, smiling up at me with her perfect white teeth. I feel myself flounder a little bit – I need to fit in, but I really, really don't have time to sit in on PTA meetings, especially ones that start at eight o'clock at night.

'Thank you for the invitation but I won't be able to make it. I'm sorry. It's got nothing to do with being shy; it's just that I simply don't have the time – I'm a freelance journalist so I work to deadlines and, as I said, my husband works away a lot. Also, I don't have anyone to look after Henry, so I can't do it. I'm so sorry.' Feeling pleased that I have dealt with it in a calm manner, while still managing to say the right thing, I look over to where Henry is waiting patiently for me by the gate, and step forward to walk towards him. Jasmine steps in front of me, blocking my path.

'Well. Of course. I didn't realise you were quite such a high flier. How wonderful for you to have such an exciting job.' She gives that funny little smile of hers. 'And of course, Henry – it must be quite trying for you, having him on your own all the time? Still, not to worry. I'm sure we can arrange another day. Lovely to see you.' Another pat on my arm and then she turns on her heel, marching out of the playground and calling

Bradley to 'come *immediately*'. He trots after her like a faithful puppy, as I look on in disbelief, sure this time she was having a dig at me. The slim woman appears by my side.

'Are you all right?' she asks, ignoring the little girl skipping about next to her.

'I'm sorry? Yes, I'm fine. Thank you. Just a little bit bamboozled by Jasmine, you know.' I give a little laugh, and look around the playground for Henry.

'I'm Olivia, Izzy's mum. I think our two have hit it off quite well.' She smiles. 'If you ever fancy a chat while we're waiting for the children to come out of the classroom, I'm always here. You can always stand with me while you wait, if you want.'

'Thanks.' Henry appears by my side, a worried look on his face.

'Are you OK, Mummy? Was Bradley's mum being mean to you?'

'No, darling, of course not. Come on, let's get over to Laurence's for our afternoon tea.' I pick up Henry's bag, give a little goodbye wave towards Olivia, and we make our way out of the playground, studiously avoiding the PTA clan of witches, holed up in the far corner.

By the time I reach Laurence's front gate, I have convinced myself that Jasmine is probably a bit of a mean girl – the way she commented on how 'some people show so early', making reference to my being

a 'high flier', which I definitely don't class myself as –
I'm just a busy mum, that's all. The best course of action
is probably to avoid her, where I can. Henry scoots up
the path and knocks the lion's-head knocker that sits
proudly on Laurence's front door, and Laurence opens it
within a few seconds, almost as if he has been waiting
for our arrival. He leans forward to kiss me 'Hello' on the
cheek, ruffling Henry's hair as he does so.

'Welcome!' Laurence booms, making Henry jump
and then giggle with embarrassment. 'I hope you two
are ready for a veritable *feast*. I've been slaving over
it all day.' He gives me a wink as I make my way into
the hallway, removing my thick winter coat and scarf.
The heating is turned up high and a welcoming blast of
warm air hits my face.

'Thank you so much for the invitation, it's very kind
of you.' I let Laurence take my coat and hang it in a
cupboard in the hallway, before he shows me through
into his living room. At first glance it appears a typical
man space – decorated in muted colours, a large leather
couch in the centre of the room angled perfectly
towards a monstrously huge television mounted on the
wall. Casting my eyes about the room I notice that there
are no knick-knacks or ornaments, nothing that shows a
personal touch, save for a double photo frame propped
up on the mantelpiece. I'm too far away to see what
the pictures are properly, and I hope I'll get a chance
to have a look – not because I'm nosey, but because

Laurence seems to have become a good friend and I am intrigued to know more about him. He comes back in the room, carrying a three-tier porcelain cake stand filled with tiny sandwiches and cakes, the entire top tier filled with Jaffa Cakes, Henry's favourites. A bubble of laughter escapes from my lips before I can stop it, and Laurence gives me a warm smile as he places the cake stand carefully onto the polished coffee table in front of the couch.

'Afternoon tea is served, ladies and gentlemen.' He gives a sweeping bow, as Henry laughs at him before catching my eye in code for 'Please Mum, can I have a Jaffa Cakes?'

'Sandwiches first,' I admonish, and after getting a nod from our host, Henry takes a tea plate and begins to pile it up with sandwiches and tiny cakes. I turn to Laurence. 'Laurence, this really is marvellous. Please tell me you didn't spend all afternoon cutting up tiny sandwiches? I can't believe you actually own a cake stand.'

'OK, I didn't. I did have help, but I would have done it all myself if I'd had to. Anything for you two. And the cake stand belongs to my ex-wife. That was the one thing she left me.' He gives me a wink and a broad grin, making my cheeks flush with what I suspect is a very unattractive blush.

'Yes, well. It's lovely. Shall we eat?' I am flustered now, and try to distract him from the fact by shoving a sandwich into my mouth. Classy.

Finally, the awkward moment passes and we ease back into the comfortable, easy conversation we found ourselves in when he came over to our house for dinner. Henry finishes eating and Laurence shows him into the other reception room, which he has kitted out as a games room. Henry isn't a big fan of video games, preferring to read his books instead, but Laurence has a huge range, including some for younger children, which puzzles me a little, and I make a mental note to somehow ask him about it later. Henry soon finds one he wants to try out, so Laurence sets him up and then takes a seat next to me on the couch.

'Everything OK, Steph? You seem a little quieter than usual.' He looks me straight in the eye, making me want to squirm away and look at the floor. He's so direct that, before I know it, I'm telling him all about Jasmine Hale and how I *think* she probably doesn't like me very much, although I'm not sure. I tell him how much speaking to Tessa on the telephone only reinforces how much I miss her now she's not here.

'Poor old Steph,' Laurence leans over and gives my hand a light squeeze, sending little bolts of lightning though my skin. 'It sounds like you've had a bit of a rough day today, but won't Mark be back soon? Surely that will help, if he's around to help with Henry and fend off horrible mothers in the school playground.' It's on the tip of my tongue to say, *No, not really*, but then I might end up elaborating on how we've been on a roller-coaster ride for the past few months, and that now we've got off it, and we are both feeling dizzy, trying to find our feet together again. The whole Melissa Davenport affair might spill out.

'Yes, it'll be fine. Let's change the subject – what about you? Shouldn't you have been working today instead of making teeny tiny food?' I smile, enjoying the light blush that stains his cheeks at my teasing.

'Technically, yes – but it turned out that making teeny-tiny food was far more fun. In all honesty, it wasn't me that made it, but I should have just let you think that for a little bit longer. Lila helped, so all credit must go to her.'

'Indeed.' I raise my teacup at him and we clink together in a toast, but I can't help feeling a tiny bit disappointed that maybe this whole thing was Lila's idea and not Laurence's. We talk for a little while longer, about everything and nothing, and I tell him how pleased I am that Henry has a new friend in Izzy, the little curly-haired girl. When he excuses himself to use the bathroom I take the opportunity to look at the photo frames on the mantelpiece. One contains a picture of a handsome, older couple, laughing together at some private joke. There is a hint of Laurence in the man's eyes and around the woman's mouth, so I can only assume they are his parents. The other photo is of a woman, strikingly beautiful, with long, sleek, dark hair. She is a little younger than me, smiling directly into the camera, confident and strong-looking, her arms around a little dark-haired boy. I wonder who she is – surely she must be the ex-wife? Someone important to him, that's for sure. I jump slightly as he re-enters the room, Henry trailing along behind him.

'Someone isn't feeling too good.' Laurence says, holding on to Henry's hand.

'Mummy, I've got a tummy ache.' Henry has turned a distinct shade of green, and I realise I should probably get him home before something nasty happens to Laurence's immaculate carpet.

'Oh dear, the Jaffa Cakes are coming back to get their revenge! Come on, let's get you home.' Laurence fetches our coats and I turn to him on the doorstep, reaching up to peck him on the cheek.

'Thank you so much, Laurence, it really was so kind of you to do this for us. You and Lila. It's been a long time since I had friends as lovely as you two.' His cheeks pink a little at the compliment and he waves me away,

'Don't be daft. Listen, I enjoyed it too. If you're game for it, and once Henry feels a little better, the funfair is in town for a few days. How about we go?'

Henry looks up in excitement, all thoughts of tummy ache disappearing.

'Can we go, Mum? Please?'

'Well, I suppose it would be OK, but only if Laurence doesn't mind? Christmas is only a couple

of weeks away, so we understand if you're too busy.'
I glance away; I don't want Laurence to feel he has to
spend time with us while Mark is away if he's got other
things he'd rather be doing.

Almost as though he has read my mind, Laurence
replies, 'Don't be silly, Steph. I'm not inviting you
because I feel like I have to spend time with you
while Mark's away – I enjoy your company, yours and
Henry's. And anyway, I secretly really want to go, so
inviting you and Henry is the perfect cover.' He laughs
and I smile at him, enjoying the flicker of warmth in my
belly that sparks at his smile.

'Then in that case, we'd love to join you. We'd hate
for you to miss out, wouldn't we, Henry?' Laurence
leans down and pecks my cheek and shakes Henry's
hand. As we start to walk back up the garden path in the
dusky twilight, a few snowflakes start to fall, making
the afternoon feel even more magical.

The magic doesn't last long as I walk up the path to
our own front door. Henry has scooted ahead and is
waiting for me, peering down at something that sits in
the corner of the open porch.

'Mum, you got something.' He kicks it at me gently
with the toe of his school shoe.

'OK, hold on, leave it there.' I bustle up the path,
digging my keys out from the pocket of my bulky
winter coat.

'Hurry up, Mummy, I still feel sick,' Henry whines as I reach the door. I get the key in the lock and open the door for him, ushering him through into the downstairs bathroom. Leaning against the wall I wait while he heaves over the toilet bowl and when it is apparent that it's only a tummy extremely full of cake making him feel poorly, I pack him off upstairs to get into his pyjamas. Remembering Henry scrubbing his toe against something in the porch, I wrap my cardigan around myself and open the front door to collect whatever parcel has been left. As I look down and register what it is, my heart starts to slam in my chest and I feel a wave of dizziness pour over me, before I slam the door shut.

CHAPTER ELEVEN

Leaning against the doorframe I take huge, deep, gulping breaths, hoping to slow my racing heart and calm myself a bit before I take another look. I can hear Henry moving around upstairs, pulling open drawers and slamming cupboard doors as he searches for his favourite pyjamas. It's no good; I have to get rid of it. I open the door again and reach out and pick it up – another posy, left again on my doorstep for me to find. Only this time, it's not a pretty little hand-tied bunch of winter flowers, colourful and designed to cheer me up. No, this time, it's a hand-tied posy of wilted, dead winter flowers, interspersed with sharp, black, prickly holly leaves and the stringy brown tentacles of blackberry brambles in winter, all tied together with a slim, black ribbon. There is a note, but as I turn it over to read it, my heart still thumping away madly in my chest, I realise it is not a nice, comforting note like last time. This one simply reads, 'Have yourself a merry little Christmas,' a line that means something shockingly significant to me.

On shaking legs, I peer out from the warmth of the porch light, out into the inky darkness that has fallen while I was seeing to Henry in the bathroom. Casting my eyes quickly about, I can see nobody around, no footprints in the light scattering of snow that has fallen, dusting the walkways and pavements with a glittery sheen. There is nothing out there, nothing to fear, I am safe in my own house, but as I look down at the dirty, decaying posy a bump of fear flutters in my belly. *Why would someone leave this on my porch, knowing I would be the one to find it? Who is it and, more importantly, what do they know about me?*

Stepping back into the warmth of the well-lit hallway, I am reaching to pull the door closed tight behind me, when a face appears out of the darkness, making me jump and utter a little shriek.

'Shit, Steph, I'm sorry.' I realise now that it is Lila looming out of the gloom, rubbing her hands together to keep warm, a rosy glow from the cold making her cheeks shine. 'Did I scare you?'

'No, well, a little. But it's not surprising. Look.' I hold out the withered and dying posy towards her, gripping it at the very ends between my finger and thumb. 'Oh yuck, what is *that*?' Lila wrinkles her nose in distaste, pulling her scarf up over her nose partially, in order to block the musty, dirty scent being emitted from the flowers.

'A little gift some kind soul left on my porch for me to find.' Tears unexpectedly spurt to my eyes and I blink rapidly to try to chase them away before they cascade down my cheeks.

'Oh, darling. Hang on,' Lila pulls her gloves on again and takes the posy from me. 'Come on, let's get you inside and talk about this properly.' She bustles her way in, stripping off hat, coat and scarf before laying the posy on the kitchen draining board and turning back to me.

'OK, so when did you find it?'

'Just now. We went to Laurence's for afternoon tea – thank you so much for that, by the way, it really was appreciated. Henry had a wonderful time.'

'Nonsense, it was all Laurence's idea. I just helped make the sandwiches. You know what men are like – they have all these grand ideas and gestures but they never quite manage to carry them through on their own.' She grins at me, before remembering about the posy and allowing a frown to cross her brow. 'This is weird, though. Any note with it? Do you think it came from the same person as last time?'

'There's a note with it that just says "Have yourself a merry little Christmas". Am I going mad? Who would leave something like this on my doorstep?' *I know though, deep down, that it must be someone who knows what happened all those years ago.* I run my hands through my hair, not caring about it sticking up all over the place.

'No, you're not going mad. But I do think that maybe this is not as sinister as you probably think.' Lila grabs my hand as I go to run it through my curls yet another time in frustration.

'What do you mean, not as sinister? Someone has left a bunch of dead flowers on my doorstep, stinking of death and decay, with a note, and I shouldn't worry about it? Surely, if someone is going to leave flowers they should be nice ones, like the last time? That was bad enough, the idea that someone was creeping around the house while I was asleep; but this is worse, Lila. I know it might not seem like a big deal to you, but to me it's a threat.' With that, a fat tear rolls down my cheek and plops onto the kitchen table. I tuck my shaking hands under my thighs.

'Maybe the same person as before did leave them,' Lila says, laying her hand on my arm. 'Maybe ...' She breaks off as Henry bumbles into the room, wearing his favourite onesie.

'Mummy, are you crying?' He peers at my face and strokes my cheek.

'No, silly boy, Mummy is just fine – come here and give Aunty Lila a hug. I haven't seen you for days, no ... weeks ... no ... years!' Lila swoops down and gathers Henry up in her arms, making him chuckle. I smile before a thought flits across my mind. *Aunty Lila?* I shrug it away, the posy making me feel on edge and uneasy about everything. Lila offers to make both Henry and myself a hot chocolate, while I busy myself making Henry's sandwiches for tomorrow's packed lunch. We can't carry on our conversation while Henry is around, so with unspoken mutual agreement we leave it for a while and enjoy making Henry laugh by making moustaches out of squirty cream. Eventually, I get Henry to bed, and ignore the tiny ping of hurt that stabs my chest when he tells me he doesn't want me to read him a story; he wants Lila.

'Sorry, Mummy, but Lila just does the voices better than you.'

I kiss him goodnight, brushing his baby-fine hair back from his forehead, and hand his storybook to Lila, who is waiting for me to leave, leaning against the doorframe with a small smile on her face. I tread lightly down the stairs and into the kitchen, flicking the kettle on and resisting the huge temptation to pour myself a glass of cold, crisp Chardonnay to take the edge off the day. The posy sits, almost malevolently, on the draining board and my stomach turns over again.

Half an hour later, Lila reappears, a flush surrounding her cheeks and a smile on her face as she bounces into the kitchen. The tea that I made sits heavily in my stomach and the smell of the posy is making me feel nauseous. She raises an eyebrow at me and I shake my head as she refills the kettle and puts it on to boil to make a cup for herself. It strikes me she seems more at home in my kitchen than I do.

'So,' she says, once she has poured her tea and is settled at the kitchen table, 'what I was trying to say earlier is that maybe it was the same person who left the posy. Maybe they left it a couple of days ago and you just didn't realise. That would explain why it was all decayed and dying when you found it.' She blows on her tea and takes a cautious sip.

'That's not possible, though. The porch is open. There's no way I wouldn't have seen it, and certainly no way Henry wouldn't have noticed. He doesn't miss a trick.'

'Did you find out who sent the last one? You could ask them if they know anything about it?'

'No, I don't have a clue. It all just feels really weird, Lila. Maybe if Mark was home it wouldn't feel so sinister, but the fact that I'm here alone with Henry and there's someone creeping around outside the house makes me feel a bit freaked out.'

'What about Laurence?' Lila eyes me carefully as she takes another sip of her steaming hot tea.

'What about him?'

'Well, did you not consider that maybe the posy was from him? It was obviously from someone who wanted to cheer you up, and if it wasn't from me, then who else could it be? Maybe he sent this one as well.'

'Maybe. Maybe the first one was from Laurence, but why not just knock on the door? I really don't understand why anyone would leave a dead posy on my doorstep, unless it was to freak me out. And the note ... well, it means something to me, that's all. It doesn't feel like a coincidence.'

'You know what, Steph?' Lila puts her cup down, the remains of her tea sloshing out onto the table. 'I think maybe you're just reading way too much into this whole thing. So what if someone left some dying flowers on your doorstep? How is that going to hurt you? Unless there's something in your life that you're keeping secret, or you've done something that you're frightened someone is going to tell people about, then I don't see any reason why anyone would do anything that could be classed as sinister or threatening towards you. Maybe you're just … a bit paranoid.'

I blink, shocked at the turn in her outlook. I thought she would be supportive of me, maybe reassure me that the posy was nothing to worry about, not accuse me of being paranoid. Remembering she doesn't know my history, the full extent of quite how ill I was, I sit there and say nothing.

'Look, Steph, I didn't mean it like that. It came out all wrong – it's just … I think maybe your hormones are a little bit up in the air and you're reading too much into it, stuff that isn't there, OK?' Lila leans over and grasps my hand between hers, clutching me tightly.

'Yes … OK. It's OK. Maybe you're right. Maybe somebody did leave them on the step a few days ago. I've been so busy; I probably just didn't notice them. Sorry – for making a big deal of it all.' I look down at the table where her hands are still tightly gripping mine, the secret knowledge of the significance of that one line written in the note lodged like a stone in my chest.

'You're sure you're OK?'

'Yes, yes, of course.' I give her a watery smile and gently tug my hand away. 'It's been a long day; I think I'm going to go to bed. Maybe I'll see you tomorrow.' I get to my feet, and Lila stands and begins to shrug her way into her coat. I see her to the door, and after she leaves I walk up the path to the recycling bin and throw the horrid posy into it. Turning to head back indoors, the security light in Laurence's front garden comes on, illuminating the path and the borders to his garden. The borders that I can't help but notice contain a neglected, brown, winter-decayed blackberry bramble bush and a large holly bush, the leaves at the bottom blackened with decay.

CHAPTER TWELVE

I wake up very early the next morning, my head feeling fuzzy and my eyes slightly puffy from the tears I shed after I went to bed. I feel almost hungover and a part of me wishes I had given in to the temptation of a small glass of wine last night; at least that would justify how crap I'm feeling right now. I ease one foot out of the covers and the icy air that's yet to be warmed by the central heating that meets my skin makes me want to curl up in a ball under the duvet and sleep the day away. But Henry needs to get to school and my appointment with Dr Bradshaw has been rescheduled for today – he conveniently had a cancellation, although I am more inclined to believe he has squeezed me in on his lunch break thanks to Mark throwing his weight around before he left.

I get up slowly, nursing my aching head and scrabbling about for some paracetamol to help ease the banging headache a fractious night's sleep has left me. Pulling open the curtains I see there has been more snow overnight, only a light sprinkling but enough to transform the world into a winter wonderland. Bare, naked tree branches glisten with silvery glitter; blades of grass are turned into icy, crunchy spikes. It's early enough that the snow is still more or less perfect, no tyre tracks in the road to turn it into slush, no footprints to mar the perfect whiteness. Except, there are. A single trail of footprints leads up my garden path, straight to my front door. My heart starts to hammer in my chest before I remember last night. *Lila*, I think, exhaling with relief, *they must be Lila's footprints from when she left the house last night.* I smile, thinking myself ridiculous; of course I am just being paranoid. I look out of the window again to enjoy the crisp freshness of the new snow, but then I realise that the footprints stop at the beginning of my garden path. There is no sign of footprints leading to either Lila's house across the street, or to Laurence's house on the left. They start at the top of my path and lead all the way to my front door.

I run down the stairs and wrench the front door open, terrified of what I am going to see on the front porch. What horror will be left there now? It doesn't matter what Lila says; I know I am not being paranoid. Someone is sneaking around my house while Mark isn't here, in the hopes of what? Frightening me? Making me feel like I'm going mad? Whatever it is they want, it's working. There's nothing there. Just a neat line of footprints leading from my top step to the end of the path. I shiver as the freezing cold air swirls about my legs, and a noise startles me.

'Mummy, what are you doing?' A sleepy-looking Henry is standing on the stairs, his hair ruffled as if he's been fighting tigers in his sleep.

'Nothing, baby. Don't worry. It's time to get ready for school. Come on.' I take his hand and lead him back up the stairs towards the bathroom, trying not to think about the disturbing footsteps.

As we leave our road to turn towards the school, Olivia comes up alongside me, cheeks red with cold. Izzy is clutching tightly to her hand, bundled up in her winter coat, and thick woollen hat and gloves.

'Izzy!' Henry is delighted to see her and manages to persuade her to let go of Olivia's hand and hold his as we slip and slide along the snow-encrusted pavement.

'Morning, Steph, how are you doing?' Olivia slips along beside me, 'Mark still away?'

I look at her curiously, as she keeps her eyes fixed on the icy walkway in front of us.

'Yes. For the moment, anyway. He'll be home soon.'

'Sooner the better, I'm sure. I struggle enough when Tim is away for one night; I'm not sure how I'd manage any longer than that. You do marvellously, though.' She smiles at me and I struggle to keep myself upright.

'These two seem to get along very well, don't they?' Changing the subject, I gesture towards Henry and Izzy as they scuff their way through the little snow banks that have built up along the edge of the path.

'Izzy is enamoured of him – that's the only way to describe it.' Olivia gives a little laugh. 'Listen, Steph, don't stay home alone while Mark's away. Why don't you pop over and have dinner with us one night? Or Henry could come for tea and you could come in for a drink when you collect him? Izzy would love it.'

'Err, OK. Maybe when I'm feeling a little less under the weather? Thank you.' She nods, and calls Izzy back to her to cross the road. I grasp hold of Henry's hand as we cross behind them, an uneasy thought ticking over at the back of my mind. *I never told her Mark worked away.*

We make it to school on time, despite the freezing roads, and I manage to drop Henry off and make my escape with only a glancing wave and beaming smile from Jasmine Hale. Feeling relieved that I don't have to deal with any of her crap today, and the exchange with Olivia making me feel more than a little unsettled, I decide to stop off for a peppermint tea on the way to my appointment with Dr Bradshaw. The morning sickness seems to have died down now and I can actually manage to inhale the aroma of coffee without needing to rush to the nearest bathroom, although I'm still not quite at the stage where I would want to drink it. I remember feeling like this with Henry, right up until the end, the thought of drinking coffee making my stomach turn.

A tiny cloud of doubt crosses my mind, as I carefully make my way up the street to the closest coffee house. Every little thing about this pregnancy that I remember from being pregnant with Henry causes a little niggle of worry to grow, like a seed, making me panic ever so slightly that I'll be the same this time around, once the baby is born. It was one of the darkest times of my life, although I can only remember it as a blur. I can't remember Henry's face clearly, as a baby; it was as though I was dealing with everything underwater. I just remember the blackest feelings of despair washing over me, and the horrifying terror that I might do something to hurt him. Relieved I am going to see Dr Bradshaw today, I enter the steamy, warm café, the smell of coffee making my stomach flip initially, before it settles again. I pick up a small muffin and join the queue to pay, noticing a woman standing in front of me. She could almost be me – she's wearing a similar coat to the one I keep for wearing to work meetings and when I go out for dinner with Mark, a smart coat, not at all like the one I wear on the school run. I resolve to dig my good coat out of the wardrobe when I get home. She is wearing an identical scarf to the one I have wrapped around my neck, and although her hair is a darker shade than mine, it is even curled in the same way. I smile to myself – Mark always says everyone has a doppelganger; how funny that mine should appear in the very same coffee house I use, the one closest to my house. The woman hands over the cash for her coffee and, as I place my order for a small peppermint tea with the barista, the woman turns to face me and, for just a moment, I'm confused.

'Lila?' She looks at me, shocked, as though I'm the last person she expects to see in the coffee house, which I suppose is not unreasonable seeing as the last time she offered me coffee, I threw up everywhere and left her standing on my doorstep.

'Steph! How are you feeling after last night? Better, I hope.' She leans forward to kiss me on the cheek and I get a waft of her perfume – Peony and Blush Suede. The perfume I usually wear.

'I'm OK. Thank you.' I don't mention the footprints. 'You look … different. Nice. You look nice.'

She tugs at the scarf around her neck, loosening it.

'You don't mind, do you? It's just I noticed your scarf and I loved it so much that when I saw this one in the shop window, I had to have it. I can take it off, if you don't want us to be matching?' Lila looks at me with eyes full of concern, biting down on her lower lip. I feel like a bitch for mentioning anything.

'No, God, of course not, it's fine. It's just a scarf. Your hair looks nice too.' She has styled her hair just like mine, which must have taken some effort seeing as I am naturally curly and her hair is straight as a die.

'Do you like it? Between you and me, I got a bit bored of poker straight all the time. You're so lucky. I'd die to have naturally curly hair like that.'

I relax and gesture towards a table that has become free, one with a comfortable couch on either side. So Lila envies my hair and my scarf. I should be flattered, I suppose, that she wants to copy my style, even though I'm probably eight years older than her and not terribly glamorous.

'I have a coat just like that too. I really should dig it out and start wearing it again, before the bump gets too big and I can't fit in it.' I take a small sip of my peppermint tea and scald my tongue in the process. It serves me right for feeling bitchy. Bloody pregnancy hormones.

'We both must have excellent taste!' Lila gives her trademark tinkly laugh and I smile weakly.

'So, really, Steph, are you OK? I was a bit worried about leaving you last night. You got yourself in a bit of a state over the flowers.'

'I'm fine. Although, there was something creepy today, when I woke up.' I catch her eye and hold it, waiting to see what her reaction is; waiting to see if she's going to tell me I'm bonkers again.

'Go on.'

'There were footprints in the snow. Not that that is so weird in itself; it's just that the footprints led from the top of my front garden path down to my front door. That's it. There were no footprints leading to or from the house in either direction. I have to admit it has freaked me out a bit, combined with the flowers.' Lila cocks her head on one side, watching me carefully.

'You know what, that is pretty creepy. I think maybe someone is just trying to have a bit of fun with you, you know. Kids, perhaps. Just ignore it; don't give them the satisfaction of freaking out.'

'Yeah, hopefully you're right,' I agree with her, even though deep down I am still convinced someone is deliberately trying to upset me, but I don't want Lila to think I'm cracking up. 'I think it's best if I ignore it … *oh.*' Sitting back, I place both my hands on my stomach.

'Steph? What is it? Is it the baby?' Lila's face is filled with alarm, her newly curled hair beginning to hang limply around her face thanks to the steamy air in the coffee house.

'Everything is fine. I just felt the baby, that's all. That's the first time I've felt it.' A broad grin sweeps across my face and I am powerless to stop it. I smooth my hands across my belly, hoping to feel that tiny fluttering, like a hundred butterflies swarming in my tummy.

'Oh, thank goodness, I thought something might be wrong. How lovely.' Lila smiles into her coffee cup, all thoughts about footprints and flowers forgotten.

I make my excuses to Lila after our drink and head off quickly towards Dr Bradshaw's office. Although I have opened up quite a bit to Lila and talked about things with her that I have never discussed with anyone other than Mark and Tessa before, I am still not ready to tell her that

I have to see a head doctor twice a month. I arrive just in time, a fresh deluge of snow beginning to fall just as I reach his office. I keep an ear out for my phone, instead of turning it off like I usually do in his office, just in case the weather worsens and Henry has to leave school early.

'Stephanie, how are you?' Dr Bradshaw's hand is warm and dry when I shake it. His beard is not quite so neatly trimmed as it was on our last appointment, and his shirt has creased where it doesn't appear to have been ironed properly. Trouble in paradise for Dr and Mrs Bradshaw, maybe? I speculate as to why he is looking so crumpled, before I realise that he has been speaking to me.

'What? Yes, sorry, I'm fine. Thank you.'

'I remember the last time we spoke you were concerned about someone leaving a gift for you while you were sleeping. Nothing else has happened like that, has it? Nothing else to cause you to feel alarmed or uneasy?' He takes up his usual position of chin resting on steepled fingers. I take a deep breath. I don't want to tell him in case he thinks I'm bonkers, but I really do need to speak to someone to see if they understand. Deciding *in for a penny, in for a pound*, I start telling Dr Bradshaw about the events of this week.

'So,' I conclude, 'don't you think that's kind of weird? The footprints and the dead flowers?'

'Well, Steph, it depends on how you look at it. You can look at it with the view that someone is out to try and frighten you, or you can look at it in a logical way. Someone left the flowers for you as a present, you never noticed them and then the cold caused them to decay before you found them. The note wasn't threatening in any way; in fact, it was wishing you a Merry Christmas. Although, given your past, that line does have some significance to you, not many people know about that, and there is the fact that it's a popular Christmas song. The footprints can be explained away by the idea that someone did come to visit you – Lila – and they are her footprints leading to and from your house.'

'But what about the fact that there were no footprints leading to my path?'

'In all fairness, Steph, you said yourself that it was early in the morning before it was fully light. It would have been quite easy to miss the footprints on the pavement from that distance away – like you also said, the pavement was full of prints by the time you left the house. Honestly, Steph, given your previous history after having Henry, and what happened during your teenage years, I really think maybe you need to come and see me more often.' Dr Bradshaw's eyes are kind and full of sympathy as he looks at me across the table. A spark of fury lights in my stomach and I swallow back the sharp refusal that comes to my lips.

'No, please, Dr Bradshaw. I don't need to come more often – you're probably right. It's all just a coincidence and I'm just reading too much into it. I shouldn't have worried you with it.' Hot tears fill my eyes and I blink furiously, conscious that I need to appear calm and reasonable.

'OK, Steph, listen to me – just come and talk to me, that's all. I don't want to have to prescribe medication, not in your condition, so if you'll agree to come and talk things over with me weekly rather than fortnightly I think we can avoid it. I'm just worried about you feeling vulnerable and I think if you can talk it out of your system it'll help, OK?'

Miserably, I nod my head. The last thing I want is to have to take medication. The last time I felt like a zombie, numb to everything. I just floated through life, not seeing, not caring, and I don't want to be like that for Henry and the new baby.

'OK, I'll come. But please, Doctor, please don't give me medication.'

Wearily I trudge home through the snow, flakes collecting in my hair and melting on my cheeks. Henry is being let out early because of the weather, so I walk straight past my house and head towards the school. I glance up as I walk past my house, briefly checking the porch to make sure no other presents have been left in my absence. Thankfully, the porch is clear and I heave a huge sigh of relief, a tiny smile flickering at the corners of my mouth as the baby turns a tiny somersault, making flutters ripple through my stomach, almost as though he or she is also relieved we don't

have any unexpected gifts awaiting us. I pass by
Laurence's, heart knocking as I see a light on in the
upstairs window. I am still undecided as to whether
to mention the dead posy to him, especially as all the
components are growing in his garden. Passing by
Lila's I see she is also home, a glowing light in the
kitchen making it seem warm and homely as the snow
keeps falling. The figure of a man stands outlined
in the kitchen doorway, gesturing with his hands, and
I see Lila enter the room, reaching up as if she is about
to peck him on the cheek. It must be the elusive Joe.
I decide that as soon as I feel a bit better, and as soon
as Mark gets home, I will invite all of them over – Lila,
Laurence and the mysterious Joe – for a nice, home-
cooked meal, a celebration of new friends and a fresh
start. I'll try to forget about all of this other nonsense,
about dead flowers and mysterious footprints. I'll say
all the right things, behave the right way and then none
of them can say I'm paranoid, or ill. I'll write it all
down in my diary and just try to forget about it. Forget
about it, move on and enjoy being a part of a new circle
of friends.

CHAPTER THIRTEEN

My plan to forget about the dead flowers and spooky footprints seems to work – I feel on edge for a couple of days, but when nothing else materialises and everything seems calm I let myself begin to relax. Lila must have been right – my hormones are all up in the air with the pregnancy and I read into it all something that wasn't there. After all, like Dr Bradshaw said, it's a very popular Christmas song. I tell myself this over and over in a bid to convince myself that they are right; that it's completely innocent. The weather stays crisp and cold, which helps with the Christmassy air of excitement that surrounds our house. Mr P. gives Henry more chocolate on our visit to the shops for advent calendars, fussing and patting at Henry's hair as he eats it, something that makes me feel slightly uneasy, but I put it down to Mr P. being overwhelmed by the Christmas spirit. Laurence helps Henry and I when we go to pick a tree – a real one, for the first time ever – and Henry decorates it while I supervise. Laurence watches, sipping at a Baileys, before lifting Henry high up to put the glittery, silver star on top. I feel a little bit wistful at that point, missing Mark and feeling he should have been the one to be there to do that, but that evening I receive an email to say they are nearly done filming in that location and he will try to call as soon as possible. He says he misses us, misses me, and wishes he were home more than anywhere else in the world. I print the email off and read it over and over at night, before sliding it between the sheet and my pillow, tears leaving wrinkled spots on the paper.

Now, it's the last week of school before the Christmas holidays start. Henry is unbelievably excited, chattering away day after day about Father Christmas, stockings and presents, aided by his new best friend, Izzy. They are inseparable and this is the happiest I have seen Henry in a long, long time. I am also excited this morning, as we make our way into the school playground, as today is the day of my twenty-week scan. I'm finally going to see my baby.

I drop Henry off and head to the hospital. I am disappointed that the appointment is for a time when Mark can't be there, but my mum has stepped in to take his place. We meet outside the entrance, Mum waiting for me, looking chic and glamorous in a camel coat with a leopard-print fur hat keeping her head warm.

'Darling. You're late. And look at you, you're so pale. Are you eating properly?' Mum smoothes my fringe away from my forehead like I'm still five years old.

'I'm fine, Mum. Honestly. And yes, I am eating properly. Like a horse, in fact.' I pull away from her slightly and gesture towards the hospital entrance, half wishing I had asked Lila to come with me instead. At least she wouldn't have told me how awful I was looking. As is so often the case in hospitals, the sonographer is running behind, something my mother can't abhor. She makes tiny comments under her breath as the clock ticks further and further around the hour, while I constantly shush her in case the receptionist hears. I'm not sure what she has to complain about really; after all, she's not the one that has been sitting with a full bladder half an hour longer than she expected. Finally, my name is called and we make our way into the ultrasound room. I heave myself up onto the bed – the last week or so my bump seems to have really started to show, ever since I first felt the baby move. The sonographer smiles at me, and smears my belly with cold gel.

'Just one second,' she says, moving the wand around my stomach as we watch the screen. 'Just one moment … I'm sorry.' She continues waving the wand around as my heart begins to thump. Why is she apologising? Is there something wrong with the baby? I look up at her anxiously as she gives me a huge grin.

'Sorry, Mrs Gordon; this one's a wiggler, that's for sure. There we go – here's your baby.' She angles the screen towards me and my eyes well up with tears. A healthy baby, thank God. My mum sniffles into a tissue, dabbing at her eyes.

'Do you want to know what you're having?' the sonographer asks and I look towards my mother. She shrugs, and then gives a tiny nod. Mark and I never seemed to get around to discussing whether we wanted to find out the sex of the baby but, seeing as how I am probably going to be doing the rest of the pregnancy on my own while he finishes putting together the programme, I think I want to know. I nod quickly and the sonographer starts pressing the wand into my belly, moving in circles.

'Here,' she says, pointing at the screen. 'Mrs Gordon, you're having a little girl.'

A little girl to complete our family. Tears fall then, running down my cheeks, as I smile and try not to think about the other baby, the one before.

My mother is as pleased as I am as we make our way out of the hospital. The morning's earlier sleet and drizzle have cleared while we have been inside and left behind a clear, blue sky that warms me despite the freezing cold temperatures. Mum fusses with her scarf and looks as though she would quite like to go home, but I don't want to leave her just yet. We don't spend enough time together as it is, and although our relationship can be very prickly at times, she is my mum and I do love her. Things have always been a bit up and down between us, especially during my late teenage years when the bad stuff happened and I found myself in a deep, dark place without much support, but since the birth of Henry we seem to have managed to keep things on an even keel.

'Fancy some lunch?' I ask her, tucking my arm through hers and steering her away from the bus stop towards the tube station. 'My treat, and then maybe a bit of shopping on Oxford Street? I've still got a couple of Christmas presents to get and I could really use your help.' If there's one thing my mum loves to do, it's shop, especially if it involves spending other people's money.

'Well, if you need my help then I suppose I had better.' Smiling, she tucks her hair into her hat and we head off towards the tube station.

Ten minutes later, we spill out of the station at Bond Street, squinting as the bright sunlight assaults our eyes. I have underestimated quite how busy Oxford Street will be, even knowing it's only a week before Christmas, and hordes of people heave in front of us, clogging the pavements with their bags. I grab my mum's hand and, pushing through the crowds trying to get into the tube station, we march towards the shops, heading for a little Italian restaurant I know, tucked away off one of the side roads where hopefully it won't be so busy. Breathing a sigh of relief as we reach the restaurant door, we are shown to a table for two next to the window, perfect for watching the world go by. The waiter hands us our menus and we struggle out of our coats, handing them to him to hang in the cloakroom.

'Gosh, I'd forgotten quite how busy town is at this time of year,' Mum whispers. 'They really are like pack animals out there. It's a good job I'll be with you, Steph, when we go shopping this afternoon. You'll need someone with sharp elbows.' I splutter a laugh, the idea of my mum elbowing people out of the way amusing me.

'Thanks, Mum, for coming with me today. It really does mean a lot.'

'Nonsense. You're my daughter, Stephanie. If poor Mark has to miss it, there's no reason why you should go alone, is there?' She busies herself with the menu, holding it close to her nose to read it, as she's too vain to wear her reading glasses. Mum is probably Mark's biggest fan – helpful seeing as Tessa and Belinda have never quite taken to him – having a tendency to tell me on more than one occasion that I am lucky to have him, and that I should hold on to him for dear life. Thankfully, she doesn't know about the Melissa Davenport affair, although I am terribly tempted sometimes just to throw it out there, just to see what she says. Probably, 'You never paid him enough attention, Steph.'

'Now,' Mum says, looking down her nose at me, 'I hope you're going to order something substantial. You have that little girl to feed.' She winks. 'And you really do look rather peaky. Is everything OK between you and Mark? You haven't upset him, have you?' I sigh, and resist the temptation to roll my eyes.

'No, Mum, I haven't upset him; I've barely even spoken to him the past few weeks, to be honest, since he left for Paraguay. But there is *something* ...' I pause, not quite sure if I want to tell her what has been going on. The way she's reacted to stuff in the past means I am always slightly on edge with her.

'What, Steph? I'm your mother, you can tell me anything.' Yes, I can, although usually I don't really want to. Mum waves the waiter away as he approaches to take our order, before calling him back and telling him she will have the house white. A bottle, please. I bite the bullet and tell Mum everything that has been happening, all about the flowers and the footprints that led to the front door.

'It's made me jumpy, uneasy. Nothing has happened for a couple of weeks now, but even so ... I just feel a bit anxious ... scared, to be honest. Do you think it's him?' I risk a look at my mum, waiting to hear what she says.

'Stephanie, don't be ridiculous. That man is long gone; they caught him, didn't they? Everything that happened was years in the past; I thought you'd got over it all? After all, you've moved on, managed to find a husband and raise a child, and you're about to have another one. What's the point of dredging all this nonsense up again? I'm sure if he'd got parole the police would have contacted you.' She picks up her menu, gestures to the waiter, and with that the conversation is over. Just like when your daughter tries to kill herself, the best thing to do afterwards is just sweep it all under the carpet and never speak of it again.

Lunch is pretty subdued after that and, as we leave the restaurant, I tell my mother that, after the excitement of today, I'm too tired to go shopping. She pecks me on the cheek, and as she goes to leave, turns back to me.

'Really, Stephanie, forget about it. He's locked away and there is nothing for you to worry about. You're seeing things that aren't there.' With that, she squeezes my arm and walks towards the station.

When I was fifteen, I was attacked. I was walking home from school, the last leg on my own after I had left Tessa at her house. There was a long way, but I chose, stupidly, to take the short cut that meant walking along the footpath through the woods. It was only a ten-minute journey, but it cut nearly twenty minutes off my walk home – I had had cross-country for PE that day, followed by a netball match after school, and I was tired. I was sensible – I didn't wear headphones while walking alone, and I kept a rape alarm in my pocket as per my mum's instructions – but that day I was dawdling along in a world of my own. Someone had said that Oliver Jackson wanted to take me to the Christmas disco and I was thinking about what I would wear. I never heard him approach, never saw his face properly, just felt a body slamming into me and the taste of sweat from a hand clamped tightly across my mouth. I was a bright girl, popular and sporty. Too bolshy for my own good, according to my mum. So when he threw me on the ground I fought him, as hard as I could, scratching and biting, trying to buck my hips in an attempt to throw him off. He liked it, laughed under his breath, and he easily held me off until, too weak to fight him any longer, I let him violate my body, hoping it would soon be over, silent tears running down my cheeks into my hair. It went on for what felt like hours before he pulled himself off me, whispered in my ear, and then sauntered off, whistling 'Have Yourself a Merry Little Christmas' under his breath. I limped home, God only knows how much later, my body broken and sore, covered in cuts and bruises, opening the door to my mum, singing as she peeled potatoes over the kitchen sink. He had said that, if I told, he would come back and kill me; that he knew where I lived and he could get me at any time. So, I pulled myself wearily up the stairs, fighting back the vomit at the back of my throat, and sat in a scorching-hot bath, scrubbing every part of me as I cried. Steph, the Steph that I knew myself to be, the bright, cocky teenager who thought she owned the world, was gone for ever. So was the relationship I had with my mother when six weeks later I discovered I was pregnant.

Lost in memories, I am home before I remember that Henry is having tea at Izzy's house. It's earlier than I thought I would be after calling off the shopping trip with Mum, so I decide to pamper myself a little before I go and pick up Henry. I've finished this week's articles ahead of deadline, and the freezing weather means my feet are like blocks of ice, so I decide to take a long, hot shower. Before, I used to relish a long, hot bath, lying in the scented water for hours with a book. It took months before I was able to enjoy soaking in a bubble bath after the attack, the simple joy of the hot water warming my bones forcing me to relive that day. That's the kind of thing my mother was never able to understand – how even the little things, like the smell of the soap that I used to scrub his smell off me, could make my stomach churn and my mouth fill with saliva. Even now there are times when I just can't face the bathtub, and today is one of them. Shaking off the cloud of depression hanging over me, after thinking back to then, to the day when I officially became broken, I slide my key into the lock and push the front door open. Immediately I can sense it – someone has been in the house. The air feels as though it has been disturbed, as if someone has just this minute breezed out of the front room. Heart hammering in my chest, I grab an umbrella that sits in the corner of the hallway, the only weapon I have to hand. Creeping my way along the hall, towards the stairs, I call out,

'Hello?' And then, I don't know why, 'Lila? Laurence? Is that you?'

There is no answer. The hairs on the back of my neck prickle, and I exhale as I reach the top of the stairs. I peer into each bedroom and the bathroom, but there is no sign that anyone has been in the house. Everything is just as I left it. I slip back down the stairs, peering into the living room as I pass it. Nothing. Breathing a sigh of relief, I mentally slap myself, giving a low chuckle under my breath and willing my knees to stop knocking together. *I just creeped myself out, that's all. Nobody has been in the house, it's just the thought of him, and talking about it with Mum today brought all the memories flooding back.* I place the umbrella back against the wall where I found it, and tugging off my coat and scarf walk into the kitchen, where my heart stops dead in my chest. There, on the draining board, is another wilted, decayed bunch of winter flowers, tied neatly together with a familiar black ribbon.

CHAPTER FOURTEEN

The shrill ring of the landline makes me jump, and I emit a tiny shriek, before turning away from the brown, withered bouquet, its musty smell making my stomach turn over and over. I race back down the hallway, almost falling over the shoes left sprawling across the floor where Henry steps out of them, my heart hammering in my chest.

'Hello?' My chest heaves and I grasp the receiver so tightly that my knuckles turn white. There is no reply from the other end of the line, just dead air hissing into my ear.

'Hello? Who's there? This isn't funny!' Hot tears burn in my eyes and I feel the grip of panic squeezing my chest, hysteria threatening just around the corner. Dead air hisses once more and I shriek angrily, slamming the receiver hard into the cradle. Immediately, the phone begins to ring again, the shrill, clanging tone going right through me. Fear and anger wash over me and I snatch up the receiver, fright making my voice stick in my throat.

'Hello?' I croak into the mouthpiece. 'What do you want? If you want to frighten me, it's worked, so please, just leave me alone!' I gulp in huge gasps of air, my chest hitching and heaving as I struggle to keep control.

'Steph? Jesus, Steph, what is it? What's going on?'

I begin to cry properly as the warm, familiar sound of Mark's voice comes tumbling down the line, dodging the hisses and crackles that always accompany our long-distance phone calls, relief making my legs feel weak. I lean against the wall, tears running down my cheeks, and take a deep breath before I can reply.

'Oh, God, Mark. Thank God it's you. I thought it was … when are you coming home? I need you to come home, Mark, please.' I slide down the wall, tears sliding into my hairline as I tip my head back.

'Steph, calm down. You need to tell me what's going on. I tried to call just now but the line was terrible; I'm lucky to get reception now. Please, tell me what's wrong.'

Pulling myself together, wiping the tears on the sleeve of my cardigan, I tell Mark everything that has happened since he's been gone – the bouquets of flowers that have decayed on the doorstep, the note, the feeling that someone has been in the house, the flowers on the draining board that prove it. After I finish speaking there is the longest silence, and I pause for a moment, thinking maybe we have been cut off. Then he says, 'Steph. You need to calm down and think about things logically. Deep breaths, come on. I know you worry about things, but I promise you; there is nothing to be afraid of. Have you been seeing Dr Bradshaw?'

'Of course I have! I told you I would and I have! I've been keeping my diary, I've done everything I promised, but I swear to you, Mark, I think someone is trying to frighten me. I know it sounds paranoid, but what other explanation could there be?' I feel the first flickers of anxiety – I should have known he wouldn't believe me, should have known he would immediately start thinking I'm spiralling downwards again.

As if he can read my mind, he says, 'OK, look, I do believe you, but try not to panic, Steph. Llewellyn Chance is locked up, right where he should be, and I'll be home soon – that's why I'm ringing. I'll be home on the twenty-fourth. It'll be late, but I'll be back, just like I promised. And you have Lila and Laurence looking after you, don't you? I know you've got a lot on your plate, but just take things one day at a time.' His voice is soothing, and I nod my head slowly before realising he can't see me.

'Yes, they've both been brilliant. They've made the time you've been away go much quicker. We do miss you, though. So much.'

'And I miss you, you know I do. Look, I'll be home for Christmas, then we will have to come back out here, just for the last few bits of filming, but we'll be done before the baby comes. I'll make sure I'm home then for a few months, OK? I'll tell them I'm taking paternity leave, or whatever. I promise, Steph, I'll stay home and take care of you.'

'OK. I'm sorry. I just panicked, that's all. I've been with my mum today.' Mark will understand this – he knows the whole story. My mother didn't know how to react after she discovered what had happened that day, and her response was to just shut down. She never wanted to speak to me about it; she never sent me for therapy. She just refused to mention it, leaving me lost, confused and alone. Another rogue tear makes its way slowly down my cheek. I know Mark is as worried as I am that things will be the way they were after I had Henry, when the dark vortex of post-natal depression pulled me in and left Mark standing out in the cold, caring for Henry on his own. Neither of us wants that. I change the subject, trying to lighten the mood, and spend the rest of the all too brief phone conversation telling Mark how I felt the baby move. He is overcome with emotion, more than I thought he would be, and I wonder if it's because he's not here to experience it, or because he is relieved I stayed with him after Melissa. I tell him about the scan and when he asks if I have found out the sex of the baby I pause.

'Do you really want to know?'

'Yes.' I can hear the smile in his voice. 'I knew you wouldn't be able to resist finding out if they asked you … so, go on … what are we having?'

He is a bit speechless when I tell him we are expecting a little girl, and I put the pause on the line down to him having to smooth the tears out of his voice, rather than the poor connection between England and Paraguay. We end the call on this note, and I feel much better than I did. Mark always has this ability to calm me down, to make me think about things a little more rationally and see the logical side of things. Another reason why we do make such a good team, when we both put our minds to it. We *will* make this work. I heave myself up from my position on the floor, and make my way slowly down the hallway back towards the kitchen. The decayed bouquet is still laid on its side, its filthy, musty smell filling the kitchen. A tiny spark of rage ignites somewhere deep down inside me, and I feel the baby do a flip, ripples fluttering through my belly. Whether someone left the posy inside or outside the house, they still left it, possibly knowing it would freak me out. Pulling on a pair of rubber gloves, I snatch it up, crushing it deep down inside the kitchen bin, throw open the windows, and spray a liberal amount of air freshener all around the kitchen in an attempt to mask the smell.

By the time I am ready to go and collect Henry from Izzy's house, the smell has disappeared and, after a hot shower, I am feeling tired, but far more together than I have all day. I push the thoughts of the posy, and the memories of the attack, to the back of my mind and try to enjoy the crunch of the thin frosting of snow under my boots as I walk over to pick Henry up. I find the house easily enough, and Olivia opens the door as soon as I walk up the path.

'Steph – you must be frozen. Come in for a cup of tea? Henry has been a delight; Izzy's had a wonderful time with him.' She pulls the front door open wide, and ushers me inside but I shake my head, too exhausted to make conversation.

'Thank you, Olivia, but I can't stop. Henry still has homework to do this evening, and I'm waiting for my husband to call. He's filming on location at the moment, so we have to schedule our calls in carefully.' I smile at her, squashing down the tiny flicker of guilt I feel at telling her a white lie. Henry *does* have homework, although not so much that I couldn't stop and have a cup of tea with her. But I'm worn out from the events of the day and longing for my bed.

'Not even one quick cuppa? OK, we'll have to arrange it properly for next time.' Olivia smiles at me, her dark hair silky and glossy where the light from the hallway hits it. She is well put together, dressed immaculately like most of the other yummy mummies who send their children to our local school, but without the snide manner so many of them have. A lot of the mothers seem to have their cliques, but I've never noticed Olivia belonging to any of them. I really should make an effort to get to know her better; she seems lovely, and it would be nice to have someone to chat to while I'm waiting for Henry. She calls Henry and Izzy, and I hear footsteps battering across the top-floor landing as they race towards the stairs. Henry rushes towards me and gives me a huge hug before following Izzy into the depths of the house to collect his school bag and coat.

'There was just one slight bit of confusion,' Olivia says, turning back to face me. 'I thought I should let you know that, when I arrived, Henry seemed to think someone else was picking him up – Lila? He said she was in the playground waiting to collect him, but when I checked with Miss Bramley she said you had definitely left instructions for Henry to be collected by me. I don't know if there was some sort of mix-up? I know what it's like when you're pregnant – my brain was like a sieve!' She gives a warm laugh and lays her hand gently on my arm. I look down at where her manicured nails rest lightly on my wrist, thinking hard as to whether I had got confused. When I don't immediately respond Olivia's hand twitches, and she abruptly pulls it away. As I raise my eyes to meet hers a look of concern crosses her face.

'Steph? Are you OK?'

'Yes, God, sorry, *yes*, I'm fine. Sorry, I was just trying to think if I had asked Lila … sorry, it's baby brain.' Aware that I am apologising repeatedly, I give a half-hearted chuckle. *What was Lila doing at Henry's school? Did I ask her to fetch him?* Before I can ponder it any further, Henry hands me his school bag, and says his thank-yous and goodbyes to Izzy and her mum.

'Thank you, Olivia, Henry really seems to have enjoyed himself.' I smile at her, hoping to smooth away any awkwardness that lingers after my confusion over Lila.

Walking back down the path, I turn to wave and Olivia makes a 'call me' sign, before shouting, 'I'll ring you! We can arrange that cup of tea!'

As we walk back along crispy, snowy streets, towards our house, Henry runs ahead, crushing small, untouched snowdrifts underfoot, before running back to me, chattering away about how much fun he and Izzy had at her house. I can't help smiling; this is the first time I've seen Henry so animated since the move and I am relieved he's finally made a friend. The thought of Lila crosses my mind, and then almost as if I'd wished her there, I see her walking towards the house from the opposite direction, still wearing the coat that matches mine.

'Lila!' I raise a gloved hand and wave at her, and at first it seems as though she doesn't see me, which is odd because I'm waving right at her, and calling her name, but then she looks up and gives me a wide grin as Henry barrels into her, throwing his arms around her waist.

'Steph! And hello, young man.' She ruffles Henry's hair and disentangles herself. 'What have you two been up to?' Losing interest, Henry runs ahead again, following a trail of cat prints in the snow.

'Not much. Henry went to tea with his new friend; I've just been to collect him. Which reminds me, there seemed to be some confusion over who was collecting Henry – I didn't ask you, did I? Only Henry seemed to think you were there to collect him.'

'Oh, he is a funny boy.' She smiles. 'I was passing the school at the end of the school day, just by coincidence. Henry saw me passing and immediately jumped to the conclusion I was there to collect him for you. Goodness knows where he got that idea from!' She gives her tinkly little laugh and I smile weakly.

'Oh, thank goodness. I was beginning to think I'd asked you *and* Olivia to collect him. That could have been embarrassing. I barely know her. She would have thought I was completely useless.'

Lila links her arm through mine as we walk towards the houses, a warm puddle of light spilling from her front porch, meaning that presumably Joe is home and waiting for her. My own porch is ominously dark where I rushed out of the house, forgetting to flick the switch that turned the outside porch light on. Feeling still slightly disturbed from the events earlier in the day, and not wanting to go into a dark, empty house on my own, I turn to Lila.

'Is Joe waiting for you inside? Do you want to come in for a cup of coffee? I think I can probably manage to make one now without vomiting everywhere.' I give her a small smile.

'Joe? Umm … no, Joe won't be waiting for me. Of course I'll come in with you. I'll even make the coffee while you bathe Henry.' Gratefully, I squeeze her hand, opening the front door and peering anxiously down into the dark corners of the porch before I step into the house.

'Steph? Is everything OK? You didn't get left anything else, did you?' Lila's tone is concerned, and she checks to make sure Henry is safely out of earshot upstairs before I answer.

'There was something,' I say. 'I came home earlier from the scan and it felt like someone had been in the house. And there was another posy, a dead one, left on the draining board. Then Mark phoned and I freaked out.'

'Oh, love.' Lila gathers me to her, pulling me into her arms and giving me a huge hug. I relax into it, soaking up her warmth and the scent of her perfume. 'Are you sure it was another one? Maybe you thought you threw the last one in the bin but you didn't? You know how it is when you're pregnant.' I stiffen at her words – Lila doesn't have any children so how could she possibly know what it's like to be pregnant and forgetful? – before realising that she is referring to *me*, not herself.

I slide out of her arms and reach for the kettle to make us a hot drink.

'I just don't know any more, Lila. I thought that it was left in the house by someone else when I wasn't here, just to frighten me, but now I'm second-guessing myself as to whether I even did throw the last one out in the first place. I did get a bit like that before, you know, after Henry, when I was poorly. I got a bit forgetful sometimes, so maybe I didn't throw it out and I forgot? But I'm sure someone had been in the house while I was gone – the air felt different, as though someone had just left the room.' I sigh, and tears threaten again. It feels as though all I've done for the past few weeks is cry. 'I genuinely don't know, Lila. To be honest, I feel as though I'm going mad.'

Lila leaves after a hot cup of tea, and making sure I'm OK – there's not really a lot else she can do, but it's comforting to have someone there to talk it all over with in Mark's absence, and I almost tell her what happened when I was a teenager – almost tell her I'm convinced Llewellyn Chance is somehow getting to me. Although I am grateful to Lila for making the time to sit with me and make sure I'm all right, I am exhausted and relieved when she stands to leave. I climb the stairs wearily, the events of the day taking their toll on me as I go up to tuck Henry into bed. I peep into his room, where he lays propped up on pillows reading the latest Tom Gates book, the lamp by his bed casting a warm glow over his features.

'Come on, pal, time to go to sleep.' I gently tug the book out of his hands, making sure to slip a bookmark in to mark his page. 'Did you have a nice time at Izzy's? You guys looked like you were having fun.' He gives a sleepy smile.

'Yeah, it was fun. I want her to come here for tea. Can we do that?'

'Of course we can. Let me speak to her mum and we can arrange it.'

'I did think Lila was getting me, though, Mummy, and I got upset. I thought I had to go home with Lila and I wasn't allowed to go to Izzy's house, because Lila was in the playground when I came out of class.'

I pause, my hand hovering over his forehead as I am about to sweep back the lock of hair that falls over one eye to one side. *Hadn't Lila said she was just passing by?*

'Are you sure she was in the playground, darling? Not waiting outside? Maybe you got mixed up because she was outside and you thought she was coming to get you?'

'*No, Mummy.*' Henry is beginning to get cross, the tiny crease in his brow that emerges when he is getting angry making an appearance. 'She was standing in the playground, waiting by the friendship stop, and when I came out I saw her. She was wearing a coat like your posh one, and when she saw me, she waved and wiggled her fingers at me, like *this.*' Henry crooks his fingers at me in a *come here* gesture. This is an entirely different story to the one Lila has told me. The friendship stop is a miniature bus stop, tucked right inside the playground, close to the school office, a place where children who are lonely can stand so the other children know they need a friend to play with. A lovely idea, but definitely carried out on school grounds. There is no way Lila can have been *just passing* if Henry saw her standing there. I tuck him in tightly, telling him not to worry about it, and kissing his forehead. He snuggles down and as I leave the room I turn back to him, his face just peeping out above the duvet cover.

'Next time, Henry, if you're not sure, or you can't remember what Mummy has told you, go and see Miss Bramley, OK? She'll know who's collecting you. Now, sleep.' I blow him a kiss and turn out the light, his comments whirling around in my head as I make my way back downstairs.

I write in my diary before bed, tugging it out from its secret hiding place between the mattress and the bed frame. I write about Lila, how she reminds me of Tessa in the way that she always knows the right thing to say or do to make me feel better about things. I write about Olivia and how I would like to be friends with her. But how did she know Mark worked away? I am still sure I never told her. I write about Henry and how I don't know if it's him or Lila that has got confused over what happened in the playground today. I write about how I wish I could just say what I wanted about things, without worrying it will be taken the wrong way, that I'll be accused of being paranoid. That they'll pump me full of medication again, and tell me it's all in my head. Exhausted, I slide the diary back into its spot and toss and turn until I do eventually fall asleep. My sleep is filled with dreams, none of them pleasant.

CHAPTER FIFTEEN

The school term is nearly finished. Henry is in a complete state of overexcitement at the idea of Christmas being just around the corner, the prospect of the approaching funfair making him giddy and hyperactive. I haven't mentioned Lila being in the playground to him again, not wanting to upset him, but I have decided that, when I next see Lila, I will challenge her about it – I have found myself in the position where I thought I could trust her, and the idea that she has lied to me makes me feel cold inside.

It's midway through December and, while the snow has finally stopped, it hasn't warmed up in any way whatsoever, so Henry and I make sure we are wrapped up warm, with thick hats and scarves covering most of our faces, as we walk up the path to meet Laurence. We have arranged to take Henry to the funfair for the final evening it's here before moving on to the next town. I wish Mark could be here to enjoy it with us, but according to his latest email his flight will arrive at

Heathrow on Christmas Eve, hopefully before Henry has to go to bed.

We make our way carefully up the front path, the flagstones glittering in the half-light, and Henry scooches his feet along, leaving long, skinny track marks behind. I go to tell him to stop, that he'll make the path slippery for other people, but before I can say anything Laurence flings his front door wide open, stepping out into the frosty air.

'Hello there, young man.' He leans down to ruffle Henry's hair as Henry laughs and twists away. 'And hello to you, too, young lady.' He smiles at me.

'Oh, stop.' I laugh, and he tucks his arm into mine as we slip and slide our way back up the icy path. We catch up during the walk to the recreation ground where the funfair is being held. I tell him about the scan, and finding out that the baby is a girl, avoiding any mention of the dead flowers and the feeling that someone had been in the house. He tells me about his latest interview, and how he's thinking of employing a gardener in the spring to help take control of the bushes that run wild in his front garden. I bite my tongue, thinking again of the first bunch of dead flowers, the ones that contained plants that could all be found in Laurence's front garden. Despite this fact, my gut instinct is that Laurence has had nothing to do with any of it – he's just too nice – and, if I'm honest, too attractive. I don't know what it is about him but he seems to have got under my skin. Maybe it's the way he listens to me without passing any judgement.

We see the lights, flashing a rainbow of colours, and hear the thud of loud music accompanying the rides before we turn the corner and see the funfair for ourselves. Henry runs ahead, unable to wait any longer, and I call to him to be careful – the last thing we need is for him to miss out because he's fallen on the slippery path. His face lights up as we arrive at the recreation ground and he turns to Laurence, eyes shining.

'Can we go on a ride? Right now?'

'How about we grab your mum a hot drink, so she doesn't get too cold while she waits for us?' Laurence looks at me, questioningly. 'Then I'll take you on whatever you want to go on.' I smile gratefully at him, the idea of a cup of hot chocolate warming my fingers against the biting chill of the cold air a welcome one. Laurence heads off to the refreshments van, the smell of candyfloss and hot dogs scenting the air, while Henry and I make our way over to the monkey swings. Henry runs on ahead again, and before I can shout at him to stop he slips on the icy pathway, careering into a small boy coming from the opposite direction. Both boys land on the hard ground with a thump, the other boy knocking his elbow hard against the tarmac. Wails fill the air and I hurry over as fast as I can, anxious to reach Henry and make sure the other child is OK. I lean over Henry, checking his face and head for bumps.

'Are you OK, darling?' I help him to his feet, giving him a quick squeeze before turning to the other boy. 'And you? Are you all right?' My heart sinks as I realise the other boy is Bradley Hale, Jasmine's son. Right on cue she appears.

'What the hell is going on here? Bradley? Are you OK?' I am leaning down to help the boy to his feet, but she pushes me roughly aside, grabbing at his arm.

'Careful, Jasmine, I think he banged his elbow. It was an accident …' Bradley stands rubbing forlornly at his elbow, a tear in his designer coat. Snot and tears stain his face and I offer him a tissue. Jasmine bats it away, pulling a tissue from her own pocket.

'Really, Stephanie, I saw exactly what happened. Henry was out of control and knocked poor Bradley to the ground. I know things must be difficult for you, what with being a single parent, but you really need to exercise some control over your son.'

'Excuse me? It was an accident, Jasmine. The ground is slippery; it could have happened to anyone. Thankfully no one is hurt. I'm sorry Bradley fell, but it really was an accident. And I'm not a single parent.'

'Accident or not, you need to learn to discipline your son. Running about like that – he's lucky Bradley wasn't seriously hurt, but I guess that's what comes of not having a father figure around. It's such a shame when parents allow their problems to affect their children's behaviour. Come on, Bradley.'

I gape at her, open-mouthed, before fury at her open hostility washes over me. I wasn't sure before if she was unpleasant or if I had read her wrong, but her reference to Mark makes me see red. *What is that supposed to mean? What does she know about Mark and me?*

'Who the *hell* do you think you are? You know, I wasn't sure before if you were making digs at me or not, but now you've just confirmed that you really are quite an unpleasant person. You think you can say things about *my son* and pass comment on *my life* just because I don't want to be part of your little clique?' The words are out before I can stop them, and a horrid sensation that feels suspiciously like guilt settles in my stomach. I shouldn't have lost my temper, shouldn't have let her get to me.

'Hey. *Hey.* What's going on?' Laurence has appeared next to me, steaming cup of hot chocolate in one hand, the other on my arm to calm me down. Jasmine tosses her hair back and allows tears to well up in her eyes.

'I'm so sorry,' she simpers up at Laurence. 'I don't know what got into her. She just started screaming at me, telling me I'm a spiteful bitch – I don't know what's wrong with her, I mean, I barely know her.' She lets one single tear snake its way down her cheek. 'The boys had a bit of a collision on the icy pavement, and she just started hollering at me, accusing me of all sorts.'

My chest is heaving and my cheeks are red, and I know I must look like a mad woman. I am speechless at the way she has turned things around, making me look deranged.

'OK. I think it's best you leave. I'll deal with Steph.' Laurence dismisses her with a wave of his hand, and she turns away, but not before giving me a little smirk as she leaves.

'Bloody hell, Steph, what was *that*? I came back from the food van and you were just screaming at her. Who is she?' He places one finger under my chin and gently tilts my head back.

'She's no one. She's a mean girl. She's the head of the PTA and I think she hates me because I won't join. She said stuff about Henry, that I need to sort his behaviour out. She said things about Mark not being here and I just lost it. I'm sorry. I've embarrassed you.'

'Listen, don't worry about her. Just let it go. You're doing a great job, and Mark will be home soon.' Laurence's dark eyes focus on mine and I feel like I could stay there all night, just swimming in those deep chocolate pools, a shiver running down my spine. 'She's not worth the hassle, OK?'

I nod, and reach for Henry's hand. He has been distracted by the hook-a-duck stall, watching kids grab at plastic ducks and walk away with the cheap plastic prizes on offer, so hopefully he hasn't paid too much attention to what just went on. Henry tugs me towards the ducks, and I dutifully hand over the money for him to have a go, and Laurence and I watch while he swipes at them, eventually snagging one and winning himself a small toy as a prize. The mood lightens, and I feel happier knowing that Laurence didn't automatically blame me for the set-to with Jasmine Hale, the way Mark would have done had he been here. Mark would definitely have thought my outburst was unreasonable, without even checking what had been said. We stroll around the funfair together, Henry switching between holding my hand and holding Laurence's, and he soon spots Izzy standing in the queue for the dodgems.

'Can we, Mum? Please?' Henry begs, pointing at the ride, hopping from foot to foot.

'OK, but I can't get on it with you.' We reach the queue, and Izzy and her mum. On seeing us arrive, Olivia leans over and gives me a kiss on the cheek, smiling warmly. She looks up at Laurence,

'Oh – you must be Mark! It's so lovely to meet you, Henry has told me all about you.'

'No, sorry. I'm Laurence …'

I butt in quickly; worried in case Olivia gets the wrong idea. It feels like I have made enough enemies at Henry's school already, and I want Olivia on my side, despite my reluctance to get to know her.

'Laurence is a friend, Olivia. Mark is still away until Christmas but I didn't want Henry to miss out on the funfair, so Laurence is here to ride with him, that's all.' A look of hurt crosses Laurence's face, and I feel like a bitch. I can never seem to get across what I want to say without it sounding wrong. We make small talk as we stand in line, and eventually the queue starts to move. Izzy and Henry reach the front and turn back to us.

'Can we ride together? Pleeeease?' Henry begs, holding tightly to Izzy's hand. I look to Olivia, but she is already nodding her assent. I'm not too happy about it, but the two children seem to take her confirmation as read, and run off to the nearest empty car.

'You don't mind, do you, Steph?' Olivia asks, slightly too late for me to make a fuss about it.

'Well, no, but ...' Laurence gives my hand a squeeze, and chimes in before I can finish, as though he instinctively knows I'm worried about Henry riding without an adult.

'I'm sure they'll be OK, and Steph is fine, aren't you? We'll be here to watch.'

Olivia smiles at him, obviously relieved she doesn't have to go on the ride.

'Listen,' she says, 'I need to make a phone call – are you guys OK to wait here and keep an eye on Izzy for me, just for a moment? I've left her little brother at home with a babysitter as he's not too well and I just want to check on him.'

'Not a problem.' I watch her walk away, mobile clamped to her ear, before turning back to Laurence.

'I'm sorry about what I said.' I scuff my boots against the frozen ground, unwilling to catch his eye. 'About you just being here to ride with Henry. I didn't mean it that way; things just come out a bit wrong sometimes.'

'It's fine, I know what you meant.' Laurence takes my hand in his and my heart starts to beat ten to the dozen, a warm flush coursing through my body. 'I wasn't offended. Look, Steph, I know how difficult things must be for you while Mark is away. I just want to let you know I'm here, OK? If you need me.'

I squeeze his hand gently, and before I know it I find myself telling him everything, even down to the attack and my fear that Llewellyn Chance is somehow trying to frighten me, and the way I'm feeling ever so slightly like I'm going mad sometimes. He listens, without commenting, without telling me not to worry, it's probably nothing, and when I finish speaking he takes a deep breath.

'Look, I know it's not the same, but I know how you feel. Not about that guy, obviously, but the way you feel like you're going mad. I felt the same, when my wife left me.' I gaze up at him, realising I'd never even thought about his wife – where she was, or why she wasn't around – and wait for him to continue.

'When Sarah left and took our son with her, I thought my world had ended, and I didn't know what to do with myself. I didn't sleep; I drank too much and ended up not knowing if everything that was going on around me was down to me or other people. I freaked out a bit, if I'm honest, so I just wanted to let you know that I know how it feels sometimes … when you feel like you're doing it all on your own and you haven't got anyone to turn to. But you do, Steph, that's what I'm trying to say. I'll look out for you when Mark isn't here.'

Before I can reply, Henry and Izzy are barrelling towards us, laughing, cheeks flushed, Henry's distress at his run-in with Bradley forgotten. Olivia appears from behind the dodgems, so I give Laurence's hand one last squeeze before dropping it and bending on one knee to give Henry a hug.

'I have to head back,' Olivia says, much to Izzy's disappointment. 'Cameron still has a temperature and he won't stop crying. I think he just needs his mum – lovely to see you though, Steph. We'll have dinner soon, yeah?' I smile and nod, doing all the right things like Dr Bradshaw would want me to.

'She seems nice.' Laurence says, watching my face.

'Hmmm. Bit full on.' That's all I say, and we each take hold of one of Henry's hands and go to find the mini roller coaster.

The rest of the evening passes quickly, full of bright lights and the smell of the fair on the air. I am aware of Laurence's closeness the entire evening, and his earlier words float through my mind on a loop, meaning I have to ask Henry to repeat himself on more than one occasion.

We walk back towards our road, Henry hyped up on sugar, our breath frosting in front of our faces in the chill evening air. Reaching our front door, I have to breathe on my cold hands before I can get the key in the lock, laughing as I fumble and drop it, before pushing the door open, Henry running upstairs to find his onesie to get warm. I lean on the doorframe, looking up at Laurence.

'Thank you for such a lovely evening. I really enjoyed myself, and so did Henry. I'm sorry about the beginning bit.' His dark eyes are drawing me in again and I mentally shake myself. *Married and pregnant, Steph.*

'Me too, and I already told you – don't worry. I know how it is, and I'm here if ever you need to talk about *anything*. Look, I like you, Steph, really like you, and if you weren't married ...' He tails off, the air thick with tension between us. Before I know what is happening his lips are pressing down on mine, sending a bolt of lightning through my body. I close my eyes, just briefly, before common sense kicks in, and I push him away, my breath coming in sharp pants.

'Oh, God, Steph, I'm sorry ... I'm so sorry.' Laurence reaches towards me and I step backwards, back over the threshold and into the house.

'Please, Laurence, just go.' He turns abruptly and marches back up the path, towards his own house, and I sag against the doorframe, tiredness washing away any excitement of the evening. At the end of her garden path Lila stands, almost as though she has been watching what just happened, but before she can say anything I step back inside and slam the front door closed, the baby fluttering in my belly like a caged bird.

Once I get Henry into bed, I run myself a bath, peering at myself in the mirror as the steam makes my reflection smudged and indistinct. *Stupid, stupid Steph can never get anything right. Now I've blown my friendship with Laurence. What was I thinking? Of course I couldn't just be friends with a guy, I would cock it up, just like I cock up all the other relationships in my life. My mum, Mark. Mark wouldn't have had an affair if I hadn't been so messed up.* My head is a tangled mess of dead bouquets, hissing long-distance lines and kisses from a man who isn't my husband. I sit on the closed toilet seat, breathing in the hot, fragrant steam and scribble into my diary, trying to make sense of how I feel about everything. It's little wonder I feel like I'm going mad.

CHAPTER SIXTEEN

Henry wakes up the next morning with a fever, his eyes bright with cold. He complains of a sore throat and earache, so I tuck him back into bed and call the school to tell them he won't be in. Foraging in the small medicine cabinet in the bathroom, I find that there is maybe a half dose left in the Calpol bottle. Sighing, I remember the last time I used it, making a mental note to buy more, but obviously that didn't happen. He needs medicine to bring his temperature down, and I can't leave him, so I call Lila and she agrees to pop over and sit with him while I run down to the shop to get more. She arrives within ten minutes, a worried look on her face.

'How is he?'

'He's OK – full of cold, but OK. Thanks so much for this, Lila, I really appreciate it. I won't be long.' I grab my coat and briskly make my way up to the shop, careful not to fall on the still-icy pavement.

Mr P. is on the till when I enter the shop – he's in his early fifties, I guess, a smattering of grey in his thick black hair, although there is none in the impressive moustache that sits on his upper lip. There doesn't seem to be any sign of a wife, or any other help in the shop – he is always sitting on his stool next to the till no matter what hour of the day it is. He smiles when he sees me.

'Hello, hello. What can I get you?' I point to the Calpol on the shelf behind the till and he reaches behind him, grabbing the largest bottle. 'Where is your little man today?'

'He's not well,' I explain, handing over the money. 'A bit of a cold, that's all. He'll be back at school soon, I'm sure.' I thank him, and race back home, eager to give my boy his medicine. Anything to make him feel better.

Lila leaves as soon as I return, making her apologies at dashing off so quickly. I wave them away and see her out, before dosing Henry up and cuddling up with him on the couch, pillow and sofa making a cosy bed for him to snooze in. I am dozing with him later on that afternoon when a shadow crosses the front window, jolting me back into wakefulness. I sit up, carefully, so that I don't disturb Henry, and slowly ease myself off the couch towards the front door. The shadow bends out of sight, as if placing something in the porch. Heart thumping, I grab the umbrella, that trusty old weapon. *It's him. Whoever has been leaving the posies. He's outside, leaving one right now.* Making sure the umbrella is in my right hand, ready to smash over the intruder's head, I take deep breath after deep breath. My heart is racing, and I can feel panic clawing at the back of my neck. Swallowing hard, I pull the door open. There is no one there. All the time I have spent psyching myself up to open the door and catch the intruder means he's left whatever he wanted to leave and has gone. I run to the end of the path and look both ways down the street but there's no one there. On the porch lies a small white carrier bag, which, when I open it, contains a football magazine and a small packet of chocolate buttons. Unsettled, and not quite sure what it means, with a queasy feeling in my stomach I throw them in the bin and go back to my spot on the couch, next to a sleeping Henry.

I hibernate for the next few days, only leaving the house to take Henry to school once he is feeling better. Choosing to spend my days indoors instead, I finish off the last couple of articles I've been sent to complete before Christmas. I buy the last few presents, the ones I didn't buy that day when I went for the scan with my mum, choosing things from different websites and arranging for them all to be delivered to the house, so I don't have to go back into town and risk running into Laurence. Cabin fever soon sets in, though, and I find myself pulling on my boots and scarf, intent on walking up to the recreation ground, hoping it will be quiet now the fairground has moved on. I am just stepping out of the front door when the telephone rings, and I dash back to answer it; but, as has often happened over the past few days, when I answer, the line is dead, a dial tone filling my ear as soon as I speak. I shrug my way back into my coat, after hanging up, and leave the house, despite a chill snaking up my back. I'm trying to convince myself that the dropped calls are only Mark trying to get through – I haven't spoken to him since I told him we were having a girl, the day I freaked out on him – but he has emailed a couple of times, just checking that we are OK, and to let me know what time his flight will be arriving on the twenty-fourth. The rational part of me knows that it is probably only Mark, but the part of me that is still a frightened fifteen-year-old girl thinks that maybe he's found me again.

Trying to explain to my mum at fifteen why there was a pregnancy test in the bin was probably the hardest thing I've ever done. She automatically assumed I had been sleeping around, and it was only after I finally told her about the attack that she actually believed I hadn't. Despite the fact that she *did* believe me, that I had been attacked, violated and ruined by a man I didn't know, the damage to our relationship was already done and was only made worse by the events that followed. She sat with me in the abortion clinic, waiting patiently for me to be given the pills that would kill the impostor inside me, and then took me home and tucked me into bed. As far as she was concerned that was the end of it – it didn't need to be spoken about again, not once the police had been to take my statement. And we didn't speak about it, not once. She wouldn't entertain the idea of any kind of therapy, the thought that people might find out what had happened more important than making sure my mental health was dealt with properly. She wouldn't consider it at all, not even when she found me unconscious on my bed, an array of empty pill packets and a bottle of vodka next to me, and the ambulance came to take me to get my stomach pumped. That's where Tessa came in. She listened to me as I cried, and relived the day over and over, trying desperately to understand what I had done wrong – what had I done that made him choose me? She told me over and over that it wasn't my fault – that there was nothing I could have done any differently. She held me as I cried for the baby I had aborted, the baby I didn't want but still felt guilty for killing. I spent as much time with Tessa and her family as I could – even though they knew what had happened, they didn't treat me any differently. They still laughed, told stories about their day, and still behaved around me as they always had. Their house was unchanged, a sanctuary I could escape to, to avoid the thick silence that had permeated my house ever since that day. When the police came to tell me they had caught him – a spotty, greasy-looking boy not much older than me, a boy I wouldn't have looked twice at had I seen him in the street – that he had done it to someone else and they had enough evidence to put him away for a long time, I saw my mother crying quietly into her apron in the kitchen. She didn't sing any more when she cooked, and we still never spoke about it.

I stride up the road towards the park, trying to shake off the memories, the darkness that is always looming close by, and decide to call Lila. I'm still not sure whether she saw what happened on the doorstep the other night and I feel as though I should at least try to explain it, in case she has the wrong impression. Nothing happened, not really, and I don't want her to think something of me that isn't true, even though she tactfully made no reference to it when Henry was poorly. I reach into my pocket for my mobile, ready to muster up the courage to call her and explain it all away, but my pocket is empty. I realise I have either left it at home, or it has fallen out on the way to the park – I left in a hurry and can't remember whether I picked it up or not. I turn on my heel and start to walk back in the direction I came. Now I have decided to call Lila and face up to what happened between myself and Laurence, I can't turn back, as I'm not sure I'll get the courage again.

As I arrive on my street, I see Lila walking back up the path from my front door, towards her own house, so I raise a hand and yell her name. She looks up and, a flush suffusing her cheeks, begins to walk towards me. She reaches me and gives me a kiss on the cheek, and although she is perfectly pleasant, I smile warily, ready to make my confession.

'Lila, listen …'

'Where have you been?' she butts in, not letting me speak. 'I haven't seen you properly for days. I was just knocking to see if you wanted to go for a cup of coffee, or peppermint tea in your case, and catch up. How is Henry feeling?' I stop, thinking that maybe she doesn't really want to speak about it, or maybe she didn't even realise what was going on. Maybe I'm just being paranoid.

'That would be lovely. I was just coming to see you. I wanted to call and see if you wanted to catch up but I think I've left my mobile somewhere.'

'Not a problem, I'm here now. Shall we go up to the café on the corner? Their lemon drizzle cake is to die for.'

Lila folds her arm through mine and we walk slowly up to the café. She chatters on as we walk, telling me how Joe has a new job, something to do with a travel magazine, which means he'll be working away a few nights a week. In fact, he won't be there for Christmas. Of course, I insist that she must spend Christmas with us, unless she is seeing Joe's family. I know she has no family, after losing her parents and brother in a car crash several years ago, and that Joe's family don't really like her, which I find hard to understand – she is so warm and friendly, and has such a kind heart, I can't really imagine anyone not liking Lila. She says she would be delighted to spend it with us. I'm not too sure how Mark will react to having Lila spend Christmas with us, but she's been so kind since he's been gone that I feel like it's the least we can do. The steamy fug of the café hits us as we step inside, a welcoming smell of fresh coffee and baking on the air, and I find us a table while Lila queues for the drinks. She is wearing the coat again, the one that looks just like mine, and from the back she could pass for me. She makes her way back to the table, carefully setting the mugs down before heading back to the till area and returning with two huge lemon cupcakes.

'Here …' She slides one plate across the table towards me. 'Have one of these. No lemon drizzle, but these are just as good. So …' She sips at her coffee. 'Have you seen Laurence lately?'

I pause, unsure of what to say. Did she definitely see what happened on the doorstep that night? I decide to wait and see if she brings it up first.

'Not since last Friday. He came with me to take Henry to the funfair. I can't go on any of the rides so I needed someone to come with me and ride with Henry.'

'It seemed like you were having trouble with him, on the doorstep on Friday. I saw you. It looked like you shoved him away – was everything OK?' *She definitely saw.*

'Um … to tell you the truth, Lila, I don't know what to think. We had a lovely evening, Henry really enjoyed himself, and then … I don't know. Laurence kissed me.' A flush of heat washes over me as I think about it again, the feel of his lips on mine. 'I pushed him away – that's what you saw. I pushed him away, he apologised, and then he left.'

'Gosh.' Lila picks up her cupcake and runs her tongue over the icing. 'That's a bit awkward. And you've not seen him since?'

'No. To be honest, I don't know what to say to him. I mean, he's so lovely, and he actually listens to me. He's been such a good friend … I'm just so confused now. I love Mark, I really do, and I pushed Laurence away, but a tiny part of me actually *liked* it.' I feel mortified now I have confessed that, actually, I did quite enjoy being kissed by someone who isn't my husband, but Lila bursts into laughter.

'Steph, honestly. Don't make everything into such a drama! It's just one kiss, and let's be serious – you're pregnant. It's not like anything is going to happen.'

'What's that supposed to mean?' Weirdly, I feel offended – something did already happen so I can't be that hideous.

'What I mean, *silly*, is that you're pregnant – you're hardly going to run off with Laurence, are you? And your hormones are all over the place; you're bound to feel more upset about things than you would normally.' She licks the rest of the icing from the top of the cupcake, much the way Henry does.

'Yes, OK. I suppose you're right. I'm overthinking things again. Do you think I should just carry on like nothing happened? I don't want to not see Laurence any more over a silly misunderstanding.'

'Absolutely.' Lila nods. 'That's all it is – don't even worry about it. Are you going to eat that?' And she swoops on my cupcake, dragging her tongue across the icing.

We walk home via the school, and on the way there I remember what Henry said about her being inside the school that day, when he thought she was there to collect him.

'Lila,' I begin, nervously, because I don't want her to think I'm accusing her of anything, and equally I really don't want to know she's lied to me. She has been such a calming influence on me lately, and she's the first person I've trusted in my life for a long time, so if I find out she's been lying to me, I'll be devastated. 'Henry says that day when you said you were outside the school … he said you were *inside*, by the friendship stop. And I just wondered … well, why did you say you were *outside* the school? When you were inside?'

Lila pulls a face at me, and I wait anxiously to hear what she has to say. I know that thinking she was there for some sinister reason is paranoid of me, but I can't help thinking the worst.

'Oh, God, honestly? I'm sorry I told you a little fib, Steph. I was there for a job interview; they've got a vacancy for a teaching assistant and I was there to see the head teacher. I didn't want to say anything, as I got made redundant in November just after you moved in, and I didn't want you to think I was a loser.' She looks at me, tears in her eyes. 'You guys have it so together, and I didn't want you to think I was just some lazy dosser with no job. I was waiting to see if I got the job before I mentioned it to you. You're so lucky, Steph. I wish I had what you have.'

I heave in a deep breath and give a little laugh as I breathe out, I am so relieved.

'Oh, Lila, don't be daft. I'm your friend; I don't care what job you have! This is fantastic news. I know Henry will be over the moon if you get it.'

She grins at me, perfect white teeth shining, and I chide myself for being so paranoid, thinking she was there to steal Henry away, or something. I should be thanking my lucky stars to have a friend like Lila.

I leave Lila at the front path and let myself back into the house, slightly anxiously, as I still can't shake off the feeling that someone has been in the house. I inch my way into the hallway, and satisfied that no one has been in, I heave a sigh of relief and strip off my coat and scarf. The phone rings as I pass the hallway table, the shrill tone piercing the air, and my heart starts to beat a little faster – *please don't let it be another dropped call.* I snatch up the receiver quickly, before the other person has a chance to ring off.

'Hello?'

'*Finally*. Darling, where the hell have you been?' Belinda's voice pours down the telephone line, her husky tones unable to mask her irritation.

'Here. I've been here – why? Did you call?'

'Only about a thousand times, sweetheart. Did you not get any of my messages? You're freelance, darling – you need to make sure you keep on top of these things. I've already had to let the Kevin Bacon interview go to Patrick, and you turned down the Melissa Davenport feature. Are you doing *anything* at the moment?' I hear a sharp intake of breath that tells me Belinda is smoking in her office again.

'Yes, well, a few bits here and there. I didn't get any messages. I'm sure I didn't – and I seem to have lost my mobile, so maybe that explains it?'

'No, darling, I called the landline and left a few messages on your voicemail. I thought you were ignoring me.' Another inhalation, and I picture her sitting at her clean, sharp desk, waving her cigarette around in one hand. 'No bother. Are you working, darling? I have a few teensy little bits coming up that I could send your way.'

'Yes, please do, Bel. Sorry, I honestly didn't get any of your messages, and things have been a little up in the air lately, but all back on track now.'

'Good. That's smashing, darling. That shit Mark still away?'

'Yes, and don't call him that, Bel. He is my husband, after all.'

'Yes, well, less said about that the better. I'll whizz you some emails over, sweetie; just make sure you respond or Patrick will be all over them and I won't be able to do anything for you, OK? And darling? Sort yourself a new mobile out.' With that, Belinda hangs up and leaves me staring speechlessly at the phone, overwhelmed by the way she zooms in and out of my life like a tornado. It's strange, though, that she says she's left messages on my voicemail. I check, and the little light that flashes when we receive a message isn't on. I dial the voicemail number, only to get the recorded message that tells me, 'You have no new messages'. Very strange. I get that creeping, crawling sensation under my skin, as though something isn't quite right again, and I try to shove it away, not wanting to get myself in a state, not now.

Henry is home from school, and sitting at the kitchen table doing his homework, so I take the time to catch up on emails, responding to the message Belinda sent over after our conversation today, and almost feeling a little excited about doing a proper interview for the first time in months. I've shut myself away lately doing articles for women's magazines, but Belinda has sent me over an interview for an actor who has recently starred in the nation's favourite soap opera – nothing too taxing, but I am quite looking forward to getting dressed up and heading into town for the day. I email Mark to let him know what's been happening (not everything, obviously), and get rid of all the junk mail. There is just one email address I don't recognise – sent from eyesonyou@hotmail.com with no subject header. Checking to make sure Henry is busy with his homework, I click on the link, my breath sticking in my throat as I read the one-line message that is written there. It reads:

'I AM WATCHING YOU. ALWAYS.'

My hands shaking, I slam the lid of the laptop closed, making Henry jump. I move to the kitchen window, peering through the blinds into the blackness of the garden outside, but it's too dark to make anything out. Trying hard to keep my breathing level and calm so as not to alarm Henry I flick the blinds closed, do the same in the dining room and front room, and then make my way upstairs to close all the upstairs curtains, checking the front door is double-locked on my way up. Shaking, I sit on the bed, head in my hands. It must be him – they must have let him out. Who else could it be? Not content with ruining my life when I was fifteen, has he come back to have another go? A knock on the door sets my heart thumping again. Reaching behind Mark's bedside table I pull out the baseball bat he keeps there 'just in case' and, calling to Henry to stay in the kitchen, make my way downstairs slowly. Picking up the phone, I call Lila, thanking God when she answers straight away.

'It's me. Can you come over?' I keep my voice low so as not to alarm Henry.

'Steph? Are you OK? Of course I can come over. Is everything all right?'

'Please, Lila, just come. I'll show you when you get here.' I hang up the phone and then position myself in front of the door, the baseball bat tucked away and hidden from view. Seeing a shadow coming up the path, I peep through the spy hole before sliding the chain across and opening the door a fraction. Lila stands there, something homemade wrapped in tin foil in her hands. I let my breath out in a slow whoosh and slide the chain off.

'Thank God it's you.' Pulling the door open, I usher her in, casting my eyes about quickly to see if anyone is loitering in the street. Satisfied it's clear, I slam the door closed and reattach the chain.

'Are you OK, Steph?' Lila looks concerned and raises her hand to feel my forehead. 'You look a bit … manic.'

'Yes. No. God, I don't know. Look, go through into the kitchen and I'll explain.'

Lila kicks her shoes off and walks through into the kitchen, ruffling Henry's hair as she sits at the kitchen table. Henry smiles at her and goes back to his colouring, before scowling at me when I tell him to go up and get ready for bed.

'Steph, what's going on? You're acting really weirdly.' Lila glances towards the stairs, where Henry is thumping his way up them as loudly as he possibly can, making me wince with every step. 'And Henry is going to notice, if you don't stop. What's wrong with you?'

I open the lid of the laptop, turning it to face her, open at the email from the unknown sender. I watch her face as she reads it.

'Oh. Gosh. When did you get this?' She peers at the screen again, hand to her mouth.

'Just now. Like, ten minutes ago. Lila, I'm scared. There's something you should know – stuff that happened to me and that I think is going to happen again.' Swallowing hard, I sit down and tell her everything that happened that night when I was fifteen: how I didn't tell anyone until I found out that I was pregnant, how my parents made me abort the baby and how I lost my grip on reality for a little while, with no therapy or professional help to get me through it. How they caught him eventually, how I had to relive it through describing him, his smell, the clothes he wore. How they think that he had probably watched me on my walk home from school every day for some weeks before taking his opportunity. I finish speaking, and Lila takes hold of my hand.

'Oh, you poor darling. What an awful, *dreadful*, thing to happen to you. But listen, he's locked away. There's no way he could get to you now, not after all this time, and I promise you, Laurence and I, we'll look after you,

OK? No one is going to get to you.' She squeezes hard, and I nod, giving her a watery smile.

'Thank you. Do you think I should call the police? Maybe I should let them know about the email?'

'No, darling. Well, you could do, but to be honest, what would they even do? You'll just get yourself all upset again for no reason.'

'They might trace it, maybe? Can't they do something where they follow the IP address or something?'

'I'm sure they can, but I doubt they'd do anything like that just for one email. Sorry, Steph. I don't want to put you off if you feel strongly about going to the police I would just worry that they won't take you seriously. Come on, you put the kettle on and I'll shut this down, so you don't have to look at it any longer.'

She spins the laptop back to face her.

'The screensaver's on. What's your password?' She peers at me over the top of the computer, and I quickly call it out to her before she busies herself closing windows as I fill the kettle. I'm sure Lila is right; he couldn't find me after all this time and the police wouldn't be at all interested, not after just one email. I firmly push thoughts of the dead flowers to the back of my mind.

I am tucked up in bed early, more or less straight after Lila leaves, a book lying unopened on my lap as I sip my tea, trying not to think about the email, when Tessa calls.

'Steph! Did you get my messages? I've been trying to call you to see how the scan went!' Her voice brings a smile to my face, and I tuck another pillow behind me to get comfortable.

'No, sorry, I've lost my mobile – Bel's been trying to get hold of me as well. I don't know what's going on; maybe something's wrong with my voicemail. And the scan was fine – she's a girl!' Tessa's squeal is piercing and I laugh at her excitement. She gabbles away for a while about all the lovely things she can pick up for little girls in New York, before turning serious.

'What about you, though, Steph? Are you OK?' Her voice is soft, and I know she's worrying about before.

'Not really.' I begin to explain to her, my oldest friend, the one who has been through everything with me, about the flowers, the feeling that someone has been in the house, and now the email. The fact that people are trying to contact me but I never seem to get any messages, and the idea that he is back, waiting to catch me unawares, making me feel like I'm going mad. I tell her about Laurence, and how I wish, just for a moment, that the kiss had carried on a little bit longer; and I tell her about Lila, who has been there for me every time I feel like I'm going crazy. When I'm done she lets out a long breath.

'Blimey, Steph. That's a hell of lot of stuff since the last time we spoke. Don't you think maybe you should phone the police? Check that he is actually still locked up? I mean, you've moved a few times since it happened. What if they've tried to contact you?' I wait for her to say something about Laurence, about how I should have let it happen, that Mark deserves everything he gets, but she doesn't.

'Have you noticed one thing, though?' She pauses, as though unsure whether to carry on or not.

'What?'

'Lila. Every time something happens to you, Steph, Lila is there to pick up the pieces. Every single time. Almost as though she knows when something is going to happen and she makes sure she's there for you, when you're frightened or upset.'

'What? Don't be so ridiculous! Lila's my *friend,* Tessa, and let's face it, she's the only one I've got right now. Why would you even suggest something like that? Unless … oh, I know.' I am furious that Tessa could even think such an awful thing about Lila.

'What? I'm not suggesting anything. I just think it's odd she always seems to be around just when you need her, that's all. I'm just saying, be a bit careful.'

'You're jealous, aren't you? You're jealous that Lila is here to help me, and support me, while you swan around New York with Pierre, leading your fabulous life, not giving two shits about me. I can't believe you'd behave like this, Tessa. You should be pleased I have someone who cares about me. You're the one who left, after all, not me.'

'I am, Steph. Jesus, stop being so paranoid. God, sorry, no, I didn't mean that.' Her voice breaks, but it is too late. She's just the same as Mark and all the others, blaming me and telling me I'm paranoid. Mad.

'Enough, Tessa. I don't want to hear it. You've made your feelings perfectly plain. I think it's best you don't contact me for a little while.' I slam the phone down, disappointed and hurt that Tessa would think that way, and reach under the mattress for my diary. Still fired up, I pick up the phone again and dial the number of the detective who dealt with my case all those years ago. Within minutes he comes back to me with the information that Llewellyn Chance can't possibly have had any contact with me. After his parole was denied three years ago, he hung himself in his cell.

Shocked and confused, the detective's words the last thing I ever expected to hear, I open my diary and write and write, about how furious I am with Tessa, with the sender of the email, the flowers, everything. How I am desperately trying to hold things together, constantly trying to make sure I do and say the right thing; how it all just feels exhausting. My writing scrawls across the page, ink blots smudging words, the nib of the pen tearing through the paper onto the page underneath. Finally, feeling wrung out and exhausted, I collapse back onto my pillows and sob until I finally fall asleep.

CHAPTER SEVENTEEN

It's the day of the interview and I'm feeling nervous, the news about Llewellyn Chance having made me feel weirdly exposed and vulnerable – if it's not him, then who is it? I had almost convinced myself it *was* him, so to hear there is no possible way he could have anything to do with it makes me feel even more worried. It's been months since I actually put myself out there and went to interview someone in person, and that, combined with the news, makes me feel even more jumpy than usual. I drop Henry at school, rushing back to get myself ready for the journey into town. Back at home I pull on soft-grey trousers, with a deep-red cashmere jumper, an outfit left over from my pregnancy with Henry, but one that is comfortable and suitable for work. I dig out my black boots with the small heel, knowing my feet will be killing me by the end of the day, and yank open the wardrobe doors to find what Henry calls my 'posh' coat. I rattle through the hangers, but no coat. Pushing them all back towards the front, I go through more slowly, inspecting each item before moving it, checking the coat hasn't fallen off it's hanger and down behind the other clothes. I reach the end and still no coat. A thought flickers across my mind, the idea that Lila is wearing a very similar coat to mine lately, and I push it away. Lila's my friend; she wouldn't steal my coat. It's madness to think someone would steal a coat. I shake my head at myself, tutting under my breath. Anyway, she hasn't ever been upstairs, apart from to tuck Henry in. It's more likely it either got lost in the house move, or that Mark took it to the dry cleaner's and forgot to tell me. Swishing through the hangers for the third time, I dig out a half-decent black jacket – it won't be warm enough, but there's no way I can turn up in my usual battered old coat. Winding a thick grey scarf round my neck, I grab my bag and head for the tube station. There's still no sign of my mobile, so I've asked the school to contact my mum if they need to for any reason. For the first time in ages I feel a bit more like my old self – it must be the idea of doing what feels like a proper day's work.

Arriving at the restaurant where the interview is to take place, I see that my interviewee has already arrived, and is seated at the table with a large glass of wine in front of him, despite the fact it's only just lunchtime. I introduce myself and allow the waiter to lead me over to the table, only spying Belinda sitting next to the soap star at the last minute. She gets to her feet, plucking her coat from the chair behind her.

'Darling, so glad you're here. I'll leave you two to it. Stephanie – I want to see you in my office tomorrow. Is that possible? I wasn't going to take a chance on leaving you a message and I was in town with Johnny anyway.' She gives me a lascivious wink and, *ewwww*, I realise she's spent the night with him, even though she's twenty years his senior. Belinda pecks me on the cheek and, ignoring Johnny completely, sashays her way through the maze of tables to the front door.

I introduce myself to Johnny, trying my hardest not to think about whatever he and Belinda got up to last night. He is nice enough, in a dim kind of way, and answers my questions without much imagination. In fact, the only time he becomes animated is when someone enters the restaurant in a flurry of activity, waiters bustling around her to take her coat, an entire entourage following her inside.

'Sorry, love.' Johnny leans to one side, laying one hand on my shoulder to push me the other way so he can get a better view. 'Now that is what you call hot stuff. No offence to your mate Belinda, but she's more up my street, that one over there.'

I turn to look behind me, only to see, to my dismay, Melissa Davenport striding into the restaurant wearing a tiny skirt and ridiculous heels. I swallow hard, beating down the vomit that rises to the back of my throat, and unclenching my hands, which have found themselves instinctively making fists. I lean behind me to grab my coat and get to my feet.

'I wouldn't if I were you, darling,' I lean down and whisper into Johnny's ear. 'She's got crabs.'

I snigger under my breath all the way home, wondering how long it'll take before someone (and I'm hoping for *heat* magazine here) picks up on the rumour that Melissa Davenport has crabs. Maybe Belinda will hear and it'll run in next week's edition of the magazine. A tiny shadow of doubt crosses my mind at the thought of seeing Belinda in her office tomorrow – I've never been summoned in before, and I'm hoping it's nothing bad. After all, surely she would just tell me if she didn't want to give me any more work? I am mulling everything over in my mind and not paying any attention to where I am going when I collide with someone going in the opposite direction.

'Gosh, I'm sorry. Are you OK?' Looking up, Laurence is in front of me, and I can't help the blush that rises, staining my cheeks a furious red.

'Laurence – God, I'm sorry; I wasn't looking where I was going. I'm fine – are you?' Awkward doesn't cover it – I don't have a clue what to say to him, and it seems he feels the same way.

'Look …'

'About the other night …'

We both begin speaking at once, and I hold up a hand.

'Please, Laurence. Let me go first. I'm sorry about the other night – it was a stupid mistake and I don't want us to fall out over it. Can we forget about it?'

'No, I'm sorry. I was an idiot. Honestly, Steph – it doesn't change the way I feel about you, but yes, I do want us to be friends. Forgotten, if that's what you want. And I'm sorry for the text messages – I just didn't know what to say.'

Feeling relieved, I take his hand. 'OK. Friends. Let's say no more about it.'

We begin to walk back towards the tube station, dawdling in the winter sunshine and chatting about the interview today and the article Laurence is working on. All too soon we reach the station, and I pull away from him.

'I'm sorry, Laurence, I'm not going home yet. I've got an appointment, but I'll see you later? Dinner? Maybe when Mark gets home?'

I want to keep our time alone together to a minimum, not because I don't trust him but because I don't trust myself. Laurence agrees, and I turn back and walk the way we just came. I have an appointment with Dr Bradshaw. It's only once I am sitting in the doctor's freezing-cold waiting room that I realise Laurence mentioned text messages – and I remember that I never told him I'd lost my mobile.

Dr Bradshaw ushers me into his only marginally warmer office, after keeping me waiting for twenty minutes in the freezing reception area. He apologises for making me wait, citing a patient emergency, and I shrug it off, not really bothered, the time spent waiting used to mull over the events of the past few days.

'So, how are things?' He looks a little bit more together than last time, and I wonder whether he and Mrs Bradshaw have reconciled their differences, or whether Mrs B. has been bumped in favour of a younger model. Either way, someone is ironing his shirts for him again.

'Steph? I asked you how things have been?'

'Sorry, Dr Bradshaw, I was miles away. Um … things haven't been great, if I'm honest. I mean, the baby is OK – I had a scan. And … well, yes. Everything is fine.'

'Well, it's good news about the baby. What kinds of other things have been happening? I'd like you to tell me what's been going on, what you've been up to.' He reaches for his battered notepad, fully prepared to start scratching away making notes. I have to tell him about the email – surely he can't put that down to my being paranoid. I have the email in my inbox.

'I had an email, from someone with an email address I don't recognise, saying they're watching me. All the time.' I blink back tears as Dr B. scratches away at his notepad. Words start tumbling out, pouring over each other as though someone has turned on a tap. 'Someone has been in the house, my coat is gone, the phone keeps ringing but when I answer there's nobody there.

I'm feeling a bit anxious, Doctor, and I don't know what to do – I feel like ...' I bite off the words '*I'm going mad*' before they can escape my mouth, cross with myself that I let so much slip. Now I'm terrified he'll want to try to give me medication, before I remember the baby and remember he can't make me take it, not if I don't want to.

'OK, Steph, calm down. There's nothing to worry about – you're safe here. Tell me about the email – did you show it to anybody else?'

'Yes, Lila. She said not to call the police, that they wouldn't do anything. And what about the other things? What about someone coming into my house while I'm not there?'

'Do you know for sure that someone was in the house? Did they move things, leave a trace?' He watches me carefully, eyes sympathetic, and I just know he doesn't believe me.

'No, it was just a kind of ... feeling. The way you can feel if somebody has just left the room. Maybe it was just my imagination, playing tricks on me. I've always had a vivid imagination, since I was a little girl.' If I downplay it enough, he'll think I'm OK, that I don't really need his help.

'Steph, honestly, I think maybe you're feeling a little fragile at the moment, vulnerable in your pregnancy, and Mark being away isn't helping. Your coat and your mobile going missing – I think it's probably a case that you've put them down somewhere and can't remember where you left them. If you really are feeling that worried, I can prescribe you something mild, something that won't affect the baby, but it's not a route I want to go down. I think with your regular appointments, and if you keep writing in your diary to handle these emotions, we can get you through this without medication. I'm here to make sure you don't go through what you went through last time, when you had Henry. OK? Perhaps you could bring your diary along next time, and we could look at it together?'

'No, I don't think so. I don't feel ready to share that just yet, if that's OK?'

He gives a sympathetic nod.

'OK, Steph, we can wait until you're ready. But perhaps get rid of the email? I don't think it would be healthy for you to keep rereading it and experiencing the emotions it's evoking in you.'

I agree – anything to get out of his office while I can – but I have no intention of deleting that email. It's the only concrete proof I have so far that I'm not making any of this up.

Inwardly seething, I force myself to walk calmly out of his office, ignoring the receptionist's call to me as I stamp past her desk, ramming my hat onto my head and yanking the door open, out onto the freezing streets. I march up the road towards the tube station, my footsteps thudding in time with my heartbeat, rage making me hot and flustered. By the time I get the train, even managing to find a seat, I am shaking and tearful. I can't go back to see Dr Bradshaw again – it's quite clear he doesn't believe a word I'm saying, obviously choosing to believe it's all in my head. Decision made, I start to calm down a little, although I decide not to mention it to Mark – he'll only worry and then we'll end up having a row. I'll just carry on leaving the house at the usual prearranged appointment times and find somewhere to sit until it's time to come back home.

By the time the train comes in, it is time to collect Henry from school, so I walk directly up the hill, chilly in my jacket now that my fury has died down. As I arrive, my heart sinks – despite the cold weather, trestle tables have been set up in the school playground, each one heaving under the weight of homemade cakes and trinkets, various PTA members standing behind them, blowing on freezing-cold hands and hopping from foot to foot to keep warm. *Shit. The PTA cake-sale fundraiser.* I remember now pulling a crumpled flier out of Henry's bag, a brightly coloured, hand-drawn poster requesting donations. I have completely forgotten all about it, and after my run-in with Jasmine at the funfair, I am anxious she'll be waiting for me, ready to haul me over the coals for it. Too late to hide, Jasmine spies me and comes striding towards me, dark hair flying out behind her and a sweet smile on her face, which I am not sure is genuine. One of her PTA pals scurries after her, an empty sweet tin holding loose change in her hands.

'Steph – how are you?' Jasmine air kisses my cheek as I stand rigidly in front of her, the other woman grinning inanely at her side. 'I didn't see a contribution for the cake stall from you. Did you, Martha? Although, luckily, Henry will still be able to benefit from the items bought with the proceeds. We do like to treat all the children equally.' The fake smile stays fixed to her face, while the other woman, Martha, shakes her head sadly.

'Look, Jasmine, I'm sorry about the other day but …'

'Sorry? Nothing to be sorry about, *dear*, all forgotten.' She turns to Martha. 'Stephanie's son and Bradley had a little *accident* at the funfair – you got a bit distressed about it all, didn't you, Steph? But it really was nothing.'

I feel the confusion cross my face – she is completely changing what was said and by whom. I open my mouth to say something but her voice cuts me off.

'Anyway, Steph, I meant to say to you – I believe you know a good friend of mine? Melissa? I'll send her your and Mark's regards, shall I?' She flashes her teeth at me again and I see red, anger coursing through me and making me lose all rationality.

'*How fucking dare you?* You complete and utter bitch!' I make a grab for her, planning on yanking that perfect dark bob right off her head. She shrieks and her minions come running, grasping me about the upper arms from behind and holding me back.

'Mrs Gordon! Mrs Gordon, *please.*' Mrs Cooper, the head teacher, is holding me still, tightly gripping my upper arms, while Miss Bramley and her entire class stand looking on in horror, including my lovely little boy. Gasping for breath I shrug her off and allow Miss Bramley to lead me back into her classroom, leaving her teaching assistant to send the children over to their parents. By the time we reach it, I am crying properly, shame and disgust at my own behaviour flooding through me.

'I'm so sorry,' I gulp, accepting her offer of a seat, a tiny child's chair on which I perch precariously. 'I just snapped … it's been an awful day and she said things that aren't … I'm sorry.' Miss Bramley hands me a tissue, and I swipe at my cheeks.

'Mrs Gordon, I do understand that you're going through a difficult time at the moment, what with Henry struggling to fit in and your husband working away, but I really can't condone this kind of behaviour, especially not in front of the children.'

I nod slowly. I do understand this, but I have to explain myself.

'Miss Bramley, Mrs Hale has said some horrid … I don't think you really understand … I mean, I'm not like this, this isn't the kind of person I am.'

'Mrs Hale has been the head of the PTA here for a very long time, Mrs Gordon, and we have never had an incident like this take place before. It is unacceptable.' Mrs Cooper stands in the doorway, arms folded across her body. 'On this occasion I won't take further action, but in future, please be aware that I will have you removed from the premises if this happens again.' With that, she turns on her heel and flounces out of the room. Miss Bramley pats my hand kindly, as another deluge of tears run down my cheeks and I sniff pathetically.

'Is there someone I can call? Someone who can walk home with you? I don't like to let you go when you're in this state.' I nod, and give her Lila's phone number.

'She's a friend, she knows Henry, she'll come and walk us home. You probably know her; she's applied for a position here.' I am wiping my face, trying to pull myself together, when Henry comes in with the teaching assistant.

'Are you OK, Mummy?' He climbs onto my lap and strokes my hair away from my face.

'Yes, darling, I'm fine. Just a silly misunderstanding. Lila's coming to walk home with us – won't that be lovely? Maybe we can stop in the park.'

Lila arrives shortly after, her hair flyaway and cheeks flushed as a result of rushing to get to the school in the shortest possible time. She glares at Mrs Cooper, who lurks in the doorway again with a sour look on her face, and takes Henry's hand before turning to me.

'Are you OK, Steph? Come on, let's get out of here and get you home.' I am too exhausted to bother with Mrs Cooper and I walk past her, head down, hopeful that Jasmine Hale and her cronies have already left. A few of them are still gathered in the playground as we leave, clearing away the remains of the fundraiser and glancing over from under their perfectly coiffed hair-dos. I avoid their gaze, leaving them to gossip about me as I walk out of the gates. We take Henry to the park, perching on the cold bench together while Henry slides down the slide over and over again.

'Want to tell me what happened?' Lila asks gently, resting a hand on mine to stop me from plucking at the threads on my jumper.

'She just started on me. And then I flipped out. Sorry, Lila, it's been a long day and I just lost my temper. I'm sorry to drag you out. I just got in a bit of a state.'

'Oh, shhhhh,' she says, before giving her tinkly little laugh. 'She really is a bitch, isn't she? Listen, sweetie, people like her always get what's coming to them. One day, she'll say something to the wrong person and it'll all blow up in her face.' I give her a small smile, before looking quickly away under the pretence of checking on Henry, not wanting her to see quite how upset I am by it all.

I invite Lila to have dinner with us, unwilling to spend the evening alone after the upsetting events of the day. She accepts, but says she will pop back to her house first and pick up the biscuits she baked earlier for Henry. While I wait for her, I make Henry a drink and get him settled in front of the television for a little while, not a usual event after school, but today I feel he needs the treat, and I need the time to get myself together again. I shove his school bag and shoes into the cupboard under the stairs and head up to my room, deciding to have one last look for my missing coat – just to prove to Dr Bradshaw that I'm not going mad, if nothing else. I scrabble through the hangers one more time, and drop to my knees and peer under the bed, knowing as I do so that it will be a fruitless search. What I see under there brings a scream to my throat, a cry that has Lila flying up the stairs, with Henry close behind her.

She pushes her way into the room, huddling down on the floor next to me, where I am sitting, throat raw from my screams, yet more tears running over my hot cheeks, my hands shaking and my stomach roiling.

'What is it, Steph? Calm down and show me.'

Henry is standing in the doorway, crying and twisting his hands together. I hold my shaking hands out to him, gesturing for him to come to me for a hug.

'Under the bed. It's another bouquet, Lila. Someone has been in and left more flowers. Under my bed.' I feel sick, the very idea that someone has been creeping around my house while I am not there making my skin crawl. Lila peers underneath, drawing back in shock when she sees I am telling the truth. Henry has edged his way into the room, and Lila quickly stands, scooping him into her arms before I can get to him.

'Come on, little fella,' she says to him, as she bustles away towards the stairs with him in her arms, 'I've got something special for you downstairs.' They leave the room and I sink back down onto the floor. I want Henry with me, but Lila seems to have control of the situation and I don't want to frighten him by shouting for her to bring him back.

'Let me get it out. Don't you touch it, Steph.' Lila is back, calm and collected, with no sign of hysteria, unlike me. She reaches under the bed and hooks the dusty, decayed bunch of flowers out with one finger, once again tied with a sleek, black ribbon, a look of distaste on her perfectly aligned features. 'Well, *this* is definitely not in your imagination.'

'I told you, didn't I? I told you someone had been in the house and no one believed me. You all just thought I was going mad. Someone is out to get me, to frighten me, and I don't know who it is, but it's working.' I still feel sick, my hand resting on my belly.

'It's OK, Steph, calm down. I'm sorry I didn't believe you before but now … I do think you're right – someone is trying to frighten you.' Her voice is grave, and I feel a flicker of fear somewhere deep inside of me. It's all very well to have these fears, but when someone else confirms them it just makes it all feel even more real.

'So I'm not going mad, am I? Someone is definitely trying to scare me.' A sense of relief washes over me. Lila believes me, which means that surely, when I tell him, Mark will believe me too. A frown crossing her brow, Lila holds the bouquet between her finger and thumb, her nose wrinkled. It is dusty, brown and withered and made from the exact same plants as the previous ones, which only makes me believe it can only be the same person who has left them each time. Lila takes a breath as if to speak, before abruptly closing her mouth and getting to her feet.

'What? Lila – what were you going to say?' She leaves the room and I heave myself to my feet and follow her. I watch as she steps outside and goes directly to the recycling bin and ceremoniously throws the bouquet into it, dusting her hands off as soon as it leaves her grip. She casts her eyes towards next door, where a warm, yellow light floods out of Laurence's living room window, his blinds open and his shadow moving backwards and forwards as he crosses the room. I close the front door behind her, and follow her into the kitchen where she takes a seat at the kitchen table, a grim look on her face.

'Lila, please, what is it? Will you just tell me?' I am exhausted and not sure if I can cope with any more drama today. I don't want to cook dinner now, or spend the evening with Lila. I just want to curl up with Henry and ignore the rest of the world.

'Steph, I don't know how to say this but ... how well do you know Laurence?'

'Not that well, not as well as I know you. Why? What does Laurence have to do with this?' My heart begins to slam in my chest; Lila is going to tell me something I really don't think I want to hear.

'It's just ... the posies. All of them have been made up of flowers and plants that grow in Laurence's garden.'

'Yes, I did notice that, but it doesn't mean anything. These plants grow all over the place. It doesn't mean that Laurence is the one who left the bouquets, does it? Why would he? He's my friend.' *She's wrong. She has to be wrong.*

'I understand that, Steph. But what I don't understand is why I saw him coming out of your house earlier today – when Miss Bramley called to say you were at the school. Steph – I think Laurence is the one who's leaving you these bouquets.'

CHAPTER EIGHTEEN

It's the last day of term – thank goodness – and I drop an overexcited Henry off at school before heading into town to Belinda's office. I keep my head down at the school gate, unwilling to make eye contact with Jasmine and her bunch of witches who congregate in their usual spot in the playground, whispering to each other. Feeling awkward, I wave Henry off as Miss Bramley gives me a weak smile, and then I turn on my heel and slink out of the playground, making my escape without having to speak to anybody.

The rush hour is over by the time I get to the tube station, so I sink gratefully into a seat and ponder what Lila said to me last night. I don't want to believe for a second that Laurence has been behind everything, not when I seem to have got so close to him. Although I'm not sure there's an alternative, now I know there is no way it could be Llewellyn Chance, as I first thought. The more I think about it, the less convinced I am that Laurence would want to hurt me – maybe I did hurt his ego by pushing him away the other night, but what kind of respectable married woman *wouldn't*? We'd agreed since then that it was all over and done with – forgotten. And I can't see how it is all connected – the flowers were left before I even really knew Laurence. The train pulls into my stop and I get off, my head a tangle of confusion. With the worry about why Belinda has called me into her office alongside the worry about whoever is taunting me, my anxiety levels are sky-high by the time I arrive. I sit in the cosy, warm reception area while I wait for Belinda, tucking my shaking hands under my thighs to hide them from her eagle-eyed secretary, Portia, a girl who never fails to miss a trick and enjoys being able to use them against you in some way.

Her phone buzzes on her desk and she waits for five minutes or so after hanging up before she turns to me. Twirling her brittle, bleached hair around one finger, she eyes me closely before saying, 'You can go in now.'

Biting my lip in order to avoid telling her how rude she is, I pick up my bag and sling my jacket over my forearm and try to stride as confidently as possible into Belinda's office, a difficult thing to do in heeled boots on the thick, plush carpet that is laid throughout.

'Ah, you made it, darling. Here, sit down.'

Belinda kicks a boot out under the desk at the chair opposite her, e-cigarette wafting in one hand.

'Bel. So, what did you want to see me about?' Nervously, I bite my lip. I might as well just cut to the chase, and get whatever it is over with.

'Honestly, Steph? I'm just worried about you. And I'm not the only person who's worried right now.' She takes a deep drag on her e-cigarette, before coughing.

'There's nothing to worry about, Bel. Honestly. I'm just a bit … I told you when we had lunch a little while ago, the pregnancy and Mark being away, it's just taken its toll a little bit. There's been a lot going on and I've been busy. That's all.'

'Bullshit.' Belinda gives me a hard glare across the table. 'Steph, we've been friends and colleagues for years. I know when you're not right – you've not replied to a single message I've sent you since we had lunch.' She sits back in her chair, quite obviously waiting for me to respond.

'I haven't *had* any messages, Bel, that's why! I've lost my mobile, there have been no messages on the house phone … unless …' I stop, not wanting to go any further as a horrid thought strikes me. 'Bel, things have been happening. Like, weird stuff. I thought somebody had maybe been in the house – maybe they've deleted my messages to make you think I don't want to speak to you?' Heart thumping, I feel triumphant – of course that's why I haven't had any messages! Belinda sighs, and leans forward on her hands, hair falling over one eye.

'Steph, why would someone want to delete your messages? It's not like they were really that important, is it? And why would you think someone was in the house?'

'Because they *were*. I could feel it, Bel, that feeling you get when someone has just left the room. Things are missing – my coat, you know the nice one I wear for work meetings? Well, it's gone; I can't find it anywhere. A picture Henry drew for me at school has disappeared – I stuck it on the fridge; it was a picture he had drawn of Mark, himself and me, and it was lovely. All of us together, with a big heading saying "My Family". I stuck it up so Mark would see it when he came home, and now it's vanished. Other little things are missing too – my tiny diamond earrings were in my jewellery box and now I can't find them; the little blanket Henry used to sleep with as a baby isn't in the box where I left it. Plus, there are the posies.'

I explain in depth to Belinda about how the flowers have been left for me, and when I'm done she pulls the e-cigarette back out of the drawer she'd stashed it in and takes a long, deep drag.

'Steph, this happened before, don't you remember? When you were poorly after you had Henry – you accused us of all sorts of things. Saying that things had been moved when they hadn't. That we had taken stuff when no one had been anywhere near it. Cutting yourself off from everyone. That's why I'm so worried now.' I shake my head, about to explain that this isn't the same; that it's different this time.

'I spoke to Tessa,' she says, and my heart sinks a little at the mention of Tessa's name. 'She says you two have had a bit of a falling out and now you're refusing to speak to her.' Feeling like a petulant child being told off by its mother, I shake my head again.

'That's not my fault, Bel. She said some horrible things about Lila, unforgivable things. She's jealous that Lila is here for me when she isn't.'

'Really, Steph? Tessa's been your friend for a very long time – do you really think she would be that petty? All these things that have been happening to you … the posies being left and things going missing … Steph, you're pregnant, it's easy to mislay things …'

'NO. Belinda, please. I am not imagining things – you're just as bad as Tessa, Dr Bradshaw … even Mark! These things have happened, and it seems like Lila is the only one I can rely on at the moment – she's the only one who believes that these things are actually happening to me. I know we've been through it all before, but I *swear*, Bel, it's different this time.' I am furious, and so disappointed that yet another so-called friend is failing to believe me.

'It's not that I don't believe you, Steph, but you have to remember, we *have* been here before, haven't we, darling? Remember how you were after Henry came along? Tessa is just worried about you – we all are.'

Belinda leans forward to take my hand, and I snatch it away fiercely.

'You don't need to worry about me, Belinda. I'm perfectly fine. I don't need your concern.' Standing, I snatch up my jacket from the back of my chair and storm out of the office, leaving Belinda staring after me.

I walk back through town towards home, not wanting to be confined in the dark, claustrophobic space of the tube. I kick through the sparse leaves that decorate the pavement, the baby swooping and swirling inside me, clearly invigorated by the anger that is coursing through my body. Belinda, of all people, I thought would have understood. Yes, I went through a tough time after Henry, and she even knows what happened to me before, but I am NOT mad, that I am sure of. Someone is trying to frighten me, and I don't know who, but I know it's not all in my head. It can't be.

I arrive at the school slightly late, the walk back from town taking longer than I had anticipated. Rushing up the hill towards the school gate I pass a few stragglers, the majority of mums having already collected their children ten minutes before, telling me I really am late. Cursing under my breath, I hurry through the gates and quickly look around the playground for Miss Bramley. She usually waits by the friendship stop, next to the school office, with any children whose parents might have been caught in traffic or are slightly delayed for whatever reason. Today, however, there is no Miss Bramley waiting outside with Henry, or any other children for that matter. I'm not too concerned – it is December, after all; no doubt she has taken the children back into the classroom to wait for the late parents in the warm. I let myself into the school, and walk down the hushed corridor to Henry's classroom. The cold has made my nose run, and I sniff as I push open the classroom door, to reveal Miss Bramley marking at her desk. There is a little girl sitting in the reading corner, a picture book open on her lap, but no Henry.

'Mrs Gordon …' Miss Bramley smiles up at me. 'Can I help you?'

I swallow hard; there is something definitely wrong with this picture.

'Where's Henry?' I demand, looking wildly around the empty classroom, just in case he is here, hiding under the table.

'Henry's been collected, Mrs Gordon. Isn't that what you'd arranged?' She gets to her feet, a look of alarm on her face.

'What? No! I didn't arrange for anyone to collect him – I'm just a bit late, that's all. I've lost my mobile; I couldn't call you to tell you.' A sick feeling swarms over me and my breath starts to come faster as panic takes hold. The teacher gives a quick glance towards the child in the reading corner, before taking my arm and leading me gently towards the corridor.

'Don't panic, Mrs Gordon, I'm sure there is a reasonable explanation – Henry is a bright boy; he wouldn't just go with anyone.'

'I can't believe you just let him *leave*. You're supposed to be taking care of him.' I can't help myself; I am shrieking at her, panic making me crazy. Mrs Cooper comes marching along the corridor, her hair an iron helmet, a scowl on her face.

'Mrs Gordon, I already warned you the other day …'

'*You!*' I turn on her. '*You're supposed to look after the children.* Someone has taken my son – and you let him go! Call the police, I'm going outside to look for him.' Mrs Cooper jolts into action, grabbing Miss Bramley's arm and talking at her urgently. Ignoring them I rush out into the playground, shouting Henry's name. Tears choke my throat, and I cry, as I can't seem to shout his name loudly enough. Turning, whirling around, desperately searching for my baby boy, Mrs Cooper appears beside me, taking hold of my arm.

'Mrs Gordon, the police have been called. The teaching assistant who took the children out seems to think someone came to collect Henry – someone he knows. He was more than happy to go with her.'

'Her? A woman took him?' I stop, confused. 'What did she look like?'

'I'm afraid I wasn't on duty. The teaching assistant saw her, and is waiting for the police to arrive so she can give a description and make a statement. I know this is difficult, but we really must try to remain calm, if we're going to find Henry quickly.'

I nod, trying to catch my breath, anything to make her let go of my arm and let me go back to searching for Henry. She backs off, and I head towards the school gate, ignoring her cries at me to stop and wait for the police. I have to go; I have to find him.

As I step out of the gate I hear the most beautiful sound I could possibly have wished for at that moment – the sound of my little boy crying, 'Mummy!' And there he is, barrelling towards me, running down the lane that leads from the school to the recreation ground.

'Oh, God, Henry, you're OK. Oh, come here.' I bend down and scoop him into my arms, tears staining my cheeks as I carry him back into the school.

'You've got him? Where was he?' Miss Bramley appears at my side, tears glistening in her eyes, fear and relief mixing together.

'Just there – just outside, running back up from the path.' I squeeze him close, covering his face with tiny kisses and inhaling his unique scent. As I look up, Lila is coming through the school gate, a smile on her face.

'Hey, I thought you were going to be late.' She grins, before the smile drops from her face at the rage reflected back at her on mine.

'What the hell do you think you're doing? You don't just turn up at the school and take someone's child! Do you know the hell you've just put me through?'

I am shaking with anger, Henry squirming in my arms. 'The police are on their way. I hope you can explain yourself.'

Shocked, Lila turns away and begins rummaging in her bag.

'Here.' She thrusts out a hand, holding her mobile phone out to me. 'You sent me a message to say you'd been held up and would be a bit late, so could I collect Henry? That's exactly what I did. I picked him up and took him to the park, and we were just on our way back home.'

I look down at the phone, reading a message that says exactly that. I can't explain it, and I am so relieved to have Henry back, I just shove the phone back at her and turn to the teachers.

'I'm sorry. There seems to have been a misunderstanding. I'm going to take Henry home now.'

Miss Bramley nods and gives my arm a quick squeeze, while Mrs Cooper looks decidedly unimpressed, and leaves to call the police to tell them Henry has been found. I walk out of the gates, holding tightly to Henry's hand, and Lila catches us shortly, slightly out of breath from jogging to catch up.

'I'm sorry, Steph, I thought I was doing what you asked me to.' She is apologetic, biting her lip, her green eyes filled with sorrow.

'All right. Just leave it, OK?' I march on, gripping Henry's hand tightly, embarrassment making me curt with her. I am mortified that I flipped out once again in front of Mrs Cooper, although I think any mother would have done the same if they'd arrived to find their child gone. Briskly, I march Henry up the garden path to our house, closing the door on Lila before she can apologise again. Henry, completely unfazed by it all, runs upstairs to play with Lego, while I lean against the front door and get my breath back. Opening it again, I look out to see Lila still standing at the end of the path, looking forlorn.

'Lila,' I call, 'I'm sorry, OK? Just a misunderstanding. I'll call you tomorrow.' She nods once, and moves on.

I settle Henry into bed early, have a hot bath to soothe away the aches and stresses of the day and climb into bed to write in my diary before I fall asleep. I write about Belinda, about my disappointment that she thinks this is like the last time, and about how panicked I felt when Henry wasn't where I thought he was. I write about how it seems to be getting harder and harder for me to keep control of my emotions, to keep up the pretence that everything is fine. I am exhausting myself every day trying to say the right things. I know now that there's little chance of anyone believing this isn't all in my head, and I realise I am pretty much alone in trying to deal with it all. Except for Laurence and Lila. They are the only ones who seem to believe these things might have actually happened. *But Laurence is also the one with all the components of the bouquets growing in his garden*, a tiny voice whispers in my ear. As I tip over the edge, into that semi-conscious world between sleeping and waking, a niggle tugs at the back of my mind. It's only as I'm falling headfirst into a dreamless sleep that I realise Lila had a text, asking her to collect Henry. But I still don't have my mobile.

CHAPTER NINETEEN

'Daddy!' Henry sprints down the hallway and throws himself into Mark's arms before Mark even manages to get one foot over the threshold. I hang back at the other end of the hallway, shyly waiting until Henry has smothered Mark with kisses. I am feeling OK – the panic over Henry going missing has calmed; I've seen Lila and sorted out the misunderstanding with her. Luckily, there are no hard feelings and we are as close, if not closer, than ever. She was understanding about my reaction, and I feel as though I can rely on her now even more than before. The past few days have been quiet, with no eerie feelings that someone has been in the house and no decayed bouquets left in the porch. I have made an effort for my husband – the last time he was home I was still in the throes of morning sickness, unable to do more than the basics required for me to leave the house. Now, though, this has passed and I have freshly washed hair, softly curled around my slightly chubbier face (now the sickness has passed, but unfortunately I still seem to be just as hungry), and I have treated myself to a soft, long, cashmere jumper that I'm wearing over black maternity tights. A slick of pink lip gloss and a touch of mascara and I look like a different woman to the bedraggled one he left behind. He staggers into the house, Henry clinging to him like a monkey, and makes his way towards me. Even now, after all these years and all the heartache we've been through, he still has the ability to make my stomach flip. *How did I ever think I could be attracted to someone else?* He leans down and gives me a soft kiss on the lips.

'Hey, you.'

'Hey. I'm so glad you're home.' He peels Henry off him and wraps me in his tanned arms. I sink into them, his warmth soothing the chilled core that has always seemed to haunt me, ever since I was fifteen. A clearing of the throat from behind Mark makes me jump and I peer over his shoulder to see Laurence, standing awkwardly in the doorway. Slipping out of Mark's arms, I give him a questioning look.

'Look who I found outside! Laurence offered to give me a hand with my bags, and it's so cold outside after Paraguay I wasn't going to say no.' Mark chuckles, and I lean forward to take the smaller bag from Laurence, careful to make sure our fingers don't touch.

'Laurence. Thank you, but I think …'

Mark talks over me, leaning over to shake Laurence's hand.

'Thanks for the hand there, mate, and for looking after these two while I've been away. If you'll excuse me though, pal, I need to reacquaint myself with my wife, if you know what I mean.' He gives a wink and I sigh inwardly. I look at the floor, in order to avoid looking at Laurence.

'No problem, Mark. Steph and Henry are a pleasure to be around.' Mark doesn't pick up on the tone of Laurence's voice, but I do, and I feel a flush wash over my cheeks, staining them red, a common occurrence whenever Laurence is around, it seems. It's all very well saying we can be friends, but I don't know how well that's going to go. Mark carries Henry through into the living room, leaving me to say goodbye to Laurence.

'Are you OK?' He looks hard into my eyes, and I nod.

'Yes, of course I am. My husband is home, isn't he?' I stare back, challenging him to say anything more. He gives a small shake of his head before turning to walk down the path.

'Well, you know where I am, if you need me.'

'Goodbye, Laurence.'

Mark and I get Henry to bed, much later than planned, as he is overwhelmed with excitement. The combination of his dad coming home, plus the fact that it's Christmas Eve is a perfect recipe for an overexcited little boy.

Eventually, though, after leaving out a plate of goodies for Father Christmas and Rudolph, setting out his stocking in front of the fire and Mark reading *The Night Before Christmas* to him three times, he is finally falling asleep. I tuck him in, and creep back down the stairs to join Mark in the living room. The fire is roaring, and he has poured himself a glass of wine, and made me a cup of peppermint tea. I curl up next to him, as best I can, on the sofa and he rests a hand on my bump.

'So, Mrs Gordon, how was everything while I was away?' He strokes my belly, and the baby swoops and swirls inside of me.

'Fine. Nothing exciting happened.'

'Are you sure? You were pretty upset when I called you last.' The last time I spoke to Mark was the day I freaked out, about the posies and everything that had been going on. We'd only been able to email since.

'No, it's all been fine. I don't know what got into me that day. Hormones, I expect.' It grates on me to say it, but after Belinda not believing me, not a lot of support from Dr Bradshaw, and feeling as though Mark didn't take it terribly seriously on the phone, I have made the decision not to tell Mark anything else. Not just yet, anyway. He didn't seem to believe me that day on the phone, even though he said otherwise, so I think the best thing to do is wait until I have enough proof to show him – like another posy. He puts his arm around me and I lean into him.

'Well, it's to be expected, I suppose. But you're sure everything is OK?' A small frown crosses his brow and I know he is worried that I will sink into a post-natal depression, just like I did with Henry.

'It's *fine*. I promise you, it won't be like before.'

'I missed you, you know. I wish I hadn't had to go.' He kisses my forehead. 'I've told them I want to stay home until after the baby has come. I don't want to leave you again.'

'I missed you too. We both did.'

'And I'm sorry, you know that? I've never regretted anything more. But we can make this work, Steph, I promise you. I'm here because I love you, and I want to be with you – no one else.' He leans over and places his mouth gently over mine, making my stomach flip.

'Me too.'

With that, he jumps up and pulls me to my feet.

'Come on, Mrs Gordon, time for bed.'

The next morning, Henry is up with the birds, despite his late night, and I know we will probably pay for it later. He's a good boy, but it doesn't stop him getting ratty when he's tired. He opens his stocking, with Mark and I beside him, making all the right noises as he opens all the little packages that Father Christmas has left for him. Stocking done, I clear away the paper before heading into the kitchen to make breakfast. It's tradition in our house that Bucks Fizz and smoked salmon and scrambled eggs are the Christmas breakfast of choice. Feeling hot, I open the kitchen window for some fresh air, before cracking the eggs for scrambling and moving to the fridge for the bottle of champagne I put in there yesterday, to chill for the Bucks Fizz. But Mark lays a hand on my arm.

'Not just yet, Steph.'

'What? Why not? I know I can't have any, but I was going to make one for you to have with your breakfast.'

'And I will, but not just yet. I need to pop out for a little while. I won't be long.' It's then that I notice he is wearing his scarf, and has his jacket slung over one arm.

'What do you mean, *you need to pop out?* It's Christmas morning, Mark, where could you possibly need to go?' I shove the champagne angrily back into the fridge.

'You'll find out. Now, I won't be long; keep Henry occupied and I'll have breakfast when I get back.' He leans across me to grab the car keys from the kitchen worktop, pecks me on the forehead and is gone. I slam the eggshells hard into the bin, unsatisfied at the tiny breaking noise they make as they hit last night's empty wine bottle. I am furious – where the hell could Mark need to go on Christmas morning? Unless … a cold feeling settles in the pit of my stomach. Surely not? The only thing I can think of is that Mark has gone to visit Melissa Davenport – are they still having an affair? His parents live in Scotland, his sister is at her in-laws and his brother moved to New Zealand years ago, so there's nobody he could possibly need to visit on this day, of all days. This was how it was before, Mark saying he just needed to pop out with no explanation of where he was going. I lower myself wearily into a kitchen chair, the hard spindles digging into my back. I lean back further, relishing the uncomfortable feeling, squashing down tears. *I will not cry.* I need to think rationally. *What will I do if they are still having an affair?* Taking a deep breath, I start to go through things logically, from explaining to Henry, to visiting estate agents to put the house on the market. I am deep in my own thoughts, so deep I don't register the bang of the front door at first, announcing Mark's arrival back home.

'Henry? Steph? Come here!' His voice rouses me, and I head into the hallway, my speech prepared and ready to deliver this evening, once Henry is in bed; the speech that says Melissa Davenport can have him and he can go now. But these thoughts are soon shoved from my mind as I see what he is carrying in his arms. A tiny, squirming bundle of curly fur, with a little black nose peeping out.

'Mark? Oh, Mark, how did you arrange this?' I hold out my arms and he places the puppy gently into them. The puppy is shaking, nervous from the journey, and I stroke him gently to calm him.

'Daddy! A puppy! A real puppy ... is he for me?' Henry is hopping from foot to foot, holding out his hands. Mark starts laughing, and leads me into the living room, where I sit with the dog on my lap, and Henry starts to stroke him.

'OK, Henry – yes, the puppy is for you. Steph, Laurence helped me – I emailed him and told him what I wanted to do and he arranged it all, so you have him to thank. Now, what are we going to call him?'

After much debate, we decide on Jasper as a name for the puppy – he is a fuzzy bundle of apricot fur, a cockapoo, apparently. Henry is happy to play with him in front of the fire, while I go back into the kitchen to finish the breakfast. Mark follows me, and I hand him the champagne to make his Bucks Fizz.

'Sorry for dashing out earlier – I had to go and collect him early before the owner's family arrived for Christmas. Are you having one of these? Steph, what's wrong?'

Tears are plopping onto the kitchen worktop, where I am whisking together eggs and milk.

'Sorry,' I sniff, 'I'm just relieved. I thought you'd gone to see Melissa.'

'Melissa? Why would I go to see Melissa?' He pulls me into his arms, 'I told you, that's all over and done with. It was a stupid mistake, one I never want to repeat, OK? We moved here for a fresh start, remember? I'm here with you because *I want you.* It doesn't matter what happens, I'll never do anything that stupid again. I love you, Steph.' I stand there, in his arms, feeling both relieved and like an idiot at the same time. A knock on the front door startles me, and I pull away.

'Shit, sorry, I forgot to tell you. I invited Lila for Christmas – you don't mind, do you? She was going to be on her own because Joe is working away on his new travel magazine job and she doesn't have any family …'

'Steph – it's fine, go and let her in!' Mark laughs and reaches past me to close the kitchen window, where a steady breeze of freezing air is streaming in, and I go to answer the door.

Christmas dinner is a triumph, if I do say so myself. Lila brings over a huge Christmas pudding, complete with a carton of custard for me, as I have to skip the brandy cream, and I roast the turkey she collected last week for me from the local farm shop. We all cram around our kitchen table, plates overfull with food, and pull crackers, wearing the paper crowns and reading out terrible cracker jokes to one another. I feel content, for the first time in what feels like months, happy to have my complete family all sitting together under one roof. My parents have gone to spend Christmas in Tenerife, my mum not terribly bothered about spending it with us, which, secretly, I feel relieved about. I'm not sure I could have coped with the stress of catering for my fussy mum as well. Dinner finished, Henry escapes the table to go and play with Jasper, and when I rise to clear the plates, Lila waves me off.

'Go and sit down, Steph – relax. You cooked this huge dinner for us, the least we can do is do the washing-up, can't we, Mark?' She looks at him, where he is still sitting at the table, paper crown at a rakish angle. I smile at Lila gratefully – they had both offered to cook the Christmas dinner, but I enjoy the cooking, even if it does give me achy feet standing at the oven for hours. The washing-up, though, I am happy for them to take over. I snuggle up on the couch, content to watch Henry and Jasper tumbling over each other on the living room rug. About to doze off, a crash startles me, and I see a sheepish-looking Henry and Jasper standing in front of the coffee table, an overturned mug leaching cold coffee onto the wood.

'Oh, Henry, be careful. Play at the other end of the room.' I heave myself to my feet, heading into the kitchen for a cloth. Entering the kitchen, I see Mark and Lila standing together, Lila passing Mark a glass to dry, a frown crossing his face.

'Everything OK?' I glance between the two of them, puzzled.

'Yes, sweetie, of course. Mark was just telling me about Paraguay.' Lila gives her tinkly laugh. 'Not a place I'll be visiting on holiday any time soon!'

'Are you OK, Steph?' Mark asks, that crease in his forehead telling me he is worried about something.

'Oh, yes. Henry was playing with the puppy and knocked over a mug. I just need a cloth to mop up the coffee he spilt.' I smile at Lila as she hands me a cloth and head back out to clean it up, leaving Mark to carry on telling Lila about his adventures abroad.

That night Lila leaves at around seven p.m., after an afternoon of Christmas telly and board games, all of us feeling stuffed and sleepy. She gives me a hug as she stands on the doorstep to leave.

'Thank you, Steph, for today. It means a lot.'

'Don't be silly – it's what Christmas is all about. Friends, family, looking out for each other.'

'I know, but … it just means a lot. You really made me feel welcome. I feel like I'm part of the family.'

'Well, you are. And thank you for the lovely gifts – you shouldn't have.'

I peck her on the cheek, satisfaction from doing good making me feel warm inside.

I bathe Henry and get him into bed early, with no need for a story, as he goes out like a light. We are all exhausted and it isn't long before Mark extends a hand to me and leads me up the stairs to our bedroom. We lie together in the inky darkness, talking softly about the day, my head resting on his chest, and I feel perfectly content. I feel safe and happy for the first time in months.

CHAPTER TWENTY

The rest of the Christmas holidays pass by, and I am relishing having both of my boys home. There is more snow, unexpected after the last bout, but I wake one morning to find a thick, crisp layer of white blanketing the world outside. I had thought Henry would be over the snow by now, but he is still just as excited as he was a few weeks ago when we had the first snowfall. When he leaps onto Mark as he sleeps, startling him into wakefulness, Mark is just as excited as he is. We pull on warm clothes, hats, scarves and thick coats, and Mark heads out to the garden shed to pull out an old sledge I have completely forgotten about. Henry is dancing from foot to foot, excited to be home from school, in the snow and with his dad, all the best possible things a little boy could wish for. I open the front door cautiously, checking the porch for any gifts that might have been left by whoever it was that left the previous ones, but there is nothing, and hasn't been since Mark came home. A voice whispers in my ear and I jump.

'What are you checking for?'

'Mark! Bloody hell, you made me jump! I was just making sure, that's all.'

'Making sure of what?' I chicken out at the last minute of telling him I was checking to see if any posies had been left. We haven't really discussed it any further since he's been home, and as nothing has happened lately I think it's best if we just leave it, so I make up an excuse about checking to see if the porch light is working. He ruffles my hair and says something about being a worrier, before shouting to Henry to hurry up, and then slipping and sliding his way up the path, dragging the sledge behind him. Henry pushes past me and slides his way up the path to meet Mark, leaving me behind to lock the front door. I smile as I watch them, skidding in the fresh snow, stopping every now and again to throw a handful at each other. I make it to the end of the path without falling over, and laugh as Mark slips, Henry taking the opportunity to cram a handful of freezing, fresh snow down the back of his shirt. As I laugh, a movement catches the corner of my eye, and I look over to see Lila watching us through her kitchen window. I raise a hand to her, about to wave her outside to see if she wants to join us, but the curtain drops back into place. Figuring she mustn't have seen me wave, I shrug, and crunch my way along the pavement to catch up with my family.

****

Mark and Henry sledge for what seems like hours –
despite my snow boots and thick socks, I still have
to stamp my feet to keep them from going numb.
The hill at the recreation park is not huge, but there
are hundreds of kids and dads sliding down and then
dragging their sledges back up. I see Izzy and Olivia
making their way cautiously up the hill, dragging a
shiny new plastic sledge Olivia has obviously bought
just for this occasion, and smile. Olivia calls me over
and I carefully pick my way through the snow.

'Mark's home, then?' She nods to where Mark and
Henry are dragging the sledge up the hill, both slipping
and sliding, Mark laughing as Henry tries to pull him
over. 'So, we need to make a plan for this dinner –
when's convenient for you guys?' I pause, feeling a
little caught on the back foot.

'Um ... I'm not really sure. Can I get back to you?
Only, I'm not sure when Mark is going back to work, or
what plans he's already made.'

'Of course – but let's make it sooner rather than later.'
She gives me a peck on the cheek and lets Izzy tug her
towards the top of the hill where Mark and Henry are
waiting. Olivia seems very nice, but I can't help feeling
she's a little intense for me, her keenness to get us
all round a dinner table making me feel a little under
pressure. *Why is she so desperate for us all to be friends?*

Olivia and Izzy reach the top and I see Henry
smiling and waving. He will be pleased to see Izzy, and

I'm sure Mark will be happy that Henry has finally made a friend. It seems like everybody is out enjoying the snow – I see a few faces I recognise from the coffee house, and then, unfortunately, Jasmine Hale stalks past me, glossy bob swinging, designer riding boots on her feet. She shoots me a look, before almost going head over heels in her impractical boots, causing a little bubble of laughter to snort out of my nose.

'Who was that?' Mark appears beside me, smelling of fresh, cold air, the tip of his nose tinted red with cold.

'Oh, nobody. Nobody important, anyway.' It gives me a tiny thrill to dismiss her that way, the way I imagine she would dismiss me. 'Just some woman from the school. Where's Henry?'

'Just coming – he was having one last ride with Izzy. I got spurned for a better offer.' He grins at me, and I know he is just as pleased as I am that Henry has a proper friend, after what felt like weeks without anyone to play with.

We walk slowly home, Henry insisting on dragging the sledge along behind him, which means we make slow progress, but he's happy. Mark decides that hot chocolate is in order, so we stop at the little convenience store and I see Mr P. seated at the till through the window.

'Wait here – I'll run in and grab some.' I take the note Mark holds out, and he grabs my hand as I take it, pulling me in for a kiss. I pull away, laughing, and head inside the store.

'Did you get my gift? I left it in the porch.' My blood goes cold as Mr P. speaks, his voice rich and low.

'Gift? What gift?' My hands are shaking and I feel sick. 'Why did you leave a gift in the porch? What do you want?' I glance outside to where Mark and Henry wait, stamping their feet against the cold.

'I left a comic and some chocolate, for the boy. You came in for medicine and said he was unwell. I wanted to make him feel better.' My breath leaves my body in a whoosh, as I remember the plastic bag left on the porch the day Henry was ill.

'How did you know where I live?'

'Your husband's newspaper – he has it delivered.'

Of course, the newspaper. Mark still has it delivered, even when he is away, saying it's too much hassle to keep cancelling and then reinstating it. Mr P. is still talking, and I take a deep breath to try to concentrate on what he is saying.

'I lost my son, many years ago. He was about the same age as your boy. I miss him dreadfully – I hope I haven't offended you?'

'What? No, no, of course you haven't. I'm sorry for your loss.' I scrabble for the change and rush out of the shop, my heart hammering in my chest. Shakily, I hand Mark the change and turn to walk home.

'Steph? Are you OK? You look awfully pale.' Mark eyes me with concern.

'I'm fine. Honestly. Just cold. Come on – let's get back.'

Passing Laurence's house, I notice that it is all shut up; his car is gone and the curtains at the top of the house have all been left drawn, even though it's not even mid-afternoon.

'Did Laurence go away?' I ask Mark, gesturing towards the empty driveway. I suppose he could have just gone to work, but there is an air of abandonment about the place, and I realise I haven't seen him, even in passing, since Christmas Eve when Mark came home.

'Yes – gone to his sister's, apparently.' Mark gives my hand a squeeze, slightly too tightly, making me wince. 'He left on Christmas Eve, straight after he helped me with the bags. He was loading his car up with stuff – presents, I suppose – when my cab pulled up. He said he was going to visit his sister, to give his nieces and nephews their presents, and that he wouldn't be back until New Year. Why do you ask?'

'No reason. I just wondered.'

I have an appointment with Dr Bradshaw marked on the calendar just after New Year, and with Mark being home I can't really miss it, despite swearing to myself I wouldn't go back there. Mark has noticed it, and says he'll catch the train into town with me, saying he'll take Henry to the aquarium as an excuse, I think, just to make sure I do actually attend the appointment. There goes my plan of sitting in a park somewhere until it's time to come home. And so this is how I find myself, on the last Tuesday of the school holidays, outside Dr Bradshaw's office, waving at my little family as they turn and walk away from me, headed for a morning of fun. I dither on the doorstep, wanting to watch them turn the corner, hoping that then I can make my escape, maybe hide in the coffee shop around the corner until it is time for me to walk towards the tube station to meet them both. Unfortunately, I dither a little too long, and Dr Bradshaw finds me on his doorstep, obviously about to do a quick cigarette or coffee run before my appointment.

'Steph! You're early.' He gives me a friendly smile. 'Head inside, into the warm.' I have to suppress a snigger at that; I've never been in such a cold building in my life. 'I'll be right there – Natalie will show you in; make yourself comfortable.' Natalie, the receptionist, is there before I can make any excuses, ushering me into the doctor's office before I can make a run for it.

I've never been alone in Dr Bradshaw's office before. I tug gently at the filing cabinet, only to find it locked (of course), and finger the leaves of the yucca plant that scowls at me from its pot by the doorway. I have just settled into a chair in front of his immaculately kept desk, no files or paper to be seen, just in case a snooping patient peeks in, no doubt, when the door flies open and he rushes in, coffee in hand.

'Apologies, Steph, I just couldn't take another cup of Natalie's awful coffee.' He crinkles his eyes at me, waiting for me to say that it's no problem. I say nothing.

'So, how are things? Mark came home for Christmas, did he?'

'Fine. Everything is fine. Yes, he came home, and it's all been fine. Nothing to report.' I know I am acting like a petulant teenager, but I don't seem to be able to stop myself. I am still sulking a little, I suppose, about the fact that he doesn't believe anything that happened *actually* happened.

'Well, that's good. So, no more sinister parcels, no more concerns about people in the house?' He couldn't make me sound madder if he tried.

'No, I told you. *Nothing*. I don't even really need to be here today; there's nothing to talk about. Unless …' A thought has struck me, and even though I don't want to talk to Dr Bradshaw about it, who else is there? Belinda doesn't believe me, Mark is already worried that this baby will send me crackers, and Tessa isn't talking to me. I felt so awful after our phone call that I emailed over a brief apology to her, in the hope she would call and we could sort things out, but nothing. She hasn't even replied to the email, and as Tessa doesn't hold grudges, I know that, this time, things are serious. The doctor and Lila are the only people I have, and the doctor doesn't understand.

'Unless?' He assumes the position – chin resting on steepled fingers – and it jolts me out of my thoughts.

'Nothing, Doctor. I'm feeling much better – right as rain.'

We discuss the pregnancy, and how things have been with Mark, until finally the bell he uses as a timer gives a quiet 'ding' and I am free to go. I stand, shrugging on my coat and the doctor also stands.

'It seems that Mark being home is a steady influence on you, Steph. Hopefully we can get through all of this without the aid of any medication, if you carry on this way. I'll see you at the next appointment.' He sees me to the door, and I scurry out, all the unsaid words swirling madly in my head.

Two days later, Henry goes back to school, Mark heads into town to the office and I am once again left to my own devices. Although I will miss them both this week, it's nice to have a little time to myself, and this first morning alone, I write in my diary how I've felt over the Christmas period. My pen scratches over the page, and the diary entry all seems quite sedate and lovely, my recounting of Christmas Day and Mark bringing Jasper home, until I reach the part about Laurence, and the seed of an idea that sprouted in Dr Bradshaw's office, the idea that has been niggling away at me since then. The idea that Lila was right – that Laurence has been behind everything that has been going on since Mark went away. After all, nothing has happened since he came back, the very same day Laurence went away.

After writing it down, I try my hardest not to think about it – Laurence isn't back yet, so, if I'm right, I have a few more days when I don't need to worry. When he does come back, if it all starts up again, then maybe I can tell Mark and he will take me seriously. I ponder it all, as I fling dirty laundry into the washing machine, and make beds, fluffing pillows and smoothing duvets. Running down the stairs, bed linen in my arms, I get a shock. Jasper is lying on the living room rug, a pool of vomit around him, shaking and scratching as if he is seriously ill. I drop the linen and rush over to him, crouching as best I can, stroking his fur,

'Shhhh, Jasper, shhhh.' *Shit*. He throws up again, dog vomit splattering my trousers. I grab a towel from the pile of dirty laundry and scoop him up, wrapping him gently in the soft fabric before shoving my feet into a pair of old trainers and running over to hammer on Lila's front door.

She opens it immediately, dressed in a designer tracksuit but with tousled hair and sleep creases on her cheek, and despite my panic over Jasper I still register that this is the first time I've ever seen her looking anything less than perfect. She takes one look at the shaking, shivering dog in my arms and snatches up a set of car keys from a glass bowl by the front door.

'Come on. Get in the car.' I don't even need to say anything; she just takes charge, not letting me even stop to think about what might be wrong with poor Jasper.

I didn't even know Lila could drive – I just assumed the car was Joe's. We don't speak much on the journey to the vet's, other than for Lila to ask what has happened and for me to tell her what I found when I entered the living room. As we pull up in the car park, Jasper gives a tiny lurch and throws up again all over the passenger footwell of Lila's car.

'Oh, God, Lila, I'm sorry. I'll clean it up when we get back, I promise.' A sniff, as a tear slides down my cheek.

'Don't worry, just get him inside. Go on. I'll go and find somewhere to park.' Lila pats my hand as I clamber ungraciously out of the car, still clutching a shivering Jasper to my chest. Once inside the vet's surgery, a kindly nurse takes one look at him and ushers us straight into an examination room. I am a wreck, sobbing and sniffling, as the vet tries to calm both Jasper and myself. I am grateful when Lila enters the room, once again taking control and explaining exactly how I found Jasper.

'Right.' The vet finishes his examination, and slings his stethoscope around his neck. 'I need to run some tests, but at the moment it's looking as though Jasper is allergic to something. We'll need to take some bloods, run some checks, and find out exactly what it is that's affected him, and then we can go from there. I've given him something to settle his stomach, but I want you to keep an eye on him over the next twenty-four to forty-eight hours. Any sign of further symptoms, or if he starts vomiting again, then bring him straight back to me.' I nod at him gratefully, wrapping Jasper back up in the warm towel, and snuggling him over the top of my bump.

'Thank you so much.' Lila twinkles up at him, before following me out of the door to settle the bill.

I am exhausted by the time we arrive home, and although I know I should invite Lila in for a cup of tea, I just can't face it. Instead, when she pulls the car up outside my house, I lean over and give her a peck on the cheek.

'Thank you, Lila, I don't know what I would have done without you today.'

'Nonsense. That's what friends are for – we're here to help each other. You give me a call if you need me.' She smiles and squeezes my hand.

'That reminds me – you will shout if you need anything, won't you, Lila? I mean, Joe still isn't back and I know what it's like when you're by yourself in the house – it gets lonely.' Lila has barely mentioned Joe since he left for wherever he's gone to work, and I wonder whether everything was all right between them before he went away.

'Don't worry, darling, honestly. I'm fine – you just make sure Jasper's OK.' Lila gives me a smile, before pulling the car smoothly away towards a parking space directly outside her own house.

CHAPTER TWENTY-ONE

After scrabbling to find the piece of paper I'd written Olivia's number on, I call her on the landline to see if she minds bringing Henry home from school. I don't want to leave Jasper in case he is ill again, but luckily she doesn't mind and they arrive not long after four p.m., Henry chattering excitedly about his school day. Olivia mentions again about dinner, but I brush her away, telling her I'll check Mark's diary this evening. She offers to come and collect Henry to take him to school in the morning, but I tell her I'm sure I'll be fine. Mark arrives home not long afterwards, having managed to sneak away from the office early for once, and once Henry is out of earshot I tell him what happened today with the puppy.

'Oh, God, Steph, I'm sorry, you should have called me! The poor thing – and you poor thing – is everything OK now?'

'Yes, well, as much as it can be. We just have to keep an eye on him; he's definitely allergic to something so I've got some special food from the vet that we need to give him, just until they can figure out what's making him sick.' I am shattered after the events of the day, and am relieved when Mark suggests a night in front of the telly, and early to bed. He goes to the bathroom to brush his teeth, and I slide my hand under the mattress for my diary, wanting to write out all the emotions of finding Jasper in such a bad way, but it's not in its usual spot. Anxious, I slide my hand further under, groping around frantically, but I can't find it. Heart thumping, I jump out of bed, lifting the corner of the mattress and peering underneath before I spot it, hidden halfway towards the middle of the mattress. Relieved, I pull it towards me and hastily scribble out an entry before sliding it back into its usual position, just under my pillow. I'm sure there's an explanation for its being shoved so far back under the mattress – maybe I moved it when I changed the bed earlier? I squash down the uneasy feeling that someone has found it and maybe read my private thoughts.

I have another day at home alone the following day, after dropping Henry at school and waving Mark off to the office. He is working late tonight, apparently going through some of the footage they took when they were in Paraguay, and deciding what they need to film on the next trip. I pass by the corner shop on my way home, lifting a hand to Mr P. as I walk by the window. I'm still not sure about him, whether his leaving a present for Henry is at all innocent, or whether I am reading too much into it. Once home, I am content, humming under my breath as I pack toys away and sort and fold laundry; after making a conscious decision, following my meeting with Belinda, that I wasn't going to take on any more work until after the baby is born – a sort of self-imposed maternity leave, if you like – I find I am enjoying being a housewife and looking after my family, although I'm sure the shine will soon wear off. I've never done it properly before – with Henry I worked right up until two days before he was born, anxiety about the birth meaning I didn't want to sit around at home, worrying about what was going to happen. The fact that there have been no more sinister goings-on, no more posies, no more things going missing, along with the reassurance from the police that Llewellyn Chance is gone for good, means I feel as though I can relax a little, and enjoy being at home. The black cloud that has been peeping over my shoulder since I was fifteen seems to have receded a little and I find myself feeling more content than I have for a long, long time, determined to enjoy these last few months with Henry before the baby comes.

Still humming, I plunge my hand into the front pocket of Mark's suit, ready to pull out whatever crap he's left in there before I drop it off at the dry cleaner's. I'm sure they must make a fortune out of all the random five- and ten-pound notes he stuffs into his pockets and forgets about. Sure enough, I pull out a handful of paper, two five-pound notes and a crumpled ten-pound note. I smooth the notes out flat and lay them on his bedside table, before carefully unfolding the paper to smooth them out. There's a business card for a man named Thomas Jolly – a lighting technician, apparently – a receipt for two cans of Red Bull from a garage, a cash-point receipt for £100, and another white slip of paper. I unfold the white slip, carefully smoothing it out so it's readable. I'm not setting out to snoop, I tell myself, but when your husband has cheated on you it's very difficult not to be tempted by random slips of paper you find in his pockets, no matter how many times he tells you it was all a mistake. Running my hand over the slip to lay it flat, I find it is a receipt from a shop named Tyler, Hancock and Jones. I rack my brains – I know that name – before it comes to me. Tyler, Hancock and Jones is the exclusive jeweller at the bottom of the High Street – one I never even glance in the window of, it's that exclusive. The receipt simply shows a product code, but the amount is staggering – £1,500. Whatever Mark has bought, it's big. With shaking hands and on legs that feel like jelly I run downstairs to the kitchen and fire up my laptop. Finding the Tyler, Hancock and Jones website I enter the product code into their search button and drum my fingers anxiously on the kitchen table as I wait for it to load. *Oh.* The picture that fills the screen is exquisite. A square cut, perfect diamond, set into a band of platinum. Simple, elegant and *beautiful*. Has Mark bought this for me? He didn't give it to me for Christmas and my birthday is months away. I have no idea what to think – after everything we've been through, the idea that Mark has bought it for me is not the first idea that pops into my head; there's always that first thought that he's bought it for someone else. A knocking at the front door startles me and I slam the laptop lid shut before scurrying over to let whoever it is in, shaking the puzzled look from my face.

'Lila! Come in.' I pull the door open wide, and Lila steps through, looking chic as ever in her coat, the one that looks suspiciously like mine, her hair sleek and styled perfectly, clutching a bundle of magazines in her arms.

'I thought you might want these.' She thrusts the magazines towards me. 'You had a stressful day yesterday, so I thought I'd bring you some trashy reading material and you could chill out for a bit – I know you won't if I don't make you!' She gives a little laugh and squeezes me in a hug, her hair like silk against my cheek.

'Thanks, Lila. I don't know what I'd do without you. Do you want a cup of tea?' We walk through into the kitchen, and she stops to fuss over Jasper, who is much better but still lies forlornly in his basket in the hope of eliciting some sympathy. Over tea we catch up, Lila telling me she has spoken to Joe and it looks as though he might be coming home soon, while I have nothing to report – which is good, in a way.

'So, nothing has happened since Laurence went away?' Lila eyes me over the top of her coffee mug, before blowing on her drink and taking a sip.

'Nothing. Which is really weird.' I sip my own drink, the menthol aroma of the peppermint soothing me. 'I mean, I just don't understand why he would want to frighten me like that – or even how he knew that it would frighten me. Only a few close friends know what happened with the attack, so it's not like he could have known I would react that way in the beginning.'

'I think that's just a coincidence – the attack, I mean. He didn't know about it, and of course you reacted more strongly than perhaps you would have normally. I would definitely keep my distance, though, if I were you. I mean … best not to encourage any sort of relationship with him, eh? And you've still got me.' I nod, a little sadly. I did really like Laurence, I still do, and part of me is still not convinced he had anything to do with anything; but if not him, then who?

'So, when does Joe get home? I bet you can't wait to see him.'

'I'm not exactly sure – he has to get a series of connecting flights, so hopefully he won't miss any.'

'You must be looking forward to seeing him, though? He's been gone for weeks, hasn't he?'

'Hmmm. Things weren't that great when he left. We'd had a few arguments – nothing major, but you know what it's like when you go through a phase like that. Everything feels a bit awkward. I'm sure we'll sort it out, though.' Lila pulls the stack of magazines towards us, flicking through the top one.

'Come on, let's have a nose at what the celebs are up to; it's got to be more exciting than a sick dog!' I lean obligingly over the magazine, getting the message that she obviously doesn't want to talk about it in any detail. What I see there takes my breath away, as though I have been thumped in the stomach.

'Oh, God.'

'Steph? What is it?' Lila looks at me with concern, a frown crossing her brow.

'Nothing, honestly, I just … I don't feel too well. I'm tired after yesterday maybe. Do you mind if we make it another day? I think I just need to go for a lie-down.' I usher her out of the door, promising that, yes, I will call her if I need anything, clicking the front door gently shut behind her.

With Lila gone, I sink back down into a kitchen chair and try to gather my thoughts. *He wouldn't, would he?* Saliva floods my mouth and I swallow it back, trying not to be sick. For there, on the front page of *heat* magazine, is a picture of Melissa Davenport, Birkin slung over one arm, striding along a London pavement. There, glittering harshly on the third finger of her left hand, is an exquisite, square-cut diamond, identical to the one I found on the jeweller's website, under a headline that shrieks, *Melissa's secret engagement!*

The afternoon passes in a daze. I lie on the couch after throwing up several times, until my mouth feels fuzzy and my stomach is sore. I drag myself out of the door when it's time to fetch Henry from school and snap at him when he asks if Izzy can come for tea, feeling like a terrible mum for being so irritable. I make fish fingers for his tea, and bathe him and get him to bed early, all on autopilot as the headline runs through my head over and over again, a wave of nausea hitting me each time I think of it. *Surely he wouldn't do this to me? Surely it hasn't been going on all this time? Has he only come back to tell me he's leaving, that he wants to marry her? Has everything he's said to me since we got here been a lie?* By the time Mark comes in, it's close to midnight and I am a wreck. He slides in through the bedroom door, into the darkness where I am lying, propped up on pillows and wide-awake. Snapping on the bedroom lamp, making him squint, I pull myself farther up the pillows, moving away as he leans over to kiss me. Reaching for the receipt I lay it flat on the bed and wait, as he pours over it.

'Shit, Steph …'

'It's too late for excuses, Mark.' I shove the magazine under his nose, the headline shrieking its damning news in bright-red font. 'I know everything. You need to leave, go to her, go on. I'm not taking any more of your shit, just go.' I planned to be cool and calm, but I can't – a huge sob heaves in my throat and tears spill over.

'Bloody hell, Steph, what the fuck is this?' He grabs the magazine, scanning the headline before tossing it aside. 'I told you *it was a mistake.* I'm not here by force – I'm here because I want to be here, with you.'

'Yeah, you've said a lot of things, Mark, over the years. How do I know what's the truth and what's a lie any more?' Tears slide down my cheeks, plopping in little fat splats onto the duvet cover.

'I'm here because I'm not me without *you*, Steph. I told you it was over – how long are you going to keep punishing me? How long before you stop being so fucking paranoid?'

'Paranoid? Seriously? I find a receipt for the *exact same ring* that the whore you slept with is wearing, and I'm *paranoid*? I'm not a fucking idiot, Mark, although maybe I am. I'm the idiot that took you back and let you get me pregnant, when all the time you just carried on behind my back!' I am properly crying now, great big ugly sobs that rack my entire body.

'Yes, Steph. You are an idiot.' His voice softening, Mark digs in his jacket pocket and throws a small, navy-blue box at me. 'I bought it for you – I was going to give it to you when the baby was born, to show you that you mean the world to me, but since you know about it you might as well have it now.' A look of disgust crosses his face. 'I know I made a mistake, and I know I hurt you, but all I want is for you to trust me again. I know this is all my fault, that my doing what I did has made you not trust me, but I thought we could get over it, start again. If you can't then maybe there's not really much point any more. You'll break my heart, Steph, but if you want me to go, I will. For you.' With that, he snatches a pillow up from the bed, and walks out of the room, shoulders hunched, leaving me sitting alone in our huge bed, diamond ring by my side, full of self-loathing.

CHAPTER TWENTY-TWO

I wake early the next morning, lying still in a small patch of sunshine that peeps through a gap in the curtains, the baby rolling over inside me, fluttering and rippling. I forget for a moment the events of the previous evening, until I stretch a hand out to Mark only to find his side of the bed smooth and unruffled, where he didn't come to bed after our argument. Rolling onto my side, I face the ring, glittering in the early morning sun and, beautiful though it is, I can't bear to look at it. I slam the lid of the ring box down, and catching sight of the time pull myself out of bed, calling to Henry to get up.

Mark is sitting at the kitchen table, sipping a cup of coffee when I enter the room. I give him a weak smile, which he doesn't return, so I busy myself with opening cupboards and fetching cereal for Henry's breakfast. I feel his eyes on me as I bustle about the kitchen and then, unable to leave it, I turn back to him, desperate to break the thick silence that hangs over us.

'Mark, I'm sorry …'

His voice cuts over mine, not letting me finish my sentence.

'Steph, I'm tired. I don't want to talk about things right now, OK? Not while Henry is home. I'm not going into the office today – I've got some calls to make and emails to send so I'll work from home. We can talk about it a bit later when Henry has gone to school.' He doesn't wait for me to reply, just throws the dregs of his coffee into the sink and pounds up the stairs, shouting to Henry to hurry up before he is late.

As soon as we enter the playground, I know that *something* is amiss, I'm just not sure what. There is a crackling electricity in the air, the way there always is when something exciting or shocking has taken place, and I see Jasmine Hale standing at the centre of a circle of concerned 'friends', tears staining her cheeks. I usher Henry towards his classroom, keeping one eye on the circle of witches surrounding Jasmine, cautiously inching my way past as she is obviously upset over something. I want to drop Henry off and get out of there fast. Avoiding eye contact with anyone, I kiss Henry goodbye and make my way back towards the school gate. I am within feet of leaving the school grounds when I hear my name being called. Heart sinking, I turn around to see Jasmine striding towards me, a look of utter rage on her face. Her mascara has run, and a tiny piece of tissue sticks to the end of her nose, which makes her look faintly ridiculous, but to laugh at her now would be suicide, judging by the look on her face.

'Is everything OK, Jasmine?' I ask, as sweetly as I can, wanting to get whatever she's got a bee in her bonnet about this time over and done with.

'OK?' she hisses, her voice a shrill squawk that runs right through me. 'OK? I cannot believe the nerve of you, Stephanie Gordon. You know exactly what you've done, and don't think I won't take this to the very end to get you dealt with properly, once and for all.'

'Sorry, Jasmine, I have no idea what you're talking about. If you'll excuse me?' Trying to disguise the fact that I am shaking, the confrontation making me feel nervous, I move to step past her but she cuts me off, one of her minions standing either side of her so there is nowhere for me to pass.

'You're going *nowhere*. Admit what you did – go on! I said you were bloody crackers after you ripped half my hair out, and this just proves it. Only mental people go round tipping paint over other people's cars.' She stands back, triumphant, hands on her hips, no sign of the crocodile tears she was bawling all over her minions just ten minutes ago. *What? I have no idea what she's talking about.*

'Really, Jasmine? Someone tipped paint over your car? I'm really sorry, but I haven't got a clue what

you're talking about. It was nothing to do with me.'
I push past her, and she snatches hold of my coat sleeve.

'I *know* it was you, I *saw* you. Don't think you'll get
away with it.' I can't help it; I see red. Jasmine Hale is
nothing more than a bully. Pregnancy has not cooled
my temper one little bit. I lean forward, right into her
face and, with hindsight, say the worst thing I could
probably have ever said in that situation.

'Jasmine, if I was going to bother doing *anything* to
you, it would be something far worse than just tipping
paint over your shitty old car.'

I march home, and by the time I reach the front door
I have calmed down considerably, enough that I can
almost laugh about her. She thinks I'm crazy, when she
goes around accusing people of throwing paint over her
car? I have no doubt her car *has* been vandalised, but
I also have no doubt a woman like her must have no end
of people who dislike her. I hear Mark on the phone as
I enter the hallway, shrugging my coat off and turning
to hang it on the hook by the front door. A slash of
colour catches my eye and there, underneath an old
coat of Mark's, is my good coat – the one I thought was
gone for good. I unhook it and look it over, checking
for any signs of damage or any sign that it hasn't been
hanging up there for the past few months while I hunted
all over for it. There is nothing – no tears or rips – only
a slight white smear on the bottom of the hem, at the

back, which could have been there for months, I wear it so rarely normally. There is a faint scent of perfume on the collar, something familiar, and although I can't quite put my finger on it, I think it must just be the smell of my perfume from previous wear. I hang it back up underneath Mark's old jacket, and go into the kitchen to make some tea to take in to Mark, as a kind of small peace offering.

He is finishing his phone call when I walk into the far end of the conservatory, into the area that we sectioned off with a small Japanese-style screen to create a kind of home office. Standing awkwardly to one side, I wait for him to finish his call before setting the tea down in front of him.

'Peace offering?' I smile at him hopefully, desperately hoping he sees how sorry I am.

'Steph, come here.' He opens his arms and I sink into them gratefully.

'I'm sorry,' I mutter into his chest.

'No, I'm sorry. It's all my fault, I know it is. I made a hideous mistake and I don't blame you for getting upset and worried about stuff, but you have to trust me, OK? When I say I want to be with you, I mean it.' I nod, feeling my hair ruffle up against his T-shirt. 'I'm worried about you, Steph. All this about posies being left and people in the house – it's not right, you know that?' I pull away, about to defend myself, about to tell him that he's wrong – that I know it sounds crazy but this stuff has actually been happening – when the shrill tone of the doorbell squawks through the house.

'Leave it.' Mark pulls me closer. 'We need to sort this out.' The bell rings again, more insistently this time, and I lean away from him.

'No, I need to answer it, it might be important.'

I rush along the hallway, leaving Mark standing in the conservatory, and throw open the door to whoever was ringing so insistently. A man and woman stand on the doorstep and somehow I can tell by their stance that they are official.

'Mrs Gordon?' I nod. 'PC Walker and PC Gilbert. Can we come in?'

'Yes, of course.' I open the door wider and show them through to the lounge. Mark appears in the doorway, a look of confusion on his face. 'Can you tell us what this is about?'

They stand together in the living room, filling the space and making me feel as though I can't breathe properly.

'There's been an allegation of criminal damage made against you, Mrs Gordon,' the man, PC Walker, states bluntly, doing his best to avoid looking at my bump.

'We need to ask you a few questions. It won't take up too much of your time,' PC Gilbert butts in, her hard stare making me feel about two feet tall.

'Hang on a minute … criminal damage?' Mark steps forward, 'What sort of criminal damage? My wife is pregnant, in case you hadn't noticed. I hardly think she looks like a criminal, do you?'

'You'd be surprised, Mr Gordon,' the woman, Gilbert, says dryly, a slight sneer crossing her features. My heart starts hammering in my chest – I didn't do anything, I know I didn't, but there is that little comment that Jasmine made in the playground – *I saw you*. I swallow hard and try to rearrange my features to hide the fear that is bubbling up inside me. I know I didn't do anything wrong, therefore I shouldn't have anything to worry about, but I can't help it – I'm frightened.

'No, this is unacceptable. You're not taking my wife anywhere.' Mark is furious, but not as furious as I am. Feeling like a rat caught in a trap, I bat away his hand as he tries to calm me down. 'Steph, what the hell is going on?'

'I didn't do anything. *I swear I didn't do anything!* What has she been saying about me?' My hands are shaking and I can't stem the tidal wave of fury that rushes over me, fuelled by the terror that they will believe whatever it is Jasmine has told them. 'Are you just going to believe what she says? Without any proof?'

'Mrs Gordon, please …' PC Walker tries to take my arm and without thinking I lash out, pushing him hard away from me, my engagement ring slicing neatly into his cheek. He staggers back, a thin line of red marring his face as I step away, my hands to my mouth.

'Oh God, I'm sorry, I'm so sorry ... I didn't mean ...' Panicked, I look to Mark, but he is standing there, useless, a look of shock on his face. PC Gilbert steps forwards and grasps my arm, hard.

'I think we'd be better off finishing this conversation down at the station, don't you? Assaulting a police officer is a serious offence, as serious as criminal damage.' She leads me towards the front door, a grim look on her face. 'We will require access to the property in order to carry out a search. I trust you don't have any issues with that?' Stunned, Mark gives a brief shake of his head.

'It'll be OK, Steph,' he says, running his hand through his hair. 'I'll come down; we can sort this out.'

'No.' I swallow back the tears that thicken the back of my throat. 'Stay here and fetch Henry. I didn't do anything, Mark, I swear I didn't.' And I let PC Gilbert lead me down the garden path to where a patrol car sits by the side of the kerb.

Three long hours later, I think I have exhausted just about every reasonable avenue I could possibly pursue, and still the police continue to question me. Jasmine Hale has reported that her car has been vandalised, a large tin of white paint thrown over it, and her private CCTV cameras that record everything within a certain radius of her house show a woman, who looks suspiciously like me, heaving a can of paint over the vehicle, sloshing it all over the roof and bonnet so that it drips a ruinous stain over the entire car, looking as though she is thoroughly enjoying what she is doing. I rub my hands over my face as I try to explain for what feels like the hundredth time that I didn't even leave the house yesterday evening.

'So I'll ask you to explain again why then, Mrs Gordon, do we have CCTV footage of you, or someone who *appears* to be you, throwing paint over the vehicle in a spiteful act of criminal damage? After all, we know the two of you have a history together – one that tells a story, wouldn't you agree? Mrs Hale has already told us that you physically attacked her in the playground.' Gilbert lays a photograph of a still image taken from the CCTV showing a woman crouched next to the car, paint tin alongside her.

'Like I already told you, Jasmine doesn't like me. We've had a few run-ins because I wouldn't join her precious PTA and then she got personal with me, but I wouldn't ever do anything like this!'

'Even though you threatened her this morning? I believe your words were, "If I was going to bother doing *anything* to you, it would be something far worse than just tipping paint over your shitty old car".'

'Yes, but that was *after.*' Abruptly, I shut my mouth, aware I am probably digging myself a bigger hole. It's no good. They don't believe me. Tears rise and begin to course down my cheeks. I'm exhausted, frightened and starting to think I'm about to be thrown in a cell for something I didn't even do. I glance at the photo one more time, something niggling in the back of my mind, before I hook it and reel it in.

'Wait,' I say, pulling the photograph towards me for a closer look, 'that coat she's wearing. It's similar to what I call my good coat – the coat I wear for work meetings and stuff – but the thing is I only found my coat this morning. I've been looking for it since we moved in and had given it up for lost, but then I found it today, hanging under Mark's jacket in the hallway. So it can't have been me, if I didn't have the coat before today!' Triumphant, I sit back in my chair, waiting for the officers to agree with me. Instead, Gilbert just raises an eyebrow, but before she can say anything another officer enters the room to tell her she has a visitor. She leaves, not bothering to excuse herself, and I sit with the other police officer in silence, the only sound the odd sniff, where I don't have a tissue. Ten minutes later Gilbert returns, throws my jacket at me and says, 'You can go.'

'Why? What happened? Do you believe me now?'

'I believe the fact that we didn't find any evidence of a paint can on your property, and I believe the lady who just saved your skin with an alibi. Now, I suggest you get out of my sight before I change my mind. Don't go far, though; we're not finished with you yet. There may be other questions we need to ask, especially if Mrs Hale persists in wanting to press charges.'

I grab my jacket from where it has landed on the floor, and scoot out of the door quickly, desperate to get away from the obnoxious PC Gilbert. Walker appears in the corridor and takes me along to the front desk, warning me to stay out of trouble as I leave. I step outside, squinting in the bright sunshine, only to see Lila waiting for me on the front steps.

'What are you doing here?' I give her a quick hug, noticing she's wearing her hair straight today and is back in her old pea-green coat.

'I came as soon as I heard. I know you couldn't have done it; I was with you all yesterday evening.' She tucks her arm through mine and we start walking back towards home.

'Not all the evening, though,' I say. 'I felt ill, remember?'

'They don't know that, do they? Anyway, they didn't find anything at your house, no paint can, no receipts, nothing. They think I'm telling the truth, and I know that *you're* telling the truth, and that's all that matters.' She gives me a huge, infectious grin that I can't help returning, even as I wonder, *if I didn't vandalise Jasmine's car, then who did?*

Mark is quiet when I get home, and doesn't ask too many questions, for which I am grateful. It's only after we've eaten and are standing side by side in the kitchen clearing away the dinner things that he brings it up.

'Steph, you didn't have anything to do with it all, did you?' He turns to face me, a faint red flush on his cheeks. I stare at him, open-mouthed, horrified that he could even think such a thing.

'Do you actually think I could do something like that?'

'No, of course not, but you haven't been yourself lately, and you have had a row with the woman, you said so yourself … and things like this happened before, didn't they? Stuff happened and you couldn't remember doing it. Look, I'm sorry, I'm out of sorts as well after yesterday evening. Forget I said anything, OK?' He kisses the top of my head as I swallow my anger back down, not having the energy to deal with another row tonight, but later that evening, as we make our way upstairs to bed, I see him pause at the coat hook and finger the bottom of my coat, where a small slick of something white stains the fabric.

CHAPTER TWENTY-THREE

Tension clouds the air over breakfast the next morning. I am hurt and more than a little upset at Mark's comment about whether or not I had anything to do with vandalising Jasmine's car. I know things like this happened before, after I had Henry – I quite often did things in the fug of post-natal depression that I didn't always remember doing – but surely Mark knows that this time it's different? There's nothing wrong with me, I'm sure of it. There is also the matter of the ring – despite apologies being made, the row about the ring still doesn't feel resolved to me. Obviously it doesn't to Mark either. As he snatches his jacket from the hook in the hallway, exposing my coat underneath, he turns to me.

'Let's have dinner tonight. I'm sure Lila will have Henry. I think we need to spend a little bit of time together, just you and me, eh? I feel like I haven't seen you properly since before I went away, what with Lila spending Christmas with us, and now all of this.

We need to talk, get things sorted out, don't you think? I don't want to carry on like this, Steph.'

'OK. I'd like that. I'll speak to Lila, if you'll book a table somewhere?'

He leans down to kiss me, properly, the way he used to kiss me before we seemed to get so bogged down by life, before everything started to go wrong. I wave him off, feeling slightly breathless, before helping Henry get ready for school, humming under my breath all the while. I'm starting to feel like maybe I can do this – there have been no more sinister presents left on the doorstep, Mark is obviously keen to make sure we are OK, and maybe, just maybe, everything is going to be all right.

I slide Jasper's harness on and we walk up to school to drop Henry off. Leaving him at his classroom, and successfully managing to avoid both Jasmine and her crew, and Mrs Cooper, who no doubt will have heard what happened yesterday, I head off back down the hill to meet Lila at the coffee house. Thankfully, it's happy to allow dogs, so I make my way inside to where Lila sits waiting, a latte in front of her and a peppermint tea in front of the other empty chair.

'Good morning.' I lean down and peck her on the cheek, before wrapping Jasper's lead around the table leg, making sure he can't escape out of the front door. He turns around three times, gives a little sigh, and collapses in an exhausted heap on my feet.

'Good morning – I got you tea, is that OK? Are you feeling OK after everything yesterday? And how's this little fella doing now? I can't believe he's allowed out already!' Lila leans down and ruffles Jasper's ears under the table.

'Yes, he's all good, I'm good – everything's going to be OK, I think.' I wave away her mention of the events of yesterday – I am too emotionally drained to talk through it all again. 'The vet called, the tests have all come back and it's not completely bad news.' I take a sip of my tea, feeling the baby push out a hand or foot against the side of my belly.

'What did he say? Is Jasper OK?'

'It turns out he *is* allergic to something. He's allergic to beef.'

'What?' Lila sputters with laughter. 'Beef?'

I can't help laughing too; her laugh is infectious and I am so relieved it was nothing more serious for poor Jasper.

'Yes, beef. Thank God it was nothing worse – apparently, it's a common thing for dogs to be allergic to. If he eats it, it'll make him really sick again, like last time, so I just have to be super careful not to let him have anything with beef in. I've got special food. Poor old Mark – he thought it was such a lovely idea to get a dog for Henry, and it's turned out to be quite traumatic.' I give a little laugh into my teacup, but Lila frowns at me.

'Don't mock him, Steph. I think you're lucky to have him. You have everything that most women could wish for. All I want is a family, my own husband, two kids and a dog. You're living the dream, even if you don't always feel like it.'

I raise my eyebrows at her. If only she knew how lucky Mark was to still have me.

'Does that include my very own stalker? Although that seems to have calmed down hugely – nothing since before Christmas.' Nothing since Laurence went away, echoes at the back of my mind, but I push it firmly away. I am still struggling with the idea that Laurence could be behind any of it. We chat for a while longer, and Lila agrees to babysit, saying she thinks Mark is right; we do need to spend some time together. I thank her again, as I seem to have done so often since I met her, for being such a good friend, to me, to Mark – to both of us. I'm grateful to have her around, especially as I haven't heard from Tessa since our row. The absence of Tessa has left a gaping hole in my heart, but Lila seems to slowly be filling it.

Lila arrives just after seven-thirty, and Henry is excited to see her. He rushes off upstairs to find a book for her to read to him, while Mark and I say goodnight to him and pull our coats on.

'Do you need me to do anything?' Lila asks, as we are about to leave.

'No, honestly, I'm just grateful you could look after Henry this evening. I've fed Jasper, so you'll just need to let him out for a wee a bit later on this evening; other than that, just get Henry to bed and hopefully asleep before we get home. And thank you, again.' I kiss her on the cheek and run out to the car where Mark is waiting, heater blasting in an attempt to warm it up.

The restaurant is quiet, being midweek, and as it has dark, comfy, leather booths, Mark and I have some privacy to discuss everything and clear the air. Once we have ordered I lean over and take his hand.

'I'm sorry, Mark. I really am, for everything that's happened recently. I'm trying to make it a fresh start, honestly. I do want us to be together and I know I have to learn to trust you again, but give me some time, OK?'

He strokes the back of my hand and looks at me closely.

'I told you, it's done. I want us to work, Steph. I want us to be together and I'm prepared to put up with whatever happens in order for that to happen. The thing I'm more concerned about is how you feel, in general. You're still seeing Dr Bradshaw, aren't you?' I nod, but don't speak. I wondered how long it would be before we got round to discussing this.

'There hasn't been anything else happening, has there? Not since I've been back?' He looks at me doubtfully and I slide my hand back.

'No, there hasn't. But Mark, these things really did happen – I've got proof! There was an email … and Lila seems to think maybe Laurence had something to do with it all. I mean …' Mark isn't listening and I break off as a shadow looms over the table. I realise to my horror that Laurence is standing next to Mark's chair. Mark stands to shake his hand, while I sit, mute, terrified in case he heard me.

'Laurence! Good to see you. When did you get back? Sit and join us for a drink.' Mark gestures to the empty chair between us, and noticing my frown gives an apologetic shrug of the shoulders, a 'What else could I do?' look on his face. Laurence lays a hand on the back of the chair.

'Only if you're sure? It looks like you're out for a romantic meal, just you guys. I don't want to impose.' Laurence eyes me quizzically and I give him a barely perceptible nod. Mark signals to the waiter and Laurence uses his being distracted to whisper to me, 'Steph, are you OK? I was worried about you over Christmas. You didn't have any more … trouble? Flowers, you know?'

'No. Nothing.' I shift uncomfortably in my seat, crossing my arms across my chest.

'It's just, I need to speak to you about it all I've got a theory about who's behind it.'

'*Are you joking?*' I hiss fiercely at him. '*I'm not discussing this with you here, so you can stop right now.*'

Before he can respond, Mark has the waiter's attention and he turns back to us, ready to catch up with Laurence after the Christmas period. I sit silently, not trusting myself to join in the conversation when all I want to do is challenge Laurence and ask him exactly what he knows about what's been going on.

After what feels like the longest drink in history, Laurence gets up and makes his excuses, making sure he turns to me to say he'll pop in and see me during the week. I nod, and decide that, when he does, I'll have to find a way to find out what he knows – and if he is the one responsible.

We get home after a pleasant enough meal, but we didn't manage to talk in any satisfactory detail about what happened while Mark was away. He gave a small nod to it when we were waiting for the bill, just saying he thinks that perhaps I got a little bit overwrought with him not being there, and that basically I made more of it than was perhaps necessary. I didn't respond, not wanting to lose my temper in front of the other diners, but when we get in the car I try to bring it up again.

'Mark … about what's been going on … I told you I have proof, and I do. I got an email, saying that someone was watching me. I can show you when we get home – then you have to believe me!'

'Steph, it's not a question of not believing you … I do believe you. It's just after everything that's happened before …' He pauses, resting his hand on my knee as we sit at a red traffic light, while I hold tight to the steering wheel. I sit there in silence, rigid and unresponsive, waiting for him to finish. The lights go green, and he moves his hand from my knee as I reach for the gear stick. 'Show me. Show me the email when we get home, then we can decide what to do.'

Lila is curled up in the armchair when we walk in, fire burning merrily, a book on her lap, looking for all the world as if she belongs in our sitting room. She rises when we come in, bringing the cold air in with us, and tells us that both Henry and Jasper were perfectly behaved for her. I thank her, and Mark tries to pay her, which once again she waves away, saying only that she thinks of us as family, and loves to look after Henry. After she has gone, I pull out the laptop, angling it towards Mark where he sits at the kitchen table. Opening up my email account, I scroll through my received emails for the one from 'eyes on you'.

'I can't find it … it was definitely here, from someone calling themselves "eyes on you".'

Backwards and forwards I scroll, up and down, before Mark pulls the laptop towards him and types the sender into the search box. Nothing. The email is gone. Mark says nothing, avoiding my eyes, before gently closing the laptop lid and heading upstairs, while I sit, nauseous and shaking, more confused than ever.

Wearily, I climb the stairs to bed after him, sliding under the duvet where he lies, his back towards me.

A few hours later, a hacking, retching sound wakes me and I drag myself into a sitting position, head cloudy with sleep and confusion. I nudge Mark, but after a bottle of red wine, followed by port, followed by an Irish coffee, he is dead to the world, so I carefully slide out of bed and into a fleecy top to investigate. Entering the kitchen, I see Jasper, lying shivering and retching in a pool of vomit, spittle foaming on his lips. *Shit.* I run back upstairs, thumping Mark hard on the arm until he wakes up.

'It's Jasper,' I whisper urgently. 'He's poorly – really, really poorly, I have to get him to a vet.'

'I'll take him.' Mark struggles into a sitting position but I hold a hand up to stop him.

'No, you'll still be over the limit. I'll take him. You stay here and look after Henry.' I grab a blanket from the end of the bed, and use it to wrap Jasper in while I drive to the emergency vet across town.

By the time we arrive Jasper has vomited again, is trembling and his ears feel burning hot to the touch. The vet takes one look at him and whisks him away while I wait anxiously in the reception area. I pace fretfully backwards and forwards until, after what feels like an interminable wait later, the vet reappears, a stern look on his face.

'Mrs Gordon, it seems as though your dog has ingested some form of toxin – a poison, if you like.'

'A poison? He's allergic to beef – that's what made him behave like this before. Could it be that? Although I don't feed him beef … I mean …' I cut off, realising I am rambling.

'Possibly. All I can tell you is that he's pretty poorly at the moment. He's on a drip to replace his lost fluids, and we need to run a few tests. We'll give you a call in the morning to let you know how he's doing. This is a very serious matter, Mrs Gordon.'

Shamefaced, I follow him through to the back room, where Jasper is lying forlornly on a blanket, drip attached, and stroke his head and tell him I'll be back for him soon. I thank the vet and head back out to the car, my mind whirling. *I know there's no beef in the house – I fed him last night myself, so what could he have eaten?*

When I get home, Mark is in the kitchen drinking tea, obviously unable to go to back to sleep. I sink down into the kitchen chair next to him and take a sip of his drink, my bones aching with tiredness.

'What did the vet say?' He stands and goes over to flick the kettle back on to make me my own tea.

'He said that Jasper has been poisoned. He's eaten something that has made him terribly poorly, but I know I got rid of all the food that had beef in, so I don't know what he could have eaten. I mean,

I fed him myself last night.' I look up as Mark doesn't respond, only to see him standing frozen over the bin, a soggy teabag on a spoon in his hand.

'Mark? What is it?'

He lays the teaspoon on the kitchen worktop and delves into the bin, pulling out an empty dog food can. One with 'WITH BEEF' written on the side in huge red letters.

'What? No! I never fed him that, Mark, I swear.' I am horrified. I know I didn't feed Jasper beef, not after it made him so poorly. *Did I?*

'You must have done, Steph – the empty can is right here!'

'It must have been Lila – she must have fed him again after we left!' I am close to tears. Poor Jasper. *I am sure I didn't feed it to him.*

'Really, Steph? Just like someone who looks like you *but wasn't you* vandalised Jasmine Hale's car? Like the email you had as "proof" that someone was after you? Come on, at least do the decent thing and accept responsibility; don't just blame it on Lila. If it was a mistake, just own up to it.' He throws the can down on the worktop and storms from the room in disgust. Tears make their way down my cheeks, and I feel slightly sick at the thought of poor Jasper, throwing up and shivering, all because someone fed him the wrong food. *Someone.* I'm sure it wasn't me. I remember feeding him and then throwing the can in the bin – so, the other can should be in the bin as well, shouldn't it? Proof that I fed him the right food, and that Lila must have fed him the wrong food by mistake. Pulling up my sleeve and wrinkling my nose, I peer into the bin, using a chopstick to move aside the other rubbish in there. An empty wrapper catches my eye – *cooking chocolate*? I push it aside, slightly puzzled, as I am *not* a baker. There is no other dog food can.

CHAPTER TWENTY-FOUR

Mark leaves the next morning to spend the rest of the week working in Bristol, a last-minute change to the schedule that apparently came through on email last night while I was poking through a dustbin full of rubbish in order to prove my innocence. We are prickly around each other as he packs an overnight bag with a few days' worth of clothes, but neither of us mentions the dog food and Jasper getting sick. I can't face the idea of another row, and when he leaves, although he does kiss me goodbye, I can't help but feel slightly relieved that I will have some time apart from him to think things over and try to get my head together a little bit. Last night, once Mark had stormed off to bed and I was done picking through rubbish, I emailed Tessa in an attempt to smooth over the cracks in our relationship. I've missed her so much, and although Lila is nearby, nothing matches up to the friendship Tessa and I have shared for the last thirty years. She's supported me through everything. She's been there, standing right by my side, for the happy occasions like Henry being born, and for the bad times as well. Tessa was the one who stepped in when I found out about Mark's affair. She came back from New York to help with Henry and cook meals when I threw him out for those few weeks. She held everything together while I fell apart, unable to even get up and face the day. Firing up the laptop I check to see if I have a reply, and see there is one email sitting unread in my inbox. Reading it, I feel sick, devastated. I wrote to Tessa, saying I didn't want to argue with her, that I needed her support more than ever right now and that she has it all wrong about Lila – Lila is a good friend. Tessa's reply is anything but the apology I was expecting in return:

To: Steph (s.gordon@hotmail.com)
From: Tessa Jackson (tjackson@lamodemag.com)
RE: Making up?
Steph,
Honestly? I love you and I never, ever thought I would say this but I'm not sure that our friendship can carry on like this. I'm pleased you've found a friend in Lila, really I am, but your previous emails have just proved how much you've changed since you met her, and in all honesty I don't think she's a good influence on you. I've supported you consistently through a lot of tough

times, and I always will; however, I can't just take the things you've said in previous emails lightly, and I'm not entirely sure I can forgive some of the things you've said. We've been friends for a long time, and I don't understand why you're letting this girl get between us. You know that if you needed me I would be back in a heartbeat, but there are some things that have been said that can never be taken back. I think maybe it's best if we just leave each other alone for a while – I'm hurting, and I'm sure you are too. Let's just have a little bit of time out, OK?
Take care,
Tessa

I sit back, shocked. *Is Tessa saying she doesn't want anything more to do with me? And what previous emails? I haven't contacted her for weeks.* I never thought Tessa would turn her back on me. I apologised to her and this is what she comes back with? I honestly thought our friendship was worth more to her than that; after all, everybody falls out occasionally, don't they? Angry tears fill my eyes and I blink them back furiously. I type out numerous angry responses, before deleting them, unwilling to send out a stream of vitriol, no matter how hurt I am feeling. Instead, I slam the lid of the laptop closed and decide to go back to bed until it's time to pick Henry up, ignoring the voice nagging in my head, telling me that going back to bed is the worst thing I could possibly do if I want to stave off the black clouds that linger overhead.

It's Friday morning, and Mark is due home later on this evening. We have spoken a few times on the phone while he's been in Bristol, and although it's been a little strained, I am looking forward to seeing him and hopefully putting it all behind us. I haven't mentioned the email from Tessa in the hope that, by not talking about it, it won't hurt so much, but I haven't deleted it either, and rereading it feels like tearing off a scab that's not ready. Jasper is home from the vet's and seems to be much better, after I have trawled through all the cupboards to make sure there are no lingering cans of food that could make him poorly. I decide to give the house a spring clean before Mark comes home, and a tap on the kitchen window as I'm mopping the floor gives me a welcome excuse for a break. Lila pokes her head round the back door.

'Are you busy? I've come to take you out for lunch. I thought we could go into town, have some lunch and maybe pick up some baby bits?' I smile, her visit the perfect excuse to leave the housework and take the rest of the afternoon off.

'That sounds perfect – the housework can wait. Let me get my coat.'

I tidy away the mop and bucket, run a brush through my hair, slick on some lip gloss and grab my coat. At the last minute, I think, *Sod it*, and pick up my good coat. It's been ages since I wore it and although I feel a little apprehensive over the coat being part of the accusation made against me by Jasmine Hale, I am determined not to let her ruin it for me.

Lila and I spend the rest of the morning strolling through town, the milder spring weather that has hit over the past few days making a walk in the weak sunshine enjoyable. We visit a couple of baby boutiques, where I pick up some essentials and Lila buys a perfect, tiny pair of pink and white bootees for the baby.

'Oh, Lila, thank you. They're perfect.' I cradle the tiny boots in the palm of my hand, then laugh as the baby kicks me hard and quickly grab Lila's hand.

'Here. Feel this.' I lay her hand on the spot where the baby is kicking me over and over, a tiny foot pressing hard against the side of my belly. A strange look crosses her face, almost twisting her features, before she smiles and pulls her hand away.

'Lovely. Come on, let's go and grab some lunch.'

We manage to snag a table at a busy bistro on the High Street, deciding at the last minute to sit on one of the small tables outside, as the weather is so lovely.

****

The snow of the previous few weeks has cleared, and now spring has definitely sprung, a mild breeze pushing along the white puffs of cloud that scud across the blue sky overhead. I lift my face up towards the sun, enjoying the warmth on my face. I think about the look that crossed Lila's face when I held her hand to my stomach, and decide I have to speak to her about it.

'I'm sorry if I made you feel uncomfortable just now,' I say, unsure as to whether I am making the right decision, bringing it up. 'You know, with the bump.' Lila gives a small smile and shakes her head.

'No, of course you didn't, it's just ...' She heaves a huge sigh and tears come to her eyes. 'Joe doesn't want children, and I'd love to have a baby. It's just not going to happen for us; Joe is adamant. It's a bit difficult for me, that's all.'

'Oh, Lila, I'm sorry, I had no idea. And I've dragged you round baby shops all morning too.' I pat her hand, feeling a little awkward. I feel awful that I've practically forced my bump on her when, all the time, she's been longing for a baby of her own.

'Don't be silly, it was my idea. You look a bit happier, Steph. I'm pleased; after all, you've had a horrible few months.'

'I'm trying. I mean, it's still not all plain sailing. I can't go too far in case the police want to talk to me again about Jasmine's car, I almost killed the dog and Tessa isn't speaking to me, but at least I can enjoy a bit of sun on my face.' As I try to make light of it all, I know that deep down I am still worried about a hell of a lot of stuff, and there's still something that doesn't sit right with me about Jasper getting so sick when I know I didn't buy food with beef in it. But the only other option is that either Mark or Lila fed it to him, and I can't see that having happened – they both love that puppy as much as I do. Either that or someone got into the house and fed it to him, and there's no way I can entertain that idea for a second, not if I don't want to drive myself crazy.

'Mark says he's staying home until after the baby is born, so hopefully we can get ourselves back on track. It's been a messed-up year.' I take a bite of my lunch to stop myself from saying anything further. Tessa is the only one who knows what Mark did and, although I trust Lila, I am too ashamed to tell her what happened.

'That reminds me!' Lila says excitedly. 'I'm sure I saw Mark on Wednesday! I was in town buying Joe a birthday present and I saw him having lunch … you'll never guess who with!' She leaves a dramatic pause, while I am frantically trying to get my head around Mark being in London on Wednesday when he told me he was leaving for Bristol on Wednesday morning.

'MELISSA DAVENPORT!' Lila sits back in her chair, triumphantly, and her excited babble about seeing a *real-life celebrity* is drowned out by the rushing in my ears. I lay my hands on the table to steady myself, before smiling weakly at Lila.

'That's … marvellous. I'm sorry, Lila, I really need to go. I have to fetch Henry. I'll catch you later?' I throw a twenty-pound note on the table to cover my meal, and rush out of the restaurant, leaving Lila sitting, mouth agape, as I rush for the exit.

I can't settle to anything for the rest of the afternoon, pacing the living room until I'm surprised there isn't a groove worn into the floorboards. Lila's words buzz round and round in my head and, although I am trying not to be hasty, I can't seem to find any way to make sense of what she saw without reaching the obvious conclusion that Mark is still lying to me, seeing Melissa behind my back. I march backwards and forwards across the window, grateful my mum was able to collect Henry and take him to hers for a sleepover. Occasionally, I stop my pacing to peer out to see if Mark is arriving home. Dusk is beginning to settle, the sky turning a beautiful shade of indigo, the sun casting a deep red hue as it sinks below the horizon, when I see Laurence coming out of Lila's house, a set look to his mouth as he walks quickly from her front door to his, not noticing me peeping out from behind the blind. I am curious as to why Laurence would be visiting Lila. I know they know each other, but I didn't realise they knew each other well enough to visit one another, and I wonder whether Lila has said anything to him about her theory of him being behind my 'gifts'. Before I can consider it any further, a cab pulls up and Mark tumbles out, dragging his overnight bag behind him. He leans down to speak to the driver, then makes his way up the front path, and I pull the front door open before he can reach for his keys.

'Steph, you're a sight for sore eyes. Come here. I'm sorry we fought.' He reaches for me and I pull sharply away. 'What is it?' A wary look crosses his face, and my heart sinks a little, the memory of that night when I first confronted him about the texts on his phone still clear in my mind.

'We need to talk.' I slam the front door shut and grab his overnight bag from him, throwing it down at the bottom of the stairs. 'I think you've got some explaining to do.'

'Me? Why? What am I supposed to have done now?' He crosses his arms in front of him, defensively.

'Does lunch in town with Melissa Davenport on Wednesday ring any bells? After you told me, *after you lied*, and said it was all over with her? You told me you were going to Bristol!' Meeting his eyes, I refuse to look away, refuse to cry. He's made me cry too many times before.

'Steph – I was in Bristol by Wednesday lunchtime; call any one of the others in the team and they'll tell you. Where have you got this idea that I was having lunch with Melissa?'

'You were *seen*, Mark. You were bloody seen by someone, having lunch in town with her. Do you still want to carry on denying it?' Shaking, knowing I'm raising my voice, I take a deep breath, trying to calm myself down. Mark rakes his hands through his hair, a desperate look on his face.

'I was in *Bristol*. I swear to you. I don't know how many times I can tell you that it was *nothing*. It's *over*, Steph. You'll believe anyone except me, won't you? Who is it that you'll believe over me?' I open my mouth to answer, when the shriek of the doorbell stops me. I yank open the front door, not caring that whoever is out there has probably heard us screaming at each other. Lila stands there, my scarf in her hands.

'Sorry,' she says, smiling apologetically and holding it out. 'You left this today. I thought you might need it.' I pull her inside, spinning her around to face Mark.

'Tell him, Lila, tell him that you saw him!' My breath is coming in huge hitches as I try to keep control of my emotions.

'What? What are you talking about, Steph?' Her face is puzzled and she pulls away in shock as I grab hold of her forearm.

'*Tell him you saw him having lunch with Melissa Davenport on Wednesday,*' I hiss, my fingers digging sharply into her arm.

'Steph, stop, you're scaring me.' She tries to pull away again, casting frantic glances at Mark. 'I didn't say I saw *Mark*. I said I saw Melissa having lunch with someone who I presumed was her producer, and was excited because I'd never seen a celebrity up close before.' She finally disentangles herself from my fingers and steps back two paces.

'*What?* No, you didn't, you didn't say that. You said you saw Mark, I know you did.' I look wildly from one to the other, Lila giving me a small, uncertain smile, while Mark just looks disgusted or disappointed, I'm not sure which.

'Steph. Maybe you got the wrong end of the stick. I mean, you're pregnant … and tired. Let's all just calm down a bit, eh?' Lila is still looking at me as though I am about to flip out at any moment.

'No, Lila, I didn't. I know what you said. Mark, she said she *saw you*.' I look at him beseechingly, willing him to believe me, but I'm already starting to doubt myself. *She did say she saw him, I'm sure she did.*

'Lila, you need to leave.' Mark takes my scarf from her, and steers her towards the front door. On the doorstep she pauses, before giving me one last glance over her shoulder and walking back down the path towards her own house. Mark turns back to me, threading the scarf through his fingers.

'Steph, this can't go on – you need help. You can't just go throwing accusations around like that; we're never going to get over this otherwise. Have you been seeing Dr Bradshaw?'

'No. Yes. I mean, I did. Please, Mark, you have to believe me, she said she saw you.'

'She couldn't have seen me, Steph, because I wasn't there.' With that, he heads up the stairs, returning with a pillow in his hands, leaving me to spend another night alone in our bed.

CHAPTER TWENTY-FIVE

Mark is sitting on the couch in the living room, pillow at one end, when I make my way downstairs the next morning, something small and black cradled in his hands. His hair is sticking up all over, like he's been running his hands through it, and I fight the urge to go over and smooth it down. He raises his head to me as I enter the room, his eyes bloodshot and ringed with dark circles where he hasn't slept. I am sure mine don't look a lot different. I try to smile, my mouth not wanting to do as I ask, and the best I can manage is a slight upturn on one side, verging on a sneer.

'Now it's your turn for an explanation.' He throws the slim, black object in his hands towards me and I catch it clumsily.

'What? Where did you get this?' It's my mobile, the one I'd given up for lost.

'It was stuffed down the back of the sofa. I could feel something digging in to me while I was trying to sleep, and there it was. But then, I'm sure you already knew that.' He looks at me and this time it is definitely disgust that crosses his face. I turn the mobile over in my hands. It's definitely mine; there's the deep scratch Henry put across the back when he drove a toy car over it, two days after I got it.

'What's that supposed to mean?' I am confused, unsure as to why he's being hostile about a mobile phone. 'I told you, I lost it, I've been looking everywhere for it. And why are you looking at me like that?'

'I suggest you check your messages.' Mark stands abruptly and walks from the room, leaving me feeling somewhat bewildered. I do as he says – clicking on the 'Received' messages icon – only to find messages from Laurence, sent after our one kiss at the funfair. The first one only apologises for what happened – nothing indiscreet there, nothing that could make Mark look at me the way he just did – but the messages that follow don't seem to make any sense. Scrolling back, and then into the 'Sent' messages folder, I see what has made Mark so angry. According to the messages log, I have messaged Laurence several times after the kiss, each message slightly more risqué than the last, including one that tells Laurence that if I weren't pregnant, I'd be leaving Mark for him. *No wonder Mark is furious.* But I know I didn't send those messages – for one thing, I'd lost my mobile by then, and for another thing, despite his faults, *I love Mark. I would never do anything to hurt him. I know how it feels to have your heart ripped out – no matter what Mark did to me I would never, ever do it to him.* I feel sick, my stomach churning, and I realise that these are the text messages Laurence was referring to when I saw him in town all those weeks ago. *But, Steph*, a little voice niggles in my ear, *no one else knew about the kiss – no one else knew that you were attracted to Laurence, so who else could have sent those messages, apart from YOU?* I am scrolling frantically down the list, reading each message with an increasing amount of horror, when a message marked to Lila stands out. Opening it, I read a message, apparently sent by me, asking her to collect Henry from school as I was running late from an appointment. Sent on the day that Henry was missing when I went to collect him. Lila was telling the truth – she did receive a message asking her to collect him. I sink back down onto the couch, feeling more confused than ever before. I was so convinced I hadn't sent those messages – I know I didn't. *So, who did?* the poisonous voice in my ear asks.

'I'm leaving.' Mark's voice makes me jump, and when I look up he's standing in front of me, his jacket on, with his overnight bag on his shoulder.

'What do you mean, you're leaving? Can't we talk about this?'

'No. Jesus Christ, Steph, I don't want to talk about how if you weren't pregnant you'd be leaving me for another man! Right now, I just need some space from you – I don't know who you are any more. One minute you're accusing me of all sorts, the next going behind my back, making up stories, lying, saying things have happened when there's just no proof. I can't take it at the moment, Steph. I'm going to stay with Paul for a couple of nights, get my head together. I suggest you take the time to think about what you really want.' He picks up his car keys from the coffee table and walks away from me. Panicking, I run after him, grabbing at the bag strap on his shoulder.

'Please, Mark, please don't go, it's you that I want, I can explain it all.' I am sobbing, clutching on to him as he opens the door. He shrugs me off, gently, before getting in the car and roaring away from the kerb. Away from me.

I call Lila. There is no one else, and I can't be on my own, not in this state. I pull the door open and she is there, standing on the doorstep, finger poised to ring the bell. I sag defeated against the doorframe, my face blotchy with tears.

'Jesus, Steph, what's going on?' Lila puts an arm round me and guides me back into the living room, where I sit, dazed, on the couch, the mobile phone on the table in front of me.

'I think Mark's left me,' I say, fresh tears sprouting to my eyes. I gesture towards the phone. 'There are messages on there to Laurence, ones that Mark thinks

I sent, but I *didn't*, I swear.' She picks it up, and scrolls through, pausing as she reads each one.

'But … there's one here to me,' she says, 'the one you sent asking me to pick Henry up that day.' She doesn't say it but the implication is there – *the day you accused me of kidnapping your son.*

'I know. I didn't send that one, either, I'm sure I didn't. At least, I don't think I did. I thought I'd lost my mobile, and now I think I'm losing my marbles.' I give a tiny laugh, before another flood of tears cascades down my cheeks.

'Don't be silly; things have just got on top of you. Mark will be back; he just needs his space. Give him time, OK. Don't call him or anything; let him call you. Good job I'm here to pick up the pieces.' She rubs my back as I cry, comforting me. 'There's something else I need to tell you – I think you should know that Joe and I have split up. The baby thing just became all too much, you know? But I'm OK; I know it'll be for the best in the long run.' Lila gives a brave sniff, as it's my turn to hug her. As I give her a squeeze and she leans her head on my shoulder, I wonder about Laurence leaving her house the previous evening. *Maybe she doesn't really think Laurence is behind everything – maybe she was warning me off Laurence because she has her eye on him? Maybe they're already together?* I'm not at all sure how I feel about anything any more.

Mark returns home early the next morning, collecting Henry and taking him straight back out to spend the day with his sister and her children, leaving me at home alone for the day to worry and wonder what's going to happen between us. Despite my attraction to Laurence, Mark is the one I want, so why would I send inappropriate messages? I wouldn't, is the answer, so that can only mean that someone else sent them. But who? The same someone who sent me dead flowers? The same person who fed Jasper something to make him hideously ill? Or is that same someone me? Head whirling, confused and feeling as though there's every chance I'm going mad, once again, I head back to my bed until Mark and Henry return home. The ringing of the phone wakes me, and I fumble for the handset.

'Hello?' My voice is slurred with sleep.

'Steph? It's Livvy – Olivia, Izzy's mum. Are you OK?'

'What? Yes, sorry. I'm not too well, I was having a nap.'

'Gosh, I'm sorry to wake you up. I just wanted to see if you two were free for dinner next week? Tim is home most evenings so any day will do for us.'

'I'm sorry, Olivia, things are … Now isn't really a good time. Can I get back to you?' I can't tell her that I don't even know if Mark is going to come home.

'Well, yes, but I did really want to get something in the diary. Tim isn't very often home in the evenings, but as this is a quiet week for him, I thought we could make some sort of plan. Not to worry, it can wait until you're better. I was just wondering – did you get the flowers I sent?' A cold chill snakes down my spine.

'No, what flowers?'

'I left you a posy, on the porch.'

I slam the phone down, my hands shaking, and the slick taste of fear bitter on my tongue. *Olivia? It was Olivia?* Rubbing my face in my hands, I start as the phone rings again, the insistent, shrill ring jolting right through me. I lift the receiver and slam it straight back down, but within a few seconds it starts ringing again, on and on until I reach down and pull the plug from its socket. Feeling claustrophobic, I get up and start pacing the room, anxiety keeping me moving. My mobile beeps and I snatch it up, only to see Olivia's name on the screen. She's left a voicemail, and I have to listen to it. I have to hear what she has to say, even though I'm scared witless.

'*Hi, Steph, I hope I haven't upset you? The phone went dead and I tried calling back but no answer. I hope you're OK – sorry you didn't get the flowers. I sent them before Christmas with a note just to cheer you up. You looked a bit down, that's all. Izzy had come home talking about Henry and I was hoping we could be friends. I'm sorry if I've done something wrong, I just wanted to give you a bit of a lift, that's all. Maybe call me back when you feel a bit better?*'

I listen to the voicemail several times, before I cry with relief. The first bunch of flowers, the beautiful little hand-tied posy, was from Olivia – nothing sinister at all, just a gesture to cheer me up when I felt crappy, because she wanted us to be friends. In too much of a state to call her back, I throw my mobile down and let the tears overwhelm me.

The slamming of the front door wakes me, and before I can get up, Mark is standing over me. I feel awkward and ashamed that he's caught me sleeping during the day, knowing his first thought will be that I am sliding back into the depression that stole my early days with Henry. I'm not, I know that, but after Olivia's phone call, her words leaving me shaking and nauseous, I took a sleeping pill. I struggle into an upright position, and switch on the bedside lamp.

'Where's Henry?' I ask, squinting slightly in the dim light.

'Downstairs. I can't leave it any longer – I need an explanation, Steph. Why did you send those messages? Is that really how you feel about us?' Mark scratches his nail along the duvet cover, avoiding my eyes.

'No, of course it isn't. I swear Mark, on Henry's life, that I didn't send those messages. I told you, ages ago, that I lost my mobile. I think … I think someone stole my phone, sent those messages, then planted the phone where you would find it, to try and break us.'

Mark huffs out a little breath, in something that could almost be a laugh.

'Who's that, then? The same person that broke into our house but never took anything? The same person that looks like you but isn't you that vandalised Jasmine Hale's car? The same person that poisoned the dog, who also wasn't you? We've had this conversation over and over again! Please, Steph, I can't take much more. I know part of the reason you are the way you are is because of me. I want to be with you, I want to help you, but I don't know if I can go through you behaving like this, not with a child in the house. You need to go back to Dr Bradshaw, and you need to get help, before it all goes too far. Otherwise I can't stay, and I'll take Henry and the new baby with me.'

I stifle a sob as his words sink in, and although I want to fight him, scream at him that that's not the way things have happened, I'm frightened he'll just take it as proof that I'm as crazy as he thinks I am, so I bite my tongue, hiding it all away, as I am so used to doing now, the diary the only place I can really be myself any more. Calmly, rationally, I lay my hand on his arm and speak.

'Mark, you don't have to believe me. I know the truth, I know that none of this is my fault, but if that's what it takes, I'll go to Dr Bradshaw, and I'll take medication and I'll do whatever it takes to make this work, OK?' Mark nods his agreement and leaves the room, still not touching me. I will make this work, but in order to do that it's not Dr Bradshaw I need. I need to find out exactly who is making me crazy, and pray to God it's not me.

CHAPTER TWENTY-SIX

Over the next few days we call an uneasy truce – Mark has moved back home after staying with Paul, a friend from work, for a couple of nights, as Henry begins to ask questions almost as though he knows something is wrong. We move carefully around one another, politely asking if the other would like a cup of tea, or where something or other is. Our conversation, when we do attempt it, is stilted and it breaks my heart that we can't seem to communicate with each other properly. I am on my best behaviour, making sure I don't mention anything to Mark about the idea that someone is trying to mess with my mind. I've accepted that it's nothing to do with Llewellyn Chance; I know he's dead and gone and the relief that comes with that knowledge is overwhelming. But I'm sure now that it's someone close to me – someone who knows me pretty well, maybe knows my innermost thoughts, someone who wishes me harm. Mark is out of the house early every day, returning late in the evening. I have no idea if he genuinely needs to work these hours, or if he's just trying to keep our time together to a minimum.

One morning I return home to find another posy on the doorstep, once again withered and decayed, a musty smell emanating from it. Looking around to see if anyone is nearby, I see that the road is empty, and with a heavy heart I pick it up between fingers and thumb and throw it directly into the recycling bin. I am exhausted – seven months pregnant and feeling completely alone. *Did Olivia leave it?* The memory of her phone call swims to the forefront of my mind. After she said she left flowers in the porch I slammed the phone down hard, heart pounding, as I realised it could literally be *anyone* trying to hurt me, and there's every chance it could be her. I grab some cardboard from the recycling pile in the kitchen and squash it down hard onto the dead bouquet, hiding it from sight. I don't want to see it, and there's no point showing it to Mark as he'll probably accuse me of sending it to myself. Unwilling to stay alone in the house after my discovery, I grab Jasper's lead and whistle to him before letting him lead me up the garden path and along the road towards the recreation ground. We are a short way from the tube station when I see a familiar copper head heading my way. Laurence is walking towards me, and my first instinct is hide away in the nearest doorway until he's gone past, but Jasper has other ideas. Laurence smiles at me, before leaning down to pet Jasper.

'Are you OK?' Concerned, he peers at me. 'You look pale, Steph, are you sure you're all right?'

'Yes, I'm fine. I think.' I blow a wayward curl out of my eyes and look away as tears form. 'I'm sorry, I just need to …' I pull Jasper away and move to walk past him but he blocks my way.

'Steph, I need to talk to you, about all this weird stuff that's been happening to you.' He looks past me, over my shoulder, and before I can turn to see what he's looking at, he starts talking again: 'It's important. I know what's been going on and I know—'

'STEPH!' A shout from behind me makes me turn, and I see Lila running towards me, waving something in the air.

'I'm sorry, Laurence, you'll have to hang on a moment.' Lila catches us up and, after a brief look at Laurence, turns to me, handing me the sheet of paper she was waving. 'Lila, what is it?'

'You're going to want to see this.' Her chest is heaving with the effort of getting her breath back, and her hair, which she has curled once again in a style similar to mine, settles around her flushed cheeks. I take the paper, feeling as though I have taken a punch to the stomach when I realise I am holding a red-top newspaper, a bold headline screaming out at me. Underneath the headline is a picture of Mark and Melissa Davenport, strolling hand in hand through a park. Mark is wearing his favourite blue shirt, one I bought him for Christmas one year, while she is wearing not an awful lot, all things considered. Scanning through the article, I read how Melissa has been spotted holding hands with producer Mark Gordon, while the journalist, if you can call them that, speculates about Mark's pregnant wife, and whether Mark is the reason for the huge diamond rock on her right hand, a replica of the one Mark bought for me. With shaking hands, I thrust the newspaper back at Lila, and swallow down the bile that threatens at the back of my throat.

'I understand now, why you thought I said I saw Mark in town having lunch with Melissa.' Lila gives me a sympathetic look and pats my hand.

'What?' I barely hear her through the rushing that pounds in my ears, a fuzzy feeling that makes me feel light-headed.

'I said ...'

'No, I heard what you said. I have to go; I have to get home.' I reel Jasper's lead in and turn on my heels and run for home, one hand holding my pregnant belly, ignoring the shouts from Lila and Laurence as they call my name.

I let myself in, dropping the lead and running straight to the downstairs bathroom, where I throw up. Sitting back on my heels I scrub my hand across my mouth and blow my nose.

'It's just like when we first met, do you remember?' I look up and Lila is standing in the bathroom doorway, no sign of the newspaper. 'Are you OK, my love? Come here, you've had a terrible shock.' She gives me a hand to help me stand, and then I follow her through into the kitchen where she puts the kettle on. 'Who do you think would have told such a terrible story? I mean, who would want to make you this upset?'

I hate myself for even thinking it, but there is only one person who knows what happened between Mark and Melissa, and only one person who doesn't have any time for me lately.

'Tessa,' I whisper. 'I think it was Tessa; she's the only one who knew what happened between those two. She hates me at the moment, but I just can't believe she would stoop this low.'

'Oh, gosh. Do you really think she did it? Well, I suppose if she's the only one who knew about it, who else could it be?' Lila places a steaming mug of tea in front of me, alongside a plate of biscuits that I push away. I couldn't eat anything even if I wanted to.

'I need to call her. I need to find out why she did this. Did she not even think about Henry? Oh, God, Henry – what am I going to say if someone talks to him? I need to call Mark. Jesus.' I push my hands through my hair, my sweaty palms pulling and tugging.

'Shh. Calm down. You call Tessa, I'll call Mark. I'll get him to come home and we can get all this straightened out, OK?' Lila crouches in front of where I sit, gently disentangling my hands from my knotty curls. I nod, and reach for the telephone, while she digs her mobile out of her handbag and leaves the room to call Mark. The international ring tone buzzes in my ear before a sharp voice says, 'Tessa Jackson'.

'Tessa, it's me.' There is a silence, almost as though Tessa is gathering her thoughts before she speaks again.

'Steph. How are you?'

'How could you do it, Tess? I know we've had our differences lately but did you not stop to think about Henry? About how he would feel about it all?' Tears thicken my throat, making it hard to speak.

'Steph, what are you talking about? Is everything OK?'

'You *know* what I'm talking about, Tessa – the newspaper article, in *The Daily*! All the details about Mark and Melissa, things that only you know about!' A sharp intake of breath, and I hear clacking as though Tessa is frantically typing.

'Oh, my God. I've got it up on screen now. I swear, I never told them anything, Steph; I haven't even spoken to anyone. Do you really think I would do something like that to you?' Her voice is quiet, calm.

'How do I know? You've accused me of sending you vile emails recently, which I never did; how do I know you're not getting your revenge? You're the only person who knew anything had happened between them. I can't trust you any more, not after this.' Without letting her speak, I slam the phone down. When I look up, Lila is standing in front of me, a small smile on her face.

'I guess that told her,' she says. 'I spoke to Mark; he'll be home soon.'

'Thank you.' I give her a weak smile, and blow my nose. 'I just can't believe that she would do that; I thought she was my friend. After everything we've been through together, I thought I could trust her with anything, but it shows she's just like everybody else.'

'Are you sure it was her? Maybe you should call the newspaper and check? See if they can confirm it? You don't want to fall out with her if she had nothing to do with it.' Lila raises her eyebrows at me and I could kiss her. I pull my laptop towards me, an idea striking. Tessa denies it, but if I can speak to the journalist who wrote the article, get them to confirm it, then I'll know for sure, and I'll know I have to cut her out of my life for good. *Maybe all of this has been Tessa all along. How do I even know she's still in New York? She could be close by; France is only an hour or two away.* Finding the article, I note the by-line, and Google for contact details. Eventually, and after tapping up another journalist who owes me a favour, I have the phone number for Peter Jenkins, the guy who has written the story. It rings twice before he picks up.

'Jenkins.'

'Mr Jenkins, you've published a story regarding my husband this morning.'

'And which story would that be?' His voice is wary, cautious, and who could blame him? After all, he is making a living by ruining people's lives.

'Mark Gordon. Listen, I'm not going to argue or scream at you; what's written is written – you can't get rid of it now. I know you have to protect your sources, but if I give you a name I just need confirmation, OK? I just need to know if it was definitely this person who gave you the story. Was it Tessa Jackson?' I hold my breath, terrified in equal measures that he will confirm or deny it.

'Sorry, Mrs Gordon. It wasn't Tessa Jackson.' I let out my breath in a huge whoosh of relief. And then he says, 'It was you.'

CHAPTER TWENTY-SEVEN

I am lying on the couch, a cool cloth on my forehead, Lila peering anxiously at me as Mark stands to one side. I try to struggle into a sitting position but Lila pushes me gently back down, making sure my head is laid on the pillow someone has so thoughtfully put there.

'Shhhh,' she soothes, 'you fainted. Luckily, Mark was just coming through the door so he carried you through into here. You did bump your head, though.' I raise my fingertips to my forehead, and sure enough, there is a small lump there. I press it gently and wince as a sharp pain crashes through my temple. I remember the baby, and place a hand on my stomach, where the baby gives a reassuring push with a hand or foot, stretching out inside me.

'That journalist … he said I told him about Mark and Melissa, but I didn't. Why would I? Why would he say that?' Remembering the picture of Mark and Melissa holding hands, I sit up and stare at him accusingly.

'Mark?' He sighs, pushing his hand through his hair, making no attempt to sit by me, or reach for me.

'It's an old picture, Steph. It was taken back in the summer; if you look, you'll see. Some pap snapped it in Regent's Park when you and Henry were up in Scotland visiting my parents in the summer holidays and I paid him two hundred and fifty quid to get rid of it.'

'I don't want to look. And I don't know anything about it – *I didn't send it.*' It sickens me, this fresh news that he paid two hundred and fifty pounds to keep his sordid little affair quiet. I see Lila cast a quick glance at Mark and he gives an almost imperceptible nod of his head. She pulls a piece of folded paper from the back pocket of her jeans.

'I found this on your computer while Mark was making you comfortable. I didn't want to snoop, I promise, but I just wanted to check. Find proof, if you like, that the journalist, that Pete guy, had got it wrong. But …' She gives a little shrug of her shoulders and hands me the square of paper. Unfolding it, my hands shake, and I am frightened of what I am about to discover. Scanning over the words quickly, my heart sinks, for I'm holding a copy of an email sent by me to Peter Jenkins, a little over twenty-four hours ago, with all the sordid details of Mark and Melissa's affair, including some things I never even told Tessa. Things that only Mark, Melissa and I know, private stuff I've poured out in my diary to avoid it overwhelming me completely. The lump on my head pounds and saliva fills my mouth, but I force away the sick feeling in my stomach, knowing that, if I'm sick, Lila will think I have a concussion and try to send me to hospital. I don't have time to go to hospital; I need to figure out what the hell is going on.

'I didn't … Mark, I swear I didn't …' The paper shakes in my hand and I lay it flat on the coffee table, getting to my feet to try to tell Mark it wasn't me. He stands before me, detached, a granite look on his face. There is no warmth about him, no affection; he's like a statue of the man I married.

'I don't want to hear it, Steph, OK? You're going to Dr Bradshaw – *today*. I'll take you there myself; at least that way I'll know you're actually going there. This has to stop – I already warned you, don't say I didn't.' Speechless, I just nod my head, wincing as a twinge ripples through my belly. Anything to convince him I didn't sabotage the little we had left to cling on to in our marriage by doing this. I figure if I go along with him, see the doctor, I can try to explain to Dr Bradshaw once and for all what's been happening and then he can tell Mark I'm not mad – it really has been happening. Lila brings me my coat, and I slowly pull it on over my shoulders. I feel exhausted, weak, wrung out. Walking out to the car, my legs feel detached from the rest of my body, and I sink gratefully into the passenger seat and strap myself in. Lila talks in hushed tones to Mark, gesturing with her hands, but even when I lower the window I can't hear what she's saying. She gives Mark a quick hug and, as he walks towards the car, I turn my face away and close my eyes.

The car journey to Dr Bradshaw's seems to take forever, hampered by London traffic and the weight of the silence that fills the car. I don't try to make any conversation and Mark only speaks to me once, when he notices that my eyes are closed, to tell me not to go to sleep in case I have a concussion. We walk into the office together after parking a couple of streets away. Natalie, the receptionist, gives me a sympathetic look as she books me in, and I curl my lip at her, just for the fun of watching her look quickly away. When Dr Bradshaw calls me, Mark gets up and I think he's coming in with me, an idea that makes my heart jump as then I can tell him the full story in front of the doctor and he'll have to believe the doctor when he says I'm not going crazy. He doesn't, though, instead telling me that he'll have to move the car to avoid getting a fine and will be back in an hour. He doesn't kiss me goodbye. Reluctantly, I make my way towards the doctor's office, where Dr Bradshaw stands in the doorway, waiting for me.

'Steph. Sit down.' He makes himself comfortable, arranging his notepad and scratchy pen just so in front of him. 'So, we seem to be having a few problems, don't we?'

'You could say that, although it's been more than a few,' I say, adjusting my scarf and smoothing my hair down over the lump on my forehead. 'More bouquets, somebody poisoned the dog – he's just a puppy! Why would someone want to do that? Someone took my mobile, and sent messages, inappropriate messages, behind my back, and then left the phone for Mark to find. Now they're saying that I emailed the newspaper and sold a story about Mark's affair, but I didn't. *I know I didn't.*'

Dr Bradshaw watches me for a moment before sliding a sheet of paper out from the slim file in front of him.

'So how can we explain this?' he asks quietly. It's a copy of the email; Mark must have given it to him, but there's something niggling me about the email, something not right.

'*I don't know,*' I hiss. 'I'm just trying to tell you what's happening; I never sent that bloody email. *Someone* is trying to get to me.'

'And the dog – why would someone want to hurt your dog? Mark says there was a can of food left in the bin of the type the dog is allergic to – the same evening you reportedly told everyone you'd already fed the dog.' I am staring at him, a memory of that evening springing to mind.

'BAKING CHOCOLATE!' I shout, slamming my hands down on the table. 'There was an empty wrapper for baking chocolate in the bin – I can't bake!

I would never even buy baking chocolate; it's extremely poisonous to dogs. Someone bought baking chocolate and fed it to Jasper to make him sick.' Dr Bradshaw makes a scratchy note in his precious notepad, before turning back to me.

'Steph, I think the best course of action is for me to prescribe some medication for you. It's a conventional antipsychotic, one that can be used when pregnant.' *Antipsychotic? I don't need antipsychotics.* Panicking, my mind races as I try to figure out the best way to play things. I try to read the typical doctor's handwriting scrawled across my file as he reaches behind him for his prescription pad. I can't make anything out as his writing is appalling, but one word is readable. *Delusional.* My palms begin to sweat and I take a deep breath. The only way to get through this is to prove to the doctor, to Mark, to everyone, that I am *not* delusional. So I thank the doctor, take the prescription and go out into the reception area, thankful to have made my escape a full ten minutes early.

I push the door onto the street open, only to find Laurence waiting outside. Flustered at the sight of him, I wrap the handle of my bag around my hand tightly and fuss with the collar on my coat.

'Laurence. What are you doing here?'

'I went to the house to see you. Lila was there; she said you were here for an appointment. I was hoping you'd come out early so I could get a chance to talk to you before Mark gets here to pick you up. Come on, there's a café just up the road. Let's grab a coffee – there are some things I need to talk to you about.'

Nervous, but curious as to what he has to say, I follow Laurence to the nearby café, careful to make sure our hands don't touch as we walk along. He pushes the café door open, a welcoming steam of coffee and butter on the air. We find a table and he comes back with a cappuccino and a hot chocolate.

'Here.' He passes me the hot chocolate. 'Listen, Steph, I've been doing some digging. There's something you need to know.'

'What? Laurence, what are you talking about?' I sip at the hot drink, wrapping my cold fingers around the mug. Another twinge pulls at my lower belly and I shift in my chair to get comfortable.

'All this stuff that's been happening to you? You're not going mad. I've been looking into it all, digging around, you know? I think I know …'

'STEPH. God, Steph, where the bloody hell were you? I went to collect you and Natalie said you left.' Mark storms into the café, a look of fear crossed with anger on his face. 'I thought you'd run off somewhere.' I stand to meet him, gesturing to where Laurence sits.

'Mark, please, Laurence was about to tell me something …'

'I don't think so, Steph. Come on.' He grabs my arm and begins to tug me towards the door, the way Henry does when he wants me to do something.

'Mark, wait, this is important.' Laurence gets to his feet, trying to make Mark listen, to let me hear what he has to say.

'*You.*' Mark glares at him. 'You stay the hell away from my wife, do you hear me?' With that he pulls me towards the door, where the car is parked outside, meaning I never do get to hear what Laurence has to say.

We pull up outside the house but there's no parking so I tell Mark to let me out while he goes to find a space, ignoring the mild cramps that tug at my stomach and the bottom of my back. My mum still has Henry and I'm hoping we can go and pick him up later, if Mark will let me. He lets me out, and slowly heads towards the end of the road, his head moving from left to right as he looks for a space. Laurence must have caught a cab home – I see him knocking on Lila's door, but when he spots me, he drops the brass door knocker and lightly jogs up the path to where I am frantically trying to get my key in the door. I am desperate to speak to him, to find out what he has to say, but I am worried that Mark will be back any minute. Plus, after the scene in the café, I am too mortified to look him in the eye.

'Steph, please, I need to speak to you.' He lays his hand on mine, over the key, and gently lowers it.

'I can't, Laurence, not right now. I banged my head.' Anything to get him off the doorstep before Mark comes back; I lift up my fringe to show him the lump.

'Look, there's other stuff, it's about Lila …'

'I said, *not now,* Laurence.' I cut him off. I don't want to hear right now about how he and Lila are getting together. It's all I can do to keep myself together at the moment; I can't listen to that, not now. I force the key in the lock and turn it hard, wrenching the door open, stumbling inside. Once inside, the door closed in Laurence's bewildered face, I heave a sigh of relief. I'll get my head sorted, then he can tell me all about his relationship with Lila, and let me know whatever he thinks he knows about what has been going on. I unwind my scarf from around my neck and wander into the kitchen. There's a cold draught blowing in from somewhere, and I shiver. The back door is swinging slightly, where someone has been through it and not shut it properly, and this is where the draught is coming from. My heart starts to bang painfully in my chest and I grab a kitchen knife from the block on the worktop. Quietly I reach the back door, and close it gently, stopping the soft banging noise as it swings to and fro. I turn to check the rest of the house, fingering my mobile in my pocket, ready to dial 999 if necessary. I sneak quietly out of the kitchen, along the hallway and into the front room, where what I see makes my blood run cold. On the coffee table are photos – the photos that stood proudly in frames along the mantelpiece, shredded into tiny pieces. Photos of me, Mark and Henry, our little family. *Just like before, when I found out about the affair.* In a rage that night, I had cut up all the photos of Mark and I together, all the ones that showed what a lying, cheating bastard he really was. Scattered across the table in slices are photos of Mark's parents and his brother on Mark's graduation day, and ones of me and Tessa on various nights out, cheeks smashed together, big grins on our faces. The front door slams and a little cry escapes my lips as I jump, nervously.

'Steph? What the bloody hell did you do?' Mark is standing in the doorway, staring in horror at the smashed photo frames, the shredded pictures, and at me standing hunched over them with a huge kitchen knife in my hand, looking every inch the mad woman he thinks I am.

CHAPTER TWENTY-EIGHT

Mark inches towards me, hand out to take the knife, as I lean over the shredded pictures, gasping as sharp pains claw at my belly.

'Mark …' I lift a hand to him, dropping the knife on the carpet. He stoops to pick it up, leaping back with a shout as a gush of water pours from between my legs. This is it. My waters have broken – the pains that have been niggling at me all day, which I have managed to ignore, are now coming in sharp, strong waves, each one threatening to take my breath away.

'Oh, God, Steph.' Mark springs into action, throwing the knife down on the table and gently guiding me to the couch. 'Come on, sit here – what shall I do?' It appears that any memories of when Henry was born have vanished from his head, as he begins to panic a little.

'Call the hospital. I think we need to go soon.' I bend double as another cramp racks my body. 'We need to time the pains …' I can barely catch my breath. I wave him towards the under-stairs cupboard, where the labour bag is kept, and he grabs it.

'I'll go and fetch the car; it's too far to walk.'

I nod weakly, already bracing myself for another contraction, praying that this won't take too long, that the baby will arrive safely, that she'll be OK even though she's early. Praying that we can begin to mend our broken relationship.

Twenty-four hours later I am propped up in my hospital bed, baby Beatrice sleeping in the cot by my side. It was a completely different labour to Henry – he took his time, but Beatrice was in a hurry and now I'm on a high, but exhausted. I lean over and examine my new daughter – she is exquisite, with a perfect peaches-and-cream complexion, long fingers and sweeping eyelashes. I wait patiently for Mark to bring Henry in. It was a mad dash yesterday evening to get here on time, so Henry has been with Lila for the night. I thank my lucky stars that Lila was around – I don't know what we would have done without her; there was barely enough time to get to the hospital as it was, and no way my mum would have got there in time to have Henry. I lie back and close my eyes, trying to catch a few minutes of sleep before Beatrice wakes up for a feed. I am just about to doze off when I hear voices in the corridor. I pull myself into a sitting position and wait for Henry to come barrelling in, which he does a minute later.

'Mummy!' He launches himself at me, making my breath whoosh out, before I snuggle him next to me on the bed, between the baby and me. He leans over the plastic cot, a look of awe on his face. I smile down at him, heart bursting to see the two of them together, meeting for the very first minute. A muffled cough grabs my attention and I look up to see Mark, face half obscured by a very large bunch of flowers.

'Hey.' I smile at him, conscious of my tired eyes and greasy hair, and smooth down my curls.

'Hey, yourself. Leave your hair, you look beautiful.' He leans over to kiss me, tickling my nose with the bouquet. 'These are from Belinda. She says she'll see you when you stop lactating.' A laugh splutters out of me and Beatrice startles in her cot. Belinda never changes.

'Did you tell Tessa?' I ask, stroking the baby's head.

'She was in a meeting. I've emailed her and left a message but, you know, it might take her a little while.'

'Listen, Mark, I need to talk to you …'

'Yoo hoo! Hello, darling. Oh, gosh, haven't you been through the mill?' My mother swoops in, all fur hat and purple nail polish. She always knows just how to make me feel terrible. 'Oh, darling, they could have let you have a shower.' She wrinkles her nose at me, before leaning over Beatrice. 'Oh, what a little dolly. Just like Henry was.' I frown at her.

'He still is, Mum. And I *did* shower.'

Mark takes over then, before I can get any more irritated with her. He scoops Bea out of the cot and hands her to my mother to coo over, while I slip Henry a chocolate bar out of the labour bag. It doesn't take long for my mum to get bored, and she soon slips her fur hat back on and leaves us to it. Mark goes to get us a cup of tea, and to chase up the doctor to see if I can be discharged, and when he comes back I grab his hand, and pull him gently down onto the bed next to me. Henry is engrossed in a chocolate bar and his handheld video game.

'Can we start again? Can we make Bea being born a fresh start for both of us?' Tears fill my eyes as I wait for him to reply.

'Oh, God, Steph, of course we can. You know there's nothing I want more than for us all to be a family – and I know I was the one who nearly ruined it for us all, but please, promise me you'll see Dr Bradshaw? We can't have any more of this stuff about people being out to get you. We've both got to work together to make this right. I need to know that you're going to drop it, just focus on us and the kids.' He strokes the back of my hand, and I watch the tears drop onto the bed cover.

'I will, I promise. I'll do whatever it takes, Mark. I just want us to be right again. How it used to be, in the beginning, do you remember?' I smile at him through my tears and he leans forward to kiss me.

'She's beautiful, isn't she?' He looks over at Bea, sleeping peacefully in her cot, unaware that she has just cemented our relationship into something more solid again. A sleek, dark head pops around the doorframe.

'I'm not interrupting, am I?' Lila asks, coming in anyway.

'Of course not.' Mark gives me a smile and pecks my lips again, the seal on our deal to start afresh, before standing and making room for her to sit next to me on the bed. But instead she heads straight to the cot, peeping in at the sleeping baby. Mark peers out of the door, while I can't take my eyes off her, feeling proud as I watch Lila drink in my beautiful newborn baby.

'Oh, Steph, you lucky thing, she's gorgeous!' Lila smiles at me, unable to tear her eyes away from Bea for long.

'Doctor's coming!' Mark announces and Lila snaps out of her daydream.

'I'll take Henry out of the way, shall I?' she says, holding out a hand to him. Henry jumps at the chance to spend more time with her, leaving Mark and I to deal with the doctor and coo over our new addition.

Mark stays home for the first few days, but before long work demands are piling up and he has to leave for the office. I am OK with that – I have to be, as part of my new resolution to make things right. Lila is across the road and has taken to coming over frequently, unable to keep away from Bea for too long, it seems. I worry that her own longing for a baby will be made worse by this, but she assures me that, all the time she is helping with Bea, it keeps her broodiness under control.

'And anyway,' she says to me one morning, once Mark has left for the office, 'you looked after me so well at Christmas; I want to return the favour. I feel like we're all family.'

I don't want to nag at Mark about work, not after we made a pact about a fresh start, and so far it seems to be working. I try not to think about what's happened before, the flowers, the email, the pictures shredded over the coffee table, but it still lurks quietly in a dark corner, ready to ambush me when I least expect it. I forgot how tiring having a baby could be, and this, alongside the battle to ignore my fears about the posies, means that, before long, I feel as though the dark clouds of depression are gathering again. The more tired I become, the harder it is not to think about it all.

I peer at myself in the bathroom mirror, toothpaste speckles dotting my reflection where Henry has brushed his teeth in the mirror and I haven't bothered to clean them off. I am tired, so tired I struggle to drag myself out of bed in the mornings to get Henry ready for school. Lila has taken to coming over early, before eight a.m., to make sure Henry is washed, fed and dressed before taking him to school for me, so I don't have to get myself and Bea up and ready. The other parents at the school all saw the newspaper article, of course they did, and no doubt I was the subject of some vicious gossip. I was more worried about the shredded photos that day, more concerned about Mark's reaction to me, poised over the pictures with a knife in my hand, and then, of course, Bea arrived. I wash my face, and tie my hair back in an effort to make myself feel a little better, before swishing the pill that Dr Bradshaw prescribed down the plughole. Mark thinks I am taking them, and after a few days of stashing them under my tongue he believes me when I say I am being a good girl. I dab a tiny bit of concealer under my eyes to try to hide the dark circles, and slide my diary out from under the mattress. The last entry is an account of the night of the shredded photos, written on my return home from the hospital, the day the newspaper destroyed the last little bit of trust Mark and I had in each other – trust we're now working overtime to rebuild. As I read it back, the writing is scrawled and messy as a result of my haste to get everything written down before Mark came back from the chemist with my prescription from Dr Bradshaw, while Bea slept in her bouncer. I cry as I reread it, the bitter taste of remembered fear on my tongue.

'*I feel as if I am truly losing my mind. The struggle to keep up appearances is exhausting, meaning I no longer know whether what I say or feel is real any more. Mark doesn't believe me, Tessa doesn't believe me. I no longer know if I believe me. I am so frightened,*

frightened that I will be all alone, frightened that this is all in my head, frightened that Mark will take Henry and Bea, Lila will leave me and I will have no one.'

Pulling myself together, trying to focus on the fact that Mark has agreed to a fresh start, I hide the diary and decide to go over to Lila's for a cup of tea. She's been a star for the past couple of weeks – taking Henry to school, dropping in bits of shopping so I don't have to go out, even cooking casseroles and bringing them over. I don't know what I would do without her, and the lure of my bed is calling me back to it, for another day under the duvet, blotting out the world. I can't have that, I need to get back to normality, so I can find out what's really going on – I have to prove to myself that none of this in my head, even though I promised Mark I would leave it. Forcing myself to do it, I grab a packet of posh biscuits out of the cupboard, pop Bea into her pram and snatch up my bag. Slinging it over my shoulder, I feel my mobile vibrate through the leather. Tempted to ignore it, I reach for my jacket but it buzzes again, so, concerned in case it is Mark checking up on me, I pull it out of the bag. There is one unread text message showing, from an unknown number. Puzzled, I open it, immediately wishing I hadn't.

'Iv got to tell you this, im sorry. The only reason mark left melissa is because she had an abortion and he wanted to keep the baby Im sorry but you should probably leave him'

The world tilts on its axis and I have to sit before I fall. *Is this never going to go away?* It's as though the minute I feel I am able to get to my feet, another wave comes and knocks me over. I reread the message, trying to absorb what the sender is telling me – that Mark only left Melissa because she had an abortion? I glance into the pram at a sleeping Bea. *Is this baby a replacement for the one he would have had with her?* I can't think straight, my thoughts colliding with each other as I rush out of the house, to Lila. She's the only one I can talk to about this, the only one left who I feel I can trust.

She opens the door immediately after I hammer the brass knocker down three times in quick succession.

'Steph, what's wrong? You look terrible.' She grasps my arm and pulls me inside, my legs shaking. I thrust the phone at her, and watch as she reads the message.

'Shit. What are you going to do?' She hands the phone back to me where I drop it into my bag as if I've been scalded. I don't want to touch it.

'I don't know,' I moan. 'This is never going to go away – I don't even know if it's true, or if it's just someone trying to get to me. Why would someone send this – unless it's true? We were supposed to be having a fresh start; you heard Mark in the hospital, didn't you?'

'Steph, you spoke about this to Dr Bradshaw, remember? There isn't anyone out to get you. Have you taken your pill?' I look at her crossly, disappointed that she still seems to be taking the view that Mark and the doctor have taken.

'Yes, of course I have. Do you think it's true? Oh God, what if it is true?' I bite the skin around my thumb hard, making it bleed.

'We'll deal with it.' She slaps my hand away from my mouth and gets up. 'I'm going to make us some tea, you're going to give me those posh biscuits and we are going to *forget* about this for ten minutes. You can't let yourself get so stressed; it's not good for any of you, and it's not fair on the children.' She heads off into the kitchen, leaving me slumped on the sofa against her enormous cushions. *It's easy for her to brush it off. How can I possibly forget, even for a minute?* A buzzing noise makes me jump, and I feel sick as I realise it is the vibration of a text arriving. I don't want to look; frightened in case it's something else come to shatter my world, but it isn't my phone. There is a text on Lila's phone from MARK. Why would Mark be texting Lila? Checking to make sure she is still busy in the kitchen I stealthily reach forward and pick up her phone. There is no password protection on it, so before I even realise what I'm doing I swipe across to open the phone and take a look. I can always say I thought it was mine. The text from Mark reads:

'Don't worry, if you can collect Henry from school today I can come home early and speak to Steph. As long as she is taking her medication it'll be OK. Mx'

Frowning, I scroll back to her sent messages to see what she has sent to Mark to warrant that reply. I find it immediately:

'Im so glad you feel the same way im scared that Henry and Bea are in danger from her iv been so worried'

What? I'm a danger to Henry? To Bea? *How dare she?* Furiously, I reread the message, something niggling at me before I see it, and then I can't unsee it. The language, the typos, the way the grammar is used … it's too familiar. Pulling my phone out of my bag I read the message that was sent to me this morning from an unknown number. It's the same – the same style, the same language, and the same childish spelling mistakes. Lila is the one who sent me the text message. Taking a shaky breath, I find the icon to mark Mark's message as unread and lay the phone back in position on the table, just as Lila comes back in carrying a tray with the tea things. Head whirling, I want to upend the tray all over her, scalding her perfect features, but I sit back, a grim smile on my face. I need proof before I can do anything, proof so that no one can say I'm making it all up.

'Here we go,' she trills, 'this will make us both feel much better.' She spies her phone and picks it up, reading Mark's message. 'Look, I have to go and pick something up for a friend; how about I get Henry for you while I'm out? Give you a chance to get yourself together. Then, when I get back, we can talk this whole thing out, OK?' She pats my hand, and I grit my teeth. I spy her laptop sitting on the desk in the alcove and an idea pings in the back of my mind.

'Do you know what, Li, that would be great, but ...' I bite my lip and force tears to my eyes. 'Would it be OK if Bea and I waited here for you two to come back? I'm scared to go home and be there on my own, especially after getting that text. No one's going to come after me here, are they?'

'Of course it's OK, darling, there's nobody here that wants to hurt you. Now, drink up.'

I leave the tea, now too terrified to drink it in case she's put something in it, and I am fully aware that this makes me sound like I really am mad. I don't want to have to trust her with Henry, but I must if I'm going to get the proof I need. Bea sleeps peacefully in her pram, her breath coming in tiny puffs. I wait for five minutes after Lila has left, just in case she's forgotten something, and then fire up the laptop. The box for a password pops up. I rack my brains, trying to think what she would use and plump for a combination of her initials and date of birth. Nothing. Pausing, I wipe away the sweat that slicks my brow and try to swallow, my mouth dry. I try another combination of her date of birth and full name but still nothing. I glance anxiously at the clock, before something tickles at the back of my mind.

The memory of Lila pulling my laptop towards her,
asking 'What's your password?' I type in HpG11103 –
my own password, a combination of Henry's initials
and his date of birth backwards. Bingo. I'm in.

I open up her emails but there is nothing of any
interest to me, nothing that relates to me, or Mark and
Henry. I check her Facebook (logged in, but no activity
for a long time) and snoop on Twitter, but she doesn't
seem to be on it. I look through her documents file, but
nothing there either, and I'm beginning to think I was
imagining it after all, when buried deep within other
files I find a folder simply called 'SG'. Heart pounding,
I open it up only to see pictures, taken without my
knowledge, of me and Henry sliding up the path in
the snow, Henry's cheeks rosy with cold, Mark and
I standing together the night Laurence first came over,
Mark's arm around me while I lean on his shoulder,
even the photo of Mark and Melissa in the park.
There are hundreds of pictures, all taken without my
noticing, little snapshots of our daily lives that she has
been hoarding behind our backs. My hands trembling,
I scroll through and find another file, one with two
Hotmail addresses and passwords. I note it down,
before opening her Internet browser and typing in the
Hotmail login. It brings up a Hotmail account called
s.gordon@hotmail.co.uk and I realise at once what
was niggling me about the email that was sent to Peter
Jenkins. The email address was wrong – mine is .com,

not .co.uk. Sure enough, when I open up the sent folder there is the email to Peter, along with ten or so other emails addressed to Tessa, each one more poisonous than the last. I give a little sob as I read through the hate she has sent to my best friend – no wonder Tessa doesn't want to know me if she thinks that's what I've sent over to her. I close it, disgust washing over me, and type in the other login details. There is only one email in the sent file – the one that reads 'I'M WATCHING YOU'. I check the clock and, with only a short window of time before she gets back with Henry, I close down the Hotmail and go to her search history. The first thing that pops up in her history is 'baking chocolate – poisonous for dogs?' *It's been her; it's been her all along.* Oh, God, the job at the school. I can't have her near Henry day after day. Horrified at the thought of her being able to get to Henry whenever she wants, I punch the number for the school into my mobile, pacing impatiently as it rings. The receptionist answers, finally.

'Yes, Mrs Gordon, can I help you?'

'The TA job.' My words tumble out over each other, 'Who got the TA job that was advertised at the end of the year? Was it Lila Frost?'

'I'm sorry, Mrs Gordon. I wouldn't be able to give that information out, even if there had been a job vacancy.'

'*Even if …?* What are you saying? That there never was a job available?'

'No, Mrs Gordon. There haven't been any teaching assistant vacancies at this school all year.'

There never was a job. That can only mean one thing – she was there, at the school, to do something to Henry that day, but Olivia being there stopped her. *Does that mean the day she took Henry she meant to keep him? Take him away from me for good? Why did she bring him back?* I can only think that someone saw her, someone who would have told me she had him. I push my shaking hands through my hair, before yanking open the drawers of her desk, searching for a reason, any reason, as to why she would want to destroy me. It doesn't take long before I find it – a slim, brown envelope taped to the back of the drawer. It seems Lila grew up reading the same Nancy Drew novels I did. Sliding my finger under the flap of the envelope, I shake out the contents, and what I see causes my stomach to lurch and bile to burn the back of my throat, the indescribable taste of fear.

Footsteps are approaching so, shaking, I shove the envelope back in the drawer and slam the laptop lid down, just as I hear Henry's voice coming up the garden path. I grab a sheet of paper from the printer and fan my flushed face to calm the heat that radiates from my cheeks, as she shoves her way through the front door, Henry tumbling in, laughing, after her.

'Steph? Are you OK?' She comes towards me, a concerned look on her face, and I shrink back, leaning against the desk.

'You …' I gasp, hot waves of fear pouring over my body. 'You did this? It was all you?'

'Steph, what …?' She gives an anxious glance towards Henry, who is watching me with wide eyes. Stepping towards me, she gives a smile that is more of a grimace, her features twisting with it. 'Steph, listen to me …'

'NO!' I shout, grappling with the strap on my bag, gesturing for Henry to come towards me. 'Get away from us. Henry, come here, darling, we're leaving.' I hold my hand out towards Henry, grasping the handle of the pram tightly with the other. He stares at me, eyes wide, before sliding his hand into Lila's. She gives me a triumphant look over the top of his head.

'Oh, dear, Steph. It seems they don't really need you that much after all, doesn't it?' A sly grin travels across her face, turning her from my friend, the girl I thought I could trust, into a snake, something poisonous and dead set on destroying everything I have.

'Henry, come to Mummy, come on.' I hold my hand out again, beckoning him towards me, desperate to get him away from her. A movement in the window behind Lila catches my eye, and I see that Mark has pulled up outside the house, obviously finished in the office for the day. 'Henry, come on, darling, Daddy's outside.'

Henry pulls his hand from Lila's and rushes to the front door, anxious to see his dad, anxious to escape the tension in the room, a tension he doesn't understand but that he knows is wrong. Lila reaches towards me, trying to stop me leaving, but I shove her away and follow him, hurriedly pushing the pram through her front door to get away. I need to get to Mark before she does; I need to tell him that it was her all along.

CHAPTER TWENTY-NINE

I am desperate to tell Mark what I found on the computer, but I'll have to wait until Henry goes to bed – he is already aware that something is wrong, and I don't want to frighten him, even though every instinct in my body is screaming at me to tell Mark everything *right now*. I slam the front door behind me, turning the key in the lock just to feel safe. Thinking about it I should have printed the emails, which I now realise is what she did. She must have printed the email off and put it in her back pocket and then pretended she'd printed it from my machine. And the threatening email – the one on my laptop – it was gone when I went to show Mark, the memory of her pulling the laptop towards her saying she would sort it out rising to the front of my mind. She must have deleted all traces of it that day, when I was in tears, terrified that someone was watching me. A flicker of rage fires up in my belly as I think about how sneaky and underhand she has been, and it battles with the feeling *Why? Why would she do this to me?*

What did I ever do to her? I wait until Henry leaves the room before I turn to Mark, unable to keep the words in any longer.

'I really do need to talk to you, Mark. I was right – it's not all in my head.' Tears are threatening and I blink them away. He lays a hand on mine.

'Not tonight, eh, Steph? Please. You promised we could have a fresh start, and it's been going well so far, hasn't it? Tomorrow, maybe.' His hair tumbles over one eye and he looks like the boy I married, before all the shit hit the fan.

'No, Mark, this can't wait. We need to talk, and we need to talk now. Either you listen to me, or I'm leaving. I'm not safe here – Henry and Bea aren't safe here.'

Mark shakes his head in disbelief.

'Really, Steph? I might have known it wouldn't last long, that you'd start it up again. I thought we agreed it was all over? That you wouldn't do this any more? I love you, but you can't keep doing this to yourself. To us.'

'I know, and I meant it, but Mark, I know who it is. I know what's been going on. *You have to listen to me!*' My voice has risen to a shriek, and even I can hear the underlying hysteria that is threatening to bubble over.

'OK, OK. Just … calm down. Let me bathe Henry and get him settled and I'll come back down and we'll talk, OK?' He eyes me warily as I nod in agreement and he calls to Henry to go upstairs.

Mark is bathing Henry and I have just laid Beatrice in her Moses basket after nursing her, when a shadow crosses the window. Immediately my heart starts racing and, worried in case it is Lila coming to visit us, I rush to the living-room window to look out. Joe is standing by his car, fiddling with what looks like a set of keys. Now is my chance. I rush outside, cardigan flapping, slippers on my feet, and call out to him.

'Yeah?' He is surly, not at all the sort of person I imagined Lila to be with.

'Joe, isn't it? You're Lila's boyfriend.' I stand in front of him, so he can't walk away, while he looks me up and down.

'Sorry, you are?'

'Steph. Steph Gordon. I live there.' I point at my house, water from the puddle-filled pavement slowly seeping through the fabric of my slippers. 'I need to speak to you about Lila. She's done some stuff, bad stuff. I think she's …' I break off as he holds his hands up to me.

'Look, Steph?' I nod. 'I don't know what she's told you, but it's nothing to do with me.'

'It *is*, though,' I shriek, desperation getting the better of me. 'You're her *boyfriend*, you have to get her to *stop*.' He frowns at me and gives a little laugh.

'Listen, love, I'm not her boyfriend. My name is Barry, not Joe. I'm the landlord; I'm renting the house to her as a favour to an old mate. I wouldn't have anything to do with her; she's fucking crackers, mate.' With that, he pushes me gently to one side, gets in his car and drives away, leaving me staring after him on the pavement.

I walk slowly back into the house, head full of this new information. Finally, there is someone out there that knows Lila isn't who she says she is. Determined to speak to Mark and tell him everything I know, I peep into the living room, but Bea isn't in her Moses basket. Thinking she must have started crying, I slowly make my way upstairs, and call softly to Mark. He answers from our room, but when I enter, Beatrice is not in his arms.

'Mark? Where's the baby?' I swallow hard, checking her cot, even though I can see through the gaps in the bars; see she's not there.

'What do you mean, *where's the baby?* She was downstairs with you.' He grabs my upper arms. 'Steph? What did you do with the baby?'

'I left her … she was in the Moses basket, and then I saw Joe outside, but it's not Joe, his name's Barry, and he's not her boyfriend.' I am gabbling, words tumbling out over one another, my teeth chattering together.

'Shut up, Steph, for Christ's sake, just shut up. *Bea!*' He lets go of me, roughly pushing me to one side before sprinting down the stairs. I follow after him, tripping over my damp, muddy slippers and grabbing the handrail as I slip on the treads. Mark races through the house, calling out for Beatrice, and I can't help the tiny bubble of hysterical laughter that pops out when I realise she can't call back.

'Steph, help me,' he pleads as he runs into the kitchen, where the back door swings open. A noise at the front of the house makes me turn and run through to the front door, tears choking me, making it hard to breathe. Yanking open the front door, she stands there, casserole pot in her hand.

'Steph? What's wrong?' Lila is there, as she always is, as soon as something goes wrong, as soon as I am upset, hurt, terrified, there she is, waiting to swoop in and make it all better. Waiting to reassure Mark, tuck Henry in, stop Bea from crying. Ready to take my place. *Just like Tessa said, always there when things go wrong, almost like she knows. Of course she knows. Why did I not notice this before?* I grab her by her coat collar, the coat that is so similar to mine it could almost be the same one, and drag her into the house.

'*Where's my baby?*' I scream at her, hard into her face. She drops the casserole dish as I twist the coat collar harder, trying to choke the information out of her.

'Stop, Steph, please stop.' She lifts her hands to me and I let go, using the fact that her hands are outstretched to scratch and claw at her face.

'STEPH!' Strong arms are around me, pulling me away from her, as I carry on swinging wildly, trying to hurt her as much as she's hurt me. 'Steph, come on.

Stop. This isn't helping. We need to call the police.' Mark wraps his arms around me and I sag into them, defeated.

'What's going on?' Lila is holding a tissue to her nose, where speckles of blood leach from the scratches on her face. Mark quickly explains to her, and she jumps into action, saying she'll help search if Mark calls the police. I stare at her, overwhelmed by the way she just walks in here and acts as though she belongs, as though she hasn't tried to tear our family limb from limb, all the while pretending she's our friend. Mark is hunting for his mobile, ready to call the police, when the doorbell rings. We go together to answer it, me pushing Lila out of the way as she tries to take my place next to Mark, only to see Mrs Beck, the elderly lady from two doors down standing on the doorstep, a tiny pink and white bundle in her arms. I grab at the bundle, crying with relief, but she holds her just out of reach. I stare at her quizzically, as she offers the baby to Mark.

'Mrs Beck – what? Where did you find her?' I ask, relief making me feel dizzy. She turns to me, giving me a hard stare.

'In your garden shed, dear. You should know; after all, you put her there. I saw you myself.'

CHAPTER THIRTY

I am woozy when I wake, groggy with a head full of cotton wool. It aches when I move it across the pillow, and my eyes are gritty and sore. It takes me a moment to remember why I feel so awful, before the memory of Beatrice in Mrs Beck's arms comes rushing back, her horrible accusation making me lose it completely. I begged and pleaded with Mark to believe me, swearing I would never do anything to harm our baby, but with Mrs Beck telling him that she saw me – 'wearing the good coat, she was' – and the dirt clinging to my slippers, where I rushed out of the house to see Joe, who is not Joe, serving as evidence I took the baby outside, in Mark's eyes I have the odds stacked against me. I try to sit up, but my head hurts too much, and I remember the doctor coming the previous evening, the GP from the practice down the road, stinging the top of my arm with a needle full of sedative. Lila sitting beside me in the dim half-light, as the drug takes hold, stroking my hair even as I try to fight against the drug, squirming away from her touch.

'Shhhhh,' she soothes as I try to push her hands away from my hair, the very thought of her touching me making me want to heave. Mark smiles at her as he sees the doctor to the door. As soon as he leaves the room, Lila leans down to whisper in my ear.

'There, Steph. Just relax and take it easy, eh? You didn't actually think you'd get away with it, did you?' I crease my brow at her in confusion, struggling to make the words come.

'Wha …? What?'

'You destroyed my life, Steph, you little bitch. I've waited a long time for this. But you know what they say – revenge is a dish best served cold. Looks like I've dished it up now, eh? It's your turn to have your life ruined – now you're going to know what it feels like to lose everything. Now, shhhhh.' Those were the last words I heard as the sedative took hold and pulled me down into a dreamless sleep.

Now, the following morning, the remnants of the sedative making my limbs feel thick and clumsy, I take a sip from the glass of water on the bedside table, and swing my legs out of bed. I need headache tablets, and the only way to get them is to go downstairs to the medicine cabinet. I remember Henry then, and strain to hear if he's in the house. I hear the faint murmurings of cartoons downstairs, and decide he must be in the living room. I slowly ease my way out of bed, body tired and sore, and sling on a dressing gown. My hair is sticking up all over, and I have crease marks on my face from the pillow. I certainly look like the definition of a mad woman.

Mark is in the living room when I walk in, Beatrice in his arms, and he coos softly to her as she watches his face intently. It makes my heart squeeze to see them together, and I don't know how I could ever have thought that Beatrice was a replacement baby. Thinking of the text angers me, and I decide to strike while the iron is hot. I have to stop Lila from destroying what we have, what we're fighting so hard to protect. Although cartoons blare from the television, Henry is nowhere to be seen, so, hoping he's out with my mum, I clear my throat softly and Mark turns to look at me.

'You're awake. How are you feeling?'

'OK – a bit groggy, maybe. Mark, we need to talk.'

'Yes, we do, you're right there. We need to sort this out, Steph. I'm worried about you; you're not yourself. Things seem to be escalating out of control. I thought we'd agreed that this was all done and dusted, that we were going to try and sort things out together.'

I take a deep breath in, my ribs hurting where I must have strained them when I lashed out at Lila yesterday, and colour comes to my cheeks when I remember the look on her face as I lunged at her. *I wish I'd hit her harder.*

'I'm not myself, Mark, I know that, but I didn't do all of this stuff, I'm telling you. Someone has been leaving things on the doorstep, has been in the house, moving things, trying to make me feel like I was going mad. I didn't feed Jasper beef – there was an empty wrapper in the bin from some baking chocolate, which is poisonous to dogs. I never took Beatrice outside and hid her. Mark, please, I'm telling you I didn't do it and I know who did.' I reach out towards him, ready to take the baby but he shifts her away from me, watching me warily.

'And who did it?'

'Lila. Lila was behind it all. I found everything on her computer. There were emails to Tessa and the one to the newspaper guy. She was the one who sent me that email saying, "I'm watching you". I found it all. There's an envelope, stuffed in the drawer of her desk. It's filled with newspaper clippings, Mark, about me. About Llewellyn Chance and what he did to me. I don't know why she has it, I don't know why she's doing this to me, but I need to find out. She's something to do with him, I just don't know what.' Tears are filling my eyes and I am trying not to raise my voice, to keep it all together. Mark gives a little laugh, adjusting Beatrice in his arms.

'She said you'd say that. She said that you'd try and blame it all on her, that you'd accused her of all sorts. She told me at Christmas that she was worried about you, that you were behaving more and more irrationally.'

'And you *believe* her?' I can't help it; my voice rises to a screech as I stare at him in disbelief. 'I'm your *wife*. How can you believe her over me?'

'Why wouldn't I, Steph? There was stuff in that email to the papers that only you and I knew about – how would she know that stuff? You vandalised someone's car, Steph. There's every chance you're going to be done for criminal damage – how is that rational behaviour?'

I scream in frustration, shoving my hands into my hair and tugging at my curls.

'She read my diary, Mark; how else do you think she knew all that stuff?' Everything was falling into place. All those times I thought she was being my friend, she was just finding ways to infiltrate herself further into my life. I grab at Mark's hand. 'Every time we let her look after Henry, she was upstairs reading my diary, rooting through my stuff. The diary was moved under the mattress and I thought it was me, I thought I moved it when I changed the bed linen, but it was *her*. I was never anywhere near Jasmine's house the night her car was vandalised – Lila bought the *exact same* coat as me, and *she* did it, to make it look like I did it. *I lost the coat*, Mark, how could I have been wearing it?'

'No, Steph, it was all you. You were the one that took the baby. Mrs Beck saw you.'

'NO!' I shout, sweeping my hand over the coffee table, crashing the two empty mugs that sit there to the floor.

'She took the baby! The back door was wide open! She wore her coat, the one the same as mine, and she put *our baby* outside! She's lying, Mark; she's got to you, just like she got to me, and I'm not letting her destroy us.' He backs away from me, jiggling Beatrice over his shoulder.

'Calm down. Come on. Look, I'll go and put Bea to bed and then I'll come back down and we can talk about this properly, OK?' I nod, and he quickly rushes from the room. Hearing his footsteps creaking up the stairs towards our bedroom, I pace anxiously, wanting to go up when I hear the baby wail, before I hear him singing to her quietly, shushing her to sleep. Pacing in front of the window, I see Laurence coming up the path, and race to the door to open it before he rings the bell and disturbs her.

'My God, Steph, you look terrible – are you OK?' He kisses my cheek and I inhale his warm, citrus-y scent. He's holding a bouquet of pink flowers that he thrusts out towards me.

'No, I'm not.' I take the flowers, and pull him inside. 'You have to help me, Laurence. I'm sorry I thought it was you … but now I know the truth.' I am babbling but I don't care. 'I have to leave; you have to help me. We'll get Beatrice and Henry and go to my mum's house. I have to get away before she knows that I know, before Mark can stop me.'

Laurence is staring at me, and I stop chattering and rub my arms, briskly, as though I have a chill.

'It's Lila, Steph. She's the one that's been doing it all, she's behind all of it.' He grabs my hands over my upper arms to stop me rubbing.

'You know? You believe me that it's her? Oh, thank God.' I almost fall, I am so relieved. 'All those things … if I had just paid attention … the baking chocolate when Jasper was sick – of course it was her! I can't bake. All those things, just so she could worm her way into my life, making me think I was going mad.' I give a hysterical little half laugh, half sob; full of horror at the idea that this could all have been prevented, if only I had just paid a bit more attention.

'I've been trying to tell you for weeks, but every time we talk you rush off. I saw her pinching flowers out of my garden, the ones that were in the posies that were left. I got suspicious after you mentioned them and started to keep an eye on her. I kept seeing her, letting herself in and out of your house when you weren't around.'

'So all those times I said I felt someone had been in the house, it's because it was true – she had been in there. She took Henry's pictures from the fridge, and his baby blanket. I couldn't find his baby blanket – she must have taken it. Oh, I feel sick.' I put my hand to my mouth, swallowing back the saliva that floods my cheeks.

'I thought maybe it was all innocent, that you'd given her a key or asked her to come in and help you out, but it was always when you weren't there. And then you said about the flowers, and I realised they were always left when she'd been in the house on her own. I asked around, did some journo work, you know? She's cracked in the head, Steph, and she's got it in for you.'

I clasp my shaking hands over my mouth; I'm so relieved it's not me, that someone else knows the truth.

'She's got an envelope, in the drawer of her desk at the house. It's full of newspaper clippings about me.'

'I was coming to that.' Laurence's face is grave, and he grasps my hand tightly. 'I delved right into her, Steph, dug up as much as I could. Her name isn't Lila, and although she gave the impression she's lived here for years, the reality is she moved in two weeks before you did. Maybe if *I'd* paid a bit of attention to what was going on around me, I could have stopped all this.' He swallows, and I give his hand a squeeze to tell him to go on, to tell me what it is he's uncovered. 'Her name is Lucy Chance. Her brother was Llewellyn Chance. She was eight when he did what he did to you, and she idolised him. After they caught him and put him away, their mother committed suicide. Their father was long gone, so Lucy was put into foster care, and grew up being shifted from one family to another, no one wanting to take her on long term. She's been planning this for years, Steph. She found you and she was watching you all this time. Your move to this house gave her the opportunity to get close to you and destroy everything you have.'

Bile rises in the back of my throat and I have to choke it down in order not to be sick all over the carpet.

'She's Llewellyn Chance's sister? Oh, God, she's done it all deliberately. This explains everything – she told me last night that I'd ruined her life, that she was going to make sure I lost everything, but I just couldn't piece it together.' It makes sense now, why she had the newspaper clippings, why she's tried to take everything from me. I knew that Chance had a sister, but she was little; it would never have crossed my mind that she would come back, that she would want revenge. 'I have to get out of here. Will you help? I need you to sort out a car, I'll need to get away.' Laurence nods and I listen hard to hear if Mark is still singing to the baby. I can hear his voice murmuring upstairs, but it sounds more like a conversation than a lullaby. Laurence kisses my cheek and squeezes my hand hard as he leaves, with promises to arrange a rental car and to come back and collect me this evening, once I've had a chance to pack my things and somehow get Mark out of the way so I can take the children and leave without him trying to stop me.

'Well, this is cosy. I saw your little friend leaving.' A voice from the doorway makes me spin round, and I see Lila's slender frame slouching against the wall.

'How did you get in?' I demand, fury washing over me.

'Mark gave me a key. He didn't know I already cut my own.' She smirks. 'He wanted me to be able to get in, in an emergency, you know, now he knows that you're a bit … mental. After all, Mrs Beck saw *you* put the baby in the garden shed, poor little mite. What kind of fucked-up mother would do something like that?' She smiles at me, swinging a door key on a loop around her finger.

'It was you! *I know it was you and I know who you are.* Get out.'

'Oh, sweetie, I'm not going anywhere. Do you know what you did to our family? With your lies and your filthy mouth? I was *eight years old,*' she spits at me. 'You said it was Llew who did that to you, and he got taken away because of it. You couldn't even pick him out in a fucking line-up, but then I only found out about that later.'

Horrified, I think back to that awful day – no, I couldn't pick Llewellyn Chance out in the line-up, but the next girl he had attacked *had.*

'The other girl. She picked him out. It wasn't my fault,' I whisper.

'You started it, Steph. You're the one who started it; she finished it. I dealt with her, don't worry about that. But you – you started it all. You destroyed our family. Do you know what happened after Llew got put away? My mum started drinking. At least a bottle of vodka a day by the time the trial was over. Dad couldn't hack it so he left – didn't even leave a note. So it was just me and my poor old alky mum. Till she tried to do two bottles of vodka in a day, and gave herself alcohol poisoning. She *died*, Steph, in a pool of her own vomit because of what you did. She did it deliberately, because she couldn't stand living with what you said about her son.'

'No. No, it wasn't my fault – they all told me it wasn't my fault.' Tears drip from the end of my chin.

'And then what happened, Steph, because of you and your fucking dirty lies? They took me away. They put me in a foster home, where my "foster dad" thought that taking care of me meant the privilege of putting his hand in my knickers whenever he got the chance. All this, because of what you did. So yeah, you ruined my life. I lost everything. And now I'm going to make sure you lose everything.' She smiles, her lips a bloodless slash across her face. 'I watched you, Steph, and I waited. Good things come to those who wait, that's what they say, isn't it? I watched you marry a man you loved, have a child; carry on living your life just like nothing ever happened.'

'It wasn't like that.' My voice gets caught in my throat, scratching its way out. 'It wasn't. I couldn't get over it for a long time – you can ask anyone, my mum, Mark ...'

Her voice cuts over mine, flat and emotionless. She is unrecognisable as the girl I thought was my friend; her pretty features twisted, made ugly by hatred.

'Then, Steph, you moved here. It was the perfect opportunity. You didn't think you could live your life without consequences, did you? See, the thing is, Steph, they don't need you any more. Mark, Henry and Bea need someone stable to look after them – someone who can give them a proper family. That's all I ever wanted, you know, a proper family. And now I get to kill two birds with one stone. I get to take away everything that you hold dear. I get to *destroy* the woman who ruined my life, and get my own ready-made family thrown into the bargain. Win-win.'

'No, you can't do that – Mark will never believe you.'

'Won't he though, Steph? He's worried about you being around the children already. You've been arrested for criminal damage, you poisoned the family dog, and you even emailed the newspapers about your husband's affair in an attempt to humiliate him. And as for what you did to that poor little baby – social services don't look kindly on mothers who harm their children. Do you really think these are the actions of a stable person?'

'It was you – it was all you! I found the emails to Tessa, and to the journalist on your computer. It was you who vandalised Jasmine's car and you who read my diary and emailed the newspaper. I didn't do any of these things.'

'Really? Where's your proof, Steph? Who's Mark going to believe? The mad woman? Or the woman who's been there to pick up the pieces every time something went wrong? You brought it on yourself, Steph, when you told people my brother raped you.'

'It wasn't my fault – none of this is my fault!' I scream, fear making me lurch towards her, desperate to stop her from taking my family away from me, when Mark appears behind her.

'Steph, please. Calm down. We need to sort this out.'

'*Get her out of here!*' I screech, lurching towards her, scratching out with my fingernails. I catch her porcelain cheek with my nail, raking a satisfying hollow into her perfect skin. She howls in pain, before pulling out a tissue and demurely dabbing at the blood that appears there, and as Mark shoves me to one side and rushes to her to check she is OK, I realise that there is no me and Mark, not any more. I can almost feel my heart snap in two.

'It's fine, just a scratch. I don't know what got into her.' She smiles up at him pathetically. 'She just went *mad.*' She catches my eye and smirks behind Mark's back.

The doorbell rings, and Mark goes to answer, leaving me alone with the poisonous bitch who has tried to destroy everything I hold dear. She pins herself flat against the wall, shrinking back as though that could stop me from killing her. My chest is heaving, my hair wild about my face, and there are two large wet patches on the front of my T-shirt where I haven't fed Beatrice, so the last person I want to see in my house is the visitor who has just arrived. Dr Bradshaw stands in the hallway, notepad in hand, with two women, who, by the way they are dressed, are obviously official. I look at Mark in confusion.

'Mark? What's going on?' He looks down at the floor, at Lila, anywhere except at me.

'I'm sorry, Steph, but it's for the best. It's just for a little while, just to get you better, and then you can come home.'

'What do you mean, *come home*? Mark, what is this?' A crashing wave of fear makes my skin prickle with goosebumps, as I go hot, then cold.

Dr Bradshaw steps forward, hushing the woman who stands next to him.

'Stephanie, this is Katie Jones; she's a social worker. And this is Alice Cotton, a psychiatrist. She's going to keep an eye on everything, OK, but we've been in discussion with Mark, as your nearest relative, and with your GP, and the consensus is that you need to go into hospital, just for a short while.' The sanctimonious prick has the nerve to bare his teeth at me in what, I think, is supposed to be a reassuring smile.

Katie Jones steps forward, a bland look on her face.

'Stephanie Gordon? We are detaining you under Section 2 of the Mental Health Act, which means for a period of time you're going to have to stay in hospital.' Her voice softens slightly. 'We're trying to help you here, Steph.' With tears sliding down my cheeks, like waterfalls that I'm powerless to stop, I turn to Mark.

'You're having me sectioned? Mark, *please*, this is all her fault – she's been out to get me since we moved here. Please, Mark, Dr Bradshaw, you have to believe me!' I am sobbing, desperate to stop this. 'Lila, tell them! Tell them it was you – Mark, she's Llewellyn Chance's sister!' I claw at his sleeve in desperation. Lila affects a puzzled look on her perfect features; features I now see carry a hint of the man who tore me apart, physically and emotionally. There is no sign of the twisted, warped hatred that sat on her features less than two minutes previously.

'I have no idea what she's talking about. I'm sorry.'

Mark sighs, scrubbing a hand across his face. He looks exhausted, worn down by the events that have taken place. His skin is grey and his stubble rasps as he runs his hand over it.

'Steph, Chance's sister disappeared years ago. No one has heard from her since she left the foster system at eighteen. The last I heard was that she'd headed overseas somewhere. Don't you think I kept an eye on it all for you? I've tried, Steph, I've tried so hard to keep us together as a family but you're sick. You're destroying us.'

I gape at him in horror, and Lila smugly looks on, taking her opportunity to whisper something into Dr Bradshaw's ear, as she gestures towards the scratch marks on her face. He looks at me, a rueful look on his face.

'I'm sorry, Stephanie, it's for the best. Really. If you co-operate now, the chances are we can get you home ASAP.' Stunned, I don't know what to say. Dr Bradshaw takes my arm and it's as though a switch has been flipped.

'*No!*' I shriek, ripping my arm away from his, shoving him backwards where he stumbles against the stone mantelpiece of the fireplace. Katie Jones makes a grab for my arm but I give her the same treatment, shoving her as hard as I can before Mark grips my upper arms tightly and holds me still. Katie looks up at me from where she lies sprawled on the carpet, the corner of the coffee table having given her head a nasty bang as she went down. There is a huge lump rising on her forehead, purple and angry, as Lila leans down to help her up.

'I won't go! Please, Mark, please don't make me go!' I shout, sobs racking through my body, making my throat hoarse and my chest heave as I fight Mark to get away. 'I won't do it any more, I promise, I won't say anything. I'll just forget that anything happened, just *please, don't take me away.*'

Dr Bradshaw gets to his feet, digging in his briefcase before walking slowly towards me, syringe in hand.

I sit in the back of Dr Bradshaw's car, Katie Jones in the passenger seat, Alice Cotton in the driver's seat, as

Dr Bradshaw gets Mark to sign the paperwork, child locks making it impossible for me to escape even if I had the energy. Whatever was in the syringe that Dr Bradshaw plunged into my arm has made me tired and woolly, and I am struggling to string my thoughts together. Laurence appears in his doorway, a small holdall in his hand that I know he is bringing to me, to help me take the children and get away, only he's too late. I try to bang on the window but my arms are like lead and I can't do it. Desperate tears slide down my cheeks, with the realisation that I can't fix this; I can't stop any of this from happening and she has won. Mark hands the doctor the pen, a desolate look on his face, and as I raise my eyes to his through the grimy window, I see tears on his cheeks that match the ones falling from my eyes, a relentless river that never seems to dry up. Dr Bradshaw gets into the seat beside me and turns to smile sadly at me.

'OK? Steph, we will get you home as soon as possible, all right? You just need to co-operate with us.'

I stare blankly at him and, as Alice pulls away from the kerb, I twist my head round to look out of the rear-view window. Mark stands, head down at the kerbside, and I see Lila appear next to him, my baby in her arms, her small white hand sliding into his.

Turn the page for an extract from Lisa Hall's debut novel

BETWEEN YOU AND ME

PROLOGUE

It happened so quickly, and now there is so much blood. More than I ever thought possible. One minute, he was shoving me backwards, into the kitchen counter, the air thick with anger and words spoken in temper that could never be taken back. The next, he was on the floor, the handle of the knife protruding from his ribs. I don't even remember picking it up, only that I had to stop him. I back away, pushing myself up against the cold, granite surface, across the room from where he lies. I feel light-headed and sick, sweat prickling along my spine. He reaches up to me with a shaky hand, slick with his own blood, and I draw back even further. He is slumped on the floor, back resting against the kitchen counter, a lock of hair falling over his brow. He is pale, a sheen of sweat shining on his forehead. A coppery, iron tang fills the air and I want to retch. Turning, I lean over the kitchen sink, where I heave and heave but nothing comes up. I wipe my mouth on a tea towel and push my shaking hands through my hair. I need to try to think calmly, rationally. I need to phone for an ambulance, and I need to get my story straight. I'll tell them that he slipped and fell on the knife, a brutal, heavy knife usually used for carving the Christmas turkey, not carving into other people. That we weren't arguing, just talking. It was an accident; one minute he was fine, the next he was on the floor. I'll tell them that I didn't see what happened – I have to protect myself. I can't tell them that I snapped. That a red mist descended and for just a few seconds I felt like I couldn't take it any more, the shouting, the aggression and the lies. That in just a split second all rationality left me and I grabbed the knife and thrust it firmly into my husband's stomach.

CHAPTER ONE

SAL

The first time you hit me it was a shock, but not a surprise. Surely, this is the natural progression of things? Starting with the little things, like wanting to know where I've been, who I've spoken to, escalating to a little push here and a shove there, until now, when a slap almost feels like a reward – and I'm thankful that it wasn't something worse, that there are no bones broken this time.

I remember the first time I saw you. Nothing on earth had prepared me for it and the sight of you hit me like a punch in the guts. Is that ironic? You stood there, in the Student Union bar, talking to a guy on your course I had seen around campus previously, a pint of Fosters in one hand. The sun was streaming in through a window behind you and you looked majestic, standing tall in a faded pair of Levi's and battered Converse, your fair hair standing out around you like an aura. I was with a group of people from my own course, planning on spending the evening with them, hashing over that day's lectures over a few drinks and then maybe heading out for a bite to eat. Once I saw you, I knew my plans had changed and that I had to pluck up the courage to approach you. How would things have turned out if I hadn't asked you if you wanted another pint? If you hadn't accepted, and we hadn't spent the entire evening holed up in one corner of the SU bar? If I hadn't answered your call the next day and accepted your invitation to lunch? If we hadn't spent the whole of that following weekend together, in your flat, ignoring your roommate, the phone, the world outside?

Maybe I would be married to someone who doesn't think it's OK to hit me. To throw things at me if I have a different opinion to the one I 'should' have. Someone who doesn't think that being happily married means the other half of the partnership towing the line at all times, no questions asked. Maybe you would be settled with someone else, someone who knows the right thing to say and the best way to handle you. Maybe you would be with someone you don't think defies you at every opportunity, although I don't, I really don't. You just think I do, regardless of what I do or what I say. Maybe both of us would be happier.

CHAPTER TWO

CHARLIE

A file the size of a house brick lands on my desk and Geoff appears, throwing himself down in the chair opposite mine.

'Another bunch of stuff for you to work through – looks like you're not going home early tonight!' he wheezes, his face bright red as he struggles to catch his breath. Geoff is the size of a house himself, his enormous belly straining at the buttons of his grubby white shirt. Geoff is a colleague, my equal, but as he's fifteen years older than me, he treats me like a five-year-old. The man has a serious lack of ambition, and a serious case of body odour.

'Honestly, Geoff? It's 8pm – surely you don't think I'm even considering going home yet?' I give a little laugh as I pull the file towards me and start leafing through it; despite the fact I still have a ton of paperwork next to me that needs going through before I can even consider leaving the office. I feel the beginnings of a migraine tapping at my temples, no doubt brought on by tiredness from a 5am start and the stress of the never-ending paperwork that comes with the case I'm working on. The pressures of being a corporate lawyer are well known – the long hours, the stressful cases that take over our lives and eat into our personal time with our families – but it is all worth it in the end. The salary and benefits make sure of that.

'Well, don't stay up too late. You don't want to leave that pretty little family of yours too much; someone else might snap them up!' Geoff heaves his massive bulk from the leather chair across the desk from me, leaning over to ruffle my hair as he leaves.

'No chance of that, Geoff.' I grin at him through gritted teeth, the thud of my headache growing louder and making me wish I could slap his meaty fingers from the top of my head. He breezes out of the room, as much as a twenty-stone, fifty-year-old corporate lawyer can, and I reach for the phone. I dial our home number, leafing through the new documents while I wait for Sal to pick up. Engaged. I hang up and redial, using the mobile number. It rings and rings, and I picture it sitting on the kitchen side where Sal always leaves it, the hideous Johnny Cash ringtone that Sal insists on blaring out. It rings out and goes to voicemail.

'Sal, it's me. Who the fuck are you talking to? Call me back.' I slam the receiver down, and lean back in my chair, grinding the heels of my hands into my eyes to relieve the pressure that beats away there. I don't need this shit – I have enough on my plate to deal with in the office, without wondering who the hell Sal is talking to at eight o'clock at night.

An hour later, when my call still hasn't been returned, and I've tried the house phone numerous times, but to no avail, I bundle up the files and stuff them into my briefcase. I can't concentrate on work all the time I am wondering why Sal isn't answering the telephone. All sorts of scenarios cross my mind, ranging from Sal knocking the phone off the hook so as not to be disturbed with some illicit lover, through to Sal on the phone to some other person (Sal's sister? Sal's mum? Someone I don't even know?), planning to leave me. I don't know what the hell Sal is playing at, but I'm not happy. I thought I had made the rules perfectly clear – if I call, Sal should answer. I spend every waking hour working my butt off to make sure I can provide for my family – I think the least Sal can do is answer the phone when I call. I smooth down my fair hair, sticking up at all angles where I've been pushing my hands through it in an attempt to calm myself while I concentrate on those bloody files Geoff dumped on me, grab my black jacket and head out the door. When I get home, Sal had better be there – and if Sal is there, I'll want to know why the bloody hell my calls this evening have gone unanswered. I'm not being ignored by anyone, least of all the person I chose to spend the rest of my life with.

ACKNOWLEDGEMENTS

A million thank-yous to my brilliant editor, Victoria Oundjian, for working her magic once again, and to the Carina team for their support and most excellent design skills.

To my agent, Lisa Moylett, for looking after me, holding my hand and encouraging all my ideas, no matter how weird they are.

To Ryan Maxwell and Ann Troup for helping me to unpick all those tricky police and psychiatric knots.

To Amy, Katie and Sarah for being my real-life and soul sisters … and for always knowing when to pour the wine.

And finally, to Nick, George, Missy and Mo – it looks like the madness isn't going to end any time soon. I love you all.